Praise for *Th*

"[*This Other Eden*] is a harrowing tale of ⟨...⟩ f
people in isolation just trying to get by ⟨...⟩ g
and meditative, a combination that is characteristic of [Ha]"

—MJ Franklin, *New York Times*

"*This Other Eden* is ultimately a testament of love: love of kin, love of nature, love of art, love of self, love of home. Harding has written a novel out of poetry and sunlight, violent history and tender remembering. The humans he has created are, thankfully, not flattened into props and gimmicks, which sometimes happens when writers work across time and difference; instead they pulse with aliveness, dream-like but tangible, so real it could make you weep."

—Danez Smith, *New York Times Book Review*

"[Harding] writes with the gravitas of a mythmaker. . . . The pace of Harding's storytelling is stately, his descriptions, even of small events, gorgeous. . . . *This Other Eden* is beautiful and agonizing—rather like the real place that inspired it."

—Claire Messud, *Harper's Magazine*

"Harding, who won a dark-horse Pulitzer Prize for *Tinkers*, again demonstrates his gifts for concision and compassion in a narrative that balances historical fact with fully drawn characters. . . . [S]ure to be a standout of 2023."

—Bethanne Patrick, *Los Angeles Times*,
"10 Books to Add to Your Reading List in January"

"Harding's gifts have found their fullest expression in *This Other Eden*. Pick any excerpt from these 200 pages and you will find that each sentence contains multitudes and works well by itself, and yet the chapters, the paragraphs, have also been sewn together into a numinous whole. . . . The novel impresses time and again because of the depth of Harding's sentences, their breathless angelic light."

—Abhrajyoti Chakraborty, *Guardian* (UK)

"*This Other Eden* is a story of good intentions, bad faith, worse science, but also a tribute to community and human dignity and the possibility of another world. In both, it has much to say to our times."

—Rachel Seiffert, *Guardian* (UK)

"Stunning. . . . You could imagine lots of ways a historical novel about this horror might be written, but none of them would give you a sense of the strange spell of *This Other Eden*—its dynamism, bravado and melancholy. Harding's style has been called 'Faulknerian' and maybe that's apt, given his penchant for sometimes paragraph-long sentences that collapse past and present. . . . [An] intense wonder of a historical novel."
——Maureen Corrigan, NPR

"Beautiful, brooding. . . . Harding paints a rich, unvarnished portrait of Apple Island and its residents. . . . Long, cascading sentences sometimes loop back on themselves to add salient details; others rush forward to encapsulate as much complexity as they can. . . . Harding's finely wrought prose shows us a community that refuses to see itself through the judgmental eyes of others, a society composed of people who give their neighbors the same latitude to go their own way that they claim for themselves. It closes on a note of determined hope, with an emblem of continuity and endurance held high above the waters that separate Apple Island from the censorious mainland."
——Wendy Smith, *Washington Post*

"With gorgeous, often antique prose, Harding takes us into the prelapsarian world of the islanders. . . . Harding has a gift for using language with intense precision that evokes his characters' points of view."
——Carolyn Kellogg, *Boston Globe*

"Frequent lyrical passages, which are as epic, forceful and sweeping as the floods the book depicts and recalls. . . . Just as wonderful are the book's frequent small touches."
——Clifford Thompson, *Times Literary Supplement* (UK)

"Tender, magical, and haunting, Paul Harding's *This Other Eden* is that rare novel that makes profound claims on our present age while being, very simply, a graceful performance of language and storytelling. Here is prose that touchingly holds its imagined island community in a light that can only be described as generous and dazzling. I have not read a novel this achingly beautiful in a while, nor one in which the fate of its characters I will not soon forget."
——Major Jackson, author of *The Absurd Man*

"There is no writer alive anything like Paul Harding, and *This Other Eden* proves it: astonishingly beautiful, humane, strange, interested in philosophy and the heart, stunningly written. It's about home, love, heredity, cruelty, and the very nature of art, so completely original it's hard to know how to describe it in a mere blurb, by which I mean: you must read this book."

—Elizabeth McCracken, author of *The Souvenir Museum*

"In boldly lyrical prose, *This Other Eden* shows us a once-thriving racial utopia in its final days, at a time when race and science were colliding in chilling ways. In the stories of the Apple Islanders—especially that of Ethan Honey, spared a destructive fate because of his artistic gifts and his fair skin—we are made to confront the ambiguous nature of mercy, the limits of tolerance, and what it means to truly be saved. A luminous, thought-provoking novel."

—Esi Edugyan, author of *Washington Black*

"Harding's third novel revisits an appalling moment in Maine history.... [A] brief book that carries the weight of history. A moving account of community and displacement."

—*Kirkus Reviews*, starred review

"Pulitzer winner Harding (*Tinkers*) suffuses deep feeling into this understated yet wrenching story.... It's a remarkable achievement."

—*Publishers Weekly*, starred review

"A superb achievement.... Harding combines an engrossing plot with deft characterizations and alluring language deeply attuned to nature's artistry. The biblical parallels, which naturally align with the characters' circumstances, add depth, and enhance the universality of the themes.... [T]his gorgeously limned portrait about family bonds, the loss of innocence, the insidious effects of racism, and the innate worthiness of individual lives will resonate long afterward."

—*Booklist*, starred review

ALSO BY PAUL HARDING

Tinkers

Enon

This Other Eden

A Novel

PAUL HARDING

W. W. NORTON & COMPANY
Independent Publishers Since 1923

For my wonderful mother, who made reading irresistible.

This Other Eden is a work of fiction. Place names and descriptions corresponding with existing or historical locations and events are used fictitiously. Apart from certain well-known historical figures, all characters in the novel are products of the author's imagination, and any resemblance to real individuals, living or dead, is entirely coincidental.

Copyright © 2023 by Paul Harding

All rights reserved

Printed in the United States of America
First published as a Norton paperback 2024

For information about permission to reproduce selections from this book, write to Permissions, W. W. Norton & Company, Inc., 500 Fifth Avenue, New York, NY 10110

For information about special discounts for bulk purchases, please contact W. W. Norton Special Sales at specialsales@wwnorton.com or 800-233-4830

Manufacturing by Lakeside Book Company
Book design by Chris Welch
Production manager: Lauren Abbate

Library of Congress Cataloging-in-Publication Data

Names: Harding, Paul, 1967– author.
Title: This other Eden : a novel / Paul Harding.
Description: First edition. | New York, NY : W. W. Norton & Company, [2023]
Identifiers: LCCN 2022058144 | ISBN 9781324036296 (hardcover) | ISBN 9781324036302 (epub)
Subjects: LCGFT: Novels.
Classification: LCC PS3608.A72535 T55 2023 | DDC 813/.6—dc23/eng/20221208
LC record available at https://lccn.loc.gov/2022058144

ISBN 978-1-324-07452-6 pbk.

W. W. Norton & Company, Inc., 500 Fifth Avenue, New York, N.Y. 10110
www.wwnorton.com

W. W. Norton & Company Ltd., 15 Carlisle Street, London W1D 3BS

1 2 3 4 5 6 7 8 9 0

Malaga Island . . . was home to a mixed-race fishing community from the mid-1800s to 1912, when the state of Maine evicted 47 residents from their homes and exhumed and relocated their buried dead. Eight islanders were committed to the Maine School for the Feeble-Minded. "I think the best plan would be to burn down the shacks with all of their filth," then Governor Frederick Plaisted told a reporter [at] the time. . . .

[In 2010], the Maine legislature passed a resolution expressing its "profound regret."

—Maine Coast Heritage Trust

1

Benjamin Honey—American, Bantu, Igbo—born enslaved—freed or fled at fifteen, only he ever knew—ship's carpenter, aspiring orchardist, arrived on the island with his wife, Patience, née Raferty, Galway girl, in 1793. He brought his bag of tools—gifts from a grateful captain he had saved from drowning or plunder from a ship on which he had mutinied and murdered the captain, depending on who said—and a watertight wooden box containing twelve jute pouches. Each pouch held seeds for a different variety of apple. Honey collected the seeds during his years as a field-worker and later as a sailor. He remembered being in an orchard as a child, although not where or when, with his mother, or with a woman whose face over the years had become what he pictured as his mother's, and he remembered the fragrance of the trees and their fruit. The memory became a vision of the garden to which he meant to return. No mystery, it was Eden. Years passed and he added seeds to his collection. He recited the names at night before he slept. Ashmead's Kernel, Flower of Kent, Duchess of Oldenburg, and Warner's King. Ballyfatten, Catshead.

After Benjamin and Patience Honey arrived on the island—hardly three hundred feet across a channel from the mainland, just under forty-two acres, twelve hundred feet across, east to west, and fifteen hundred feet long, north to south, uninhabited then, the only human trace an abandoned Penobscot shell berm—and after they had settled themselves, he planted his apple seeds.

Not a seed grew. Benjamin was so infuriated by his ignorance that over the next year he crossed to the mainland whenever he could spare some time and sought out orchards and their owners in the countryside beyond the village of six or seven houses, called Foxden, that stood directly across the channel from the island, and traded his carpentry skills for seeds and advice about how they grew and how to cultivate the trees and their fruit.

Benjamin and Patience and their sons and daughters and grandsons and granddaughters and great-grandchildren kept more and more to the island as time passed, but in the final years of the eighteenth century it was not as dangerous as it came to be later for Black man to range the land. Any able-bodied adult who kept peace and lent a hand surviving was accepted. So the story went among his descendants. So, Benjamin rambled around and found farms where he could help raise a barn or split shingles or clear an acre for crops and came home with seeds that quickened and struck roots and elaborated themselves into the shapes of his remembered paradise.

Roxbury Russets, Rhode Island Greenings, Woodpeckers, and Newtown Pippins. Benjamin Honey kept an orchard of thirty-two apple trees that began to bear fruit in the late summer of 1814, a decade after he planted them. Pippins were perfect for pies, Woodpeckers for cider. Children bit sour Greenings on dares and laughed at one another when their eyes watered and mouths puckered. Russets were best straight from the tree.

Benjamin Honey surveyed his orchard in the cooling air and sharpening, iridescent, ocean-bent sunset light, the greens and purples deepening from their radiant flat day-bright into catacombs of shadowed fruit and limb and leaf. It felt as if his mother were somewhere among the rows. She might step from behind a tree in a white Sunday dress that took up the shifting light and colors and smile at him. He inhaled the perfume, salted, as everything on the island, and took a bite of the apple he held.

ON THE FIRST day of spring, 1911, Esther Honey, great-granddaughter of Benjamin and Patience, dozed in her rocking chair by the woodstove in her cabin on Apple Island. Snow poured from the sky. Wind scoured the island and smacked the windows like giant hands and kicked the door like a giant heel and banked the snow up the north side of the shack until it reached the roof. The island a granite pebble in the frigid Atlantic shallows, the clouds so low their bellies scraped on the tip of the Penobscot pine at the top of the bluff.

Esther drowsed with her granddaughter, Charlotte, in her lap, curled up against her spare body, wrapped in a pane of Hudson's Bay wool from a blanket long ago cut into quarters and shared among her freezing ancestors and a century-old quilt stitched from tatters even older. The girl took little warmth from her rawboned grandmother and the old woman practically had no need for the heat her grandchild gave, no place, practically, to fit it, being so slight, and so long accustomed to the minimum warmth necessary for a body to keep living, but each was still comforted by the other.

Esther's son, Eha—Charlotte's father—rose from his stool and one at a time tossed four of the last dozen wooden shingles onto the embers in the stove. The relief society inexplicably had sent a pallet of the shingles to the settlement last summer. There was no need for them. Eha and Zachary Hand to God Proverbs were excellent carpenters and could make far finer cedar shingles than these. But as with each of the past four years, summer brought food and goods from the relief society, and some of the supplies were puzzling to the Apple Islanders, like the shingles, or a horse saddle, once, for an island that only had a handful of humans and three dogs on it. With the food and stock also came Matthew Diamond, a single, retired schoolteacher who under the sponsorship of the Enon College of Theology and Mission traveled from somewhere in Massachusetts each June to stay in his summer home—visible on the mainland in clear weather 300 yards across the channel, in the village of Foxden—and row his boat to Apple Island each morning, where he preached, helped with a kitchen garden here, a leaky roof there, and taught lessons in the one-room schoolhouse he and Eha Honey and Zachary Hand to God Proverbs had built.

Useless spalt anyway, Eha said, closing the woodstove on the last of the shingles.

Tabitha Honey, Eha's other daughter, ten years old, two years older than her sister Charlotte, scooted on her behind across the cold floor to get closer to the stove. She wore two pairs of stockings, three old dresses, a donated wool coat the society had sent, and the one pair of shoes she owned, boy's boots passed down from her big brother, Ethan, when he'd outgrown them. They were too big for her and she'd stuffed the toes and heels with dry grass that poked out of the split soles like whiskers. Tabitha wore another square of the Hudson's Bay blanket wrapped over her head and shoulders.

C'mere, Victor, Tabitha said to the cat curled behind the stove. Tch, tch, c'mere, Vic. She wanted the cat for her lap, for some warmth. Victor raised his head and looked at the girl. He lowered his head back down and half-closed his eyes.

I hope you catch fire, you no-good hunks, Tabitha said.

Ethan Honey, fifteen, Eha's oldest child, sat on a wooden crate across the room, in the coldest corner, drawing his grandmother and little sister with a lump of charcoal on an old copy of the local newspaper that Matthew Diamond had given him last fall the day before he closed up his summer house and returned to Massachusetts. The boy's nose was red, his lips purple. His fingers and hands were mottled white and blue, as if the blood were wicking into clots of frost under their skin. He concentrated on his grandmother and sister and their entwined figures came into finer and finer view across the front page of the *Foxden Journal*, seeming to hover above the articles about the tenth annual drill and ball, six Chinamen deported, a missing three-masted schooner, ads for fig syrups, foundries, soft hats, and black dress goods.

Tell us about the flood, Grammy, Tabitha said, still eyeing the cat.

Charlotte lifted her head from her grandmother's breast and said, Yes, tell us again, Gram!

Ethan looked from his drawing to his grandmother and sister and back. He said nothing but wanted as much as his sisters for his grandmother to tell the story about the hurricane that had nearly sunk the island and had nearly swept away his whole family.

Eha went from the stove to the corner opposite where Ethan drew and tipped a basket sitting on a shelf toward him and looked into it.

I'll fix these potatoes and there's a little salt fish left, he said. A can of milk, too.

You want to hear about the flood? That old flood? Again? Esther Honey said.

Yes, Gram, please!

Please, Gram, tell us!

Well, that old flood was almost a hundred years ago, now, she began. Way back in 1815.

A HURRICANE STRUCK in September of 1815, twenty-two years after Benjamin and Patience Honey had come to the island and begun the settlement, by which time there were nearly thirty people living there, in five or six houses, including the first Proverbs and Lark folks, the ones from Angola and Cape Verde, the others from Edinburgh—Patience herself from Galway, Ireland, originally, before she met Benjamin on his way through Nova Scotia and went with him—and three Penobscot women, sisters who'd lost their parents when they were little girls. A surge of seawater twenty feet high funneled up the bay, sweeping houses and ships along with it. When the wall of ocean hit, it tore half the trees and all the houses off the island, guzzling everything down, along with two Honeys, three Proverbs, one of the Penobscot sisters, three dogs, six cats, and a goat named Enoch. The hurricane roared so loudly Patience Honey thought she'd gone deaf at first, that is, until she heard the tidal mountain avalanching toward them, bristling with houses and ships and trees and people and cows and horses churning inside it, screaming and bursting and lowing and neighing and shattering and heading right for the island. Then she knew all might well be lost, that this might well be the judgment of exaltation, the sealed message unsealing, that after they'd all been swept away by the broom of extermination there'd be so few trees left standing a young child would be able to count them up, and their folks would be scarcer than gold. But not all gone. Not everyone. Patience knew. Some Honeys would persist, some Proverbs survive. A Lark or two might endure. So, for reasons she could never afterward explain, she snatched the homemade flag she'd stitched together from patches of the stars and stripes and the Portuguese crown and golden Irish harp shaped like a woman, who looked so much like a figurehead and always reminded her husband of the one on the front of the ship he'd been a sailor on, that had sunk off the coast and brought him to the island in the first place, and the faded, faint squares embroidered with Bantu triangles and diamonds and circles that he'd carried with him everywhere, that he showed her meant man and woman and marriage and the rising sun and the setting sun, that he always said were his great-grandfather's, although she in her heart of hearts didn't think that that could be true, and tied it like a scarf around her throat, and she took Benjamin by the hand and dragged him from their shack out into the whirlwind. She swore it was a premonition, because no sooner had she and her husband passed out the door than the house broke loose from its pilings and tumbled away behind them, bouncing and breaking apart into straw like a bale of hay bouncing off a rick and into the ocean. Now that she stood in the open, facing the bedlam, her legs would not work. She was sure that this was the Judgment and what was to be was to be; it was useless to try to outrun the outstretched arm of the Lord.

Benjamin roared to her over the roaring storm, The tree, the tree! And he pointed to the tallest tree on the island, the Penobscot pine, at the top of the bluff. Benjamin pointed and leaned his face toward his wife's and pointed.

Up the tree!

Wind plastered his shirt and the rain lashed and streamed down his face and ran from his hair and lightning broke across the sky and thunder blasted against the earth and sea and he roared again over the roaring storm, The tree! And Patience thought of their grown children and their young grandchildren and cried to her husband, The children! And Benjamin looked beyond his wife and there were their children and grandchildren, drenched and shouldering their way against the winds and lashing rains, the ocean rising now up to the windows of the Larks' old shack and pouring into it through the broken panes, and the largest surging waves thundering nearly up to where his own house had stood not two minutes before and sucking all the earth right off the very rocks and into the black and gray and brooding jade Atlantic, and he cried, Go to the tree! And he ran toward his grown children and young grand-children and grabbed two soaking little ones from their mothers and carried one each under his arms and ran toward the tree. And the wind roared and spun and they staggered against it, now nearly blown toward the bluff, now nearly blown back away from it. When they reached the tree, one of Benjamin and Patience's sons, I think she always said it was Thomas, stood on Benjamin's shoulders and the other sons and daughters climbed up the two men and reached the lowest branches of the old tree and once they got their footing as best as they could in the middle of bedlam, the others tossed the waterlogged children up to them one by one. Once Patience had climbed into the tree, and Thomas followed her up from Benjamin's shoulders, Benjamin himself scaled the trunk like the mast of a ship and roared once more: As high as ye can climb! And all the Honeys in that old tree climbed with all their strength, the children screaming and crying, the men and women screaming and crying, until the whole soaked clan clung together and to the trunk in a trembling, grasping cluster at the top of that swaying, bending, mighty old tree snapping back and forth in the wind like a whip. And right then they all heard a greater thunder rumble from the clamor and the whole island quaked under them, telegraphing their extinction. And at that moment, Patience Honey, holding one of her grandbabies tight as could be against her side with one arm, and clenching the tree with the other, looked to the south, down the bay, and there she saw that piled ocean, all the trees and buildings and shrieking people and wagons and sloops and schooners churning in its saltwater guts, and an old sea captain named Burnham in his pilot coat rowing a dinghy on the blazing crest of it all, smoking a pipe, bowl-downward to keep the water out, crying for mad joy at this last rapturous pileup, and all of it, that great massif of water and ruin speeding right for the Honeys in their tree, which now seemed like a twig, a toothpick, a drenched blade of grass set against the immensity of that mountain range of ocean and demolition. What was always so eerie about it afterward, Patience always said, what was so terrifying about it that made her bowels feel as if they'd turned to sand, was how quiet it all seemed, like a breath drawn and held, right before it hit, how breathtakingly fast but nearly silent and so just plain beautiful it was, all those people and trees and ships and horses cartwheeling past within the billows. It wasn't silent, really, but more, so loud it was too big to hear. I could not hear it for that second, because it was just too big a sound for my ears to hear.

The water hit the south shore of the island first and swallowed it whole and smooth. Then it hit the jagged bedrock spine running up the middle of the island and broke over it hissing like a saw blade. When it struck the slope of the bluff it exploded across the horizon in front of the islanders in the tree, hung up and suspended for a moment in an apocalyptic entablature, that Patience afterward always said looked in that instant before it all collapsed back together and swept along how the parted sea must have appeared to the poor Israelites. I was pretty well given up on it all and in that tree holding it so hard the bark cut into my arms and gave me these scars and holding that baby so hard against me I thought I'd crack it, drenched to the marrow and screaming and trying not to let go, but when that tower of ocean and ruination burst apart in front of me, in a blink, but deep as my soul, I saw a broad, dry avenue running through the middle of the sea, and it was thronged with shepherds and sheep and old ladies on donkeys, litters of children curled up asleep on hay in the beds of rickety carts. The parted ocean towered on both sides, sheer, smooth, and monolithic. And inside the water, a pell-mell cavalcade of Egyptian men and horses and chariots scrolled past, tumbling heel over headdress, fetlock over cannon, bumper over shaft. Most of the men wore linen tunics, but some wore leopard skins and feathers and had elaborate headdresses. Some of them were tethered to their chariots by leather reins and held longbows. Arrows and spears twirled among the men and horses and cars. Their black-lined eyes stared wide open, but they were all clearly drowned. And I knew what it was like when God parted the sea. And I knew that Moses was way up there at the front of the line. Not like the idea of Moses, but the man himself. The very man, Moses. When God opened the ocean. Then the waters collected all the relic and rubble back up and swept over the rest of the island. The water churned and rose and rose up the Penobscot pine laden with the Honeys.

Patience looked down through the branches and limbs and watched the seething waters rise over her children's and grandchildren's feet, billow up their skirts and rise over their midriffs and up their exposed throats then into their sputtering mouths, and she watched their hair soak up the boiling waters, and she watched the waters swill Benjamin up, too, and she watched her daughter, Charity Honey, wrench free from the tree and tumble away in the wreckage clutching her baby son, David, in her arms, and the waters reached her feet and she felt something deep down in the bottom of the tree crack and give and the tree bowed and she was in the swift and roaring waters up to her waist. Then the tree levered itself back upright. Though it seemed not to swallow at her quite as greedily as it first had, the water still rose, and it reached Patience's collarbone and Patience always said she could still just see the top of Benjamin's head below her in the water, serene, almost, almost becalmed, tiny bubbles of air rising from his hair. And it was then, just as the water touched it at her throat, that Patience remembered the old flag she'd sewn for Benjamin from the bits and pieces of other flags and national rags and bedraggled patches, not long after they'd married and first settled their now drowning island, still tied around her neck. She always said later, I just decided right then that if we were all going to Judgment, I was going to fly our little flag until the last possible second. So, I hoisted that baby up even more and pressed it between the tree and my breast harder than I ever otherwise would have dared and freed my hand and somehow unknotted the flag from my neck and held it in my hand and held my hand up just as high as I could get it, and the wind took the flag up and snapped it and practically tore it from of my grasp but I kept hold and there it flew. Then the water rose over the baby, who'd gone past wailing and just stared, wedged between my body and the tree, dumbfounded at the pandemonium, wide-eyed and quiet as it burbled under, and the water reached my mouth and covered my face and went over my head, and still I held that foolish flag as high as I could, and the water rose up my shoulder, and the water rose up to my raised elbow, and the water rose up my forearm, and the water reached my wrist, and so there was just my one hand holding that motley little tattered flag sticking up above the surface of the flood, and the waters rose up my fingers, and just as my hand was about to disappear and that flag and all us Honeys be swallowed up in the catastrophe, the water stopped rising.

The surge struck the innermost of the bay, spilled onto the mainland, dumping the foremost of the ruin it had plowed along the way onto a campsite called Little Shell Cove, where a hundred years later campers still turned up trinkets from the calamity, and the cauldron of wrath doubled back on itself and withdrew, quaffing the people, creatures, pie safes, pews, and catboats it had failed to devour the first time caterwauling off toward the horizon.

The water stopped rising and seemed to pause. It was as if my hand and the sputtering flag were at the center of a great whirlpool guzzling the island down its throat but then the eddying slowed and stopped then began to unwind.

Patience Honey clung to the Penobscot pine under the water, the baby in her arms limp, eyes closed then, asleep against her breast inside the bosom of the sea. Patience looked down the length of the tree, into the garbled dark. Bodies clung to it below. Benjamin. Her cousin and best friend, Shekhinah Goodfellow. Deeper down, the island appeared to move. It began to revolve around the tree, like a dark stone wheel around a wooden axle. It was a whale—circling, nosing at Patience and the other fugitives newly arrived in his kingdom, until he caught sight of an ancient great white shark cruising through the schoolhouse, trolling for drowned children and spinster marms. The whale launched after its prehistoric nemesis and the monsters jetted away from the shallows of the newly drowned world back into the proper abyss.

I could no longer hold my breath. Just as I had to give out and inhale the Atlantic into my lungs and swallow it into my guts like a last meal of seawater soup, the whirlpool began to uncoil from around my hand and the flag and the water began to lower. My arm seemed to rise out of the water, then my head and body, along with the Penobscot pine, too, which rose like the mast of a wrecked ship unsinking. The ship—I mean, the island—and I surfaced and rose above the water and the wind dashed against my face and I gasped at the air and lost hold of the tree.

PATIENCE SHUCKED HERSELF from the mud and sand in which she lay face down at the base of the tree, the infant under her unrecognizable, not even clearly boy or girl, just a naked, wrung-out, be-slimed little pup squashed into the humus. She poked a finger in its mouth to unplug the earth from its throat. Its nose was clogged, too, so she sealed her mouth over the baby's whole face and sucked as hard as she dared and the muck uncorked and spattered into her mouth. She spat to the side and watched the child. The infant belched a ladleful of seawater, opened its eyes, which seemed as if they did not see, opened its mouth and for a moment lay petrified and silent. It barked and gurgled and gathered its breath and shrieked. The baby shrieked and shrieked and Patience thumbed gunk from its eyes and ears and looked at her husband.

Benjamin was pressed into the mud and debris, face up, staring at the low clouds sizzling and flashing overhead. Patience knew what he was thinking. She saw his hope and heart draining into the ocean with their lost children and grandchildren and with his apple trees, those trees that he had labored so long and so hard at because they reminded him of the one place he remembered being with his mother when he was a little boy. Grief overtook her and as she began to panic and cry hysterically and scrambled up, looking for who else was left, the baby still howling, too, she looked at her husband, who had come from nowhere and taken her away from nowhere to try to find somewhere, together, who she had loved the moment she first saw him, and she knew she had to fetch him back from the brink of the pit.

It's still Apple Island! she screamed, sobbing the name over wind and wailing child and through her own wailing that now felt like it was erupting straight out of her heart, spouting from her in gouts as she searched in every direction for her children and their children.

It's Apple Island! It *is* Apple Island!

Benjamin Honey looked at his wife crying to him—fierce and true. But she was wrong. His orchard, so fair in appearance, was a folly; his half-remembered Eden no sooner restored than carried off by a little wind and rain.

ESTHER FINISHED THE STORY of the flood. Halfway through the telling she always found herself saying, *I* held the baby, *I* couldn't hold my breath, which scared and thrilled everyone listening, nearly conjuring as it did their common, first mother. And so there the last of the Honeys were—fourth, fifth, and sixth generations' distillate of Angolan fathers and Scottish grandpas, Irish mothers and Congolese grannies, Cape Verdean uncles and Penobscot aunts, cousins from Dingle, Glasgow, and Montserrat, the wind thumping, the snow swirling, their stomachs growling, their toes and fingers burned black to icicles, crowding the cooling woodstove, the girls asleep, Ethan paused at his drawing—imagining that old local calamity—Eha, too, quieted, calmed, thoughtful, thrilled and hallowed by the story they all knew as well as the one from the Bible. Better, even.

Noah had his ark. The Honeys had Apple Island.

After another moment of quiet, Eha said, Dinner, and Grammy Esther roused sleeping Charlotte from her lap and Ethan woke Tabitha, sprawled on the floor, and the Honeys ate around the now cooling wood-stove and the wind and snow whistled and whirled outside.

Esther recited a bit of Scripture, Yet the dogs eat of the crumbs from the master's table.

Each child received a strip of salted cod, half a potato, and two roasted chestnuts, the last from the previous fall, to celebrate the coming spring. Eha removed the plug of tobacco tucked in his cheek, placed it gently on his knee, and ate his half potato in two bites. He closed his eyes, sighed two hymnal notes, and replaced the chew in his mouth. Grammy did not eat. She smoked her pipe and drank her tea, black as oil, smelly as tar, from a chipped china cup with no handle.

The first sundown of spring came over Apple Island. Light had been lingering later each evening, but the storm made for early dark. Eha could check his trap for a lobster after the storm. The children could scoop clams at low tide, midnight, Lotte holding the lantern in the dark, singing ghost songs, Ethan and Tabby digging in the icy sand.

Like his father and grandmother, Ethan, at fifteen, already had the habits into which all the islanders grew, of smoking or chewing tobacco or both and drinking mulchy black tea to nip morning, noon, and suppertime pangs if not real hunger. Hunger wore everyone to exhaustion, the family wrapped and huddled around the stove heads bowed, meager dinner almost making things worse.

TWO OTHER FAMILIES—the McDermotts, and the Larks—lived on Apple Island besides the Honeys, as well as old Annie Parker, who lived alone, and Zachary Hand to God Proverbs, who lived by himself, too, mostly inside a hollow tree although he also had a shack he'd built for himself years before. The three families lived within sight of one another on the north end of the island, in homes built on top of beds of crushed shells just above the beach. Annie Parker and Zachary Hand to God lived on the south end of the island, Annie on the west side, Zachary on the east. As night came and spring commenced beyond the borders of the spinning blizzard, all the souls on Apple Island hunkered in their homes and held out for fairer seasons.

THE LARKS LIVED not a quarter mile from the other families on the north end of the island but may as well have been camped on the Moon. Theophilus and Candace Lark were called cousins but the other adult Apple Islanders knew it was most likely that they were half-brother and sister and very possibly downright brother and sister. They had been the last of the Lark family, and the last of the island's variety of traits inherited from African fathers and Irish mothers, Penobscot grandmothers and Swedish grandpas almost seemed to have drained out of their clan, terminating, nearly, in the two wan, peaked cousins probably siblings, who had colorless hair and colorless eyes and who, after their parents passed within two days of one another in the winter of 1899, out of loneliness and grief continued their family together, having nine children, four of whom lived, all of whom inherited their parents' pale, colorless features and fragile constitutions, and all of whom were slightly harder of hearing, slightly nearer sighted, slightly more asthmatic, wholly more sensitive to sunlight than their parents, to such an extent that, except for Millie, who attended three hours of school each summer weekday, the Lark children were nocturnal and rarely up and about before sunset.

Theophilus and Candace managed to stave off starvation for themselves and their children like everyone else. Theo was a competent fisherman and seamster and fished for cod and flounder and did the mending for the laundry the McDermott sisters, Iris and Violet, took in from the mainland. The Lark children were largely left to themselves. Winters, they clustered together on the floor like a litter, often enough one, two, or all three of the semi-stray island dogs nestled among them, in a nest of rags and hay and old scraps of newspaper and canvas and the blanket sent by the relief society. Summer nights, the children wandered over the island alone or in pairs or a trio or the whole quartet, in the flour-sack dresses they wore, boys and girls alike, glowing under the moon against the dark earth, to appearances wandering aimlessly, spread across the meadows and woods like the ghosts of Apple Island's lost children. When Eha Honey came across the children late at night after he'd been clamming with a tide, they wordlessly encircled him and he, anticipating, gave each of them a littleneck clam, or periwinkle, or whelk. Sometimes he gave them oysters from his wire basket, which he shucked with his scrimshaw rigging knife, careful not to spill the broth. The girls poked the frilled, layered meat and slid it around the smooth insides of the carapaces. The boys sipped from the shells like teacups.

Theophilus Lark had been a decent fisherman, too, but when the relief society began sending food and supplies—a bowl or two here, a wooden spoon and a colander there (the colander disappeared the same day it arrived; the children swiped it so they could scoop sand and seaweed and shells and creatures from tide pools and watch the thin strings of water squirt from the holes)—he spent more and more time around the shack, puttering and fussing as if tending house. He fell without a thought to caring for the kitchen utensils, which he rubbed with his rag and lined up on the top of the pear crates they sometimes used for cleaning fish on. He wore a threadbare gingham dress and an old, dirt- and oil-stained apron that he carefully folded once over and tied around his waist as solemnly as if it were a Freemason's habit. The dress had been his mother's, the apron his grandfather's. Theophilus's grandfather had been a clerk in a shop on the mainland, in some small town Theophilus could not remember the name of. Theophilus's and Candace's mother had once told them that whenever a female customer entered the shop, their grandfather met the customer right there at the entrance, before she'd even closed the door behind her—Wearing this very apron I got on now, their mother had said—and he'd ask her, What lack ye, ma'am? Every time, just like that, What lack ye, ma'am?

So Theophilus poked around the shack and brooded over the pile of sleeping children like a mother robin, wearing the dress and shopkeeper's apron, and whenever any islander passed by he paused at his aimless chores or rose from the chair outside the door and came to the edge of the dirt yard and wrung his hands in an old red rag he took from the apron's front pocket, nodded at the passerby and said, What lack ye, Mr. Diamond? What lack ye, Eha Honey? To the children he asked, What lack ye, my little salted cods? What lack ye, my little oysters?

Candace Lark never liked housekeeping and was no good at it anyway. A particular squalor surrounded the Larks' shack when she had been in charge of domestic order. Much of that had been due to the children, who arrived one after another for eight years, counting the five that didn't live. But even considering mothering and scant means and the necessity of staying home while Theophilus fished, Candace lacked instinct for tending her kids and shack.

Candace was relieved at first that she no longer had to make a show of keeping house. Then she grew bored. Theophilus fiddled with the utensils and the children slept most of the day and were free to come and go as they liked all night, so she grew irritated by her brother's fussiness with the bowls and spoons and mug. It was as though he were playing shopkeeper. She kept silent because he meant well and she loved him, but watching him hum and wipe out the inside of the mug with his rag and hold it up to the light and look inside it and blow into it as if to get the last of the dust out of it then rub the inside with the rag again then hold it up and look inside it again made her want to snatch the mug and smash it on a rock and shout, The blasted Christing mug is *clean*!

So she began to fish.

One morning, Theophilus sat outside working his rag around the wooden bowl when Candace emerged from the shack wearing his leaky waders, carrying his handline, hooks, and leaders.

Going fishing, she said. Theophilus nodded.

Looks so, he said. Want I should—

No. Dory set?

Yep.

See you sundown.

Candace spent the day on the water, learning to keep her balance standing in the unsteady, narrow dory, and bobbing the line up and down, jigging for what exactly she did not know. She used some leftover chum Theophilus had in a bucket that smelled so horrendous when she took the cover off she gagged and nearly gave up. But she turned away and took a deep breath and wiped the tears streaming down her face and figured the stench was probably good for attracting fish. She baited the gangs of hooks on both lines and dropped them into the water and began to joggle them up and down. Eha passed at a distance in his peapod and Candace waved and he waved back.

The ocean teemed, lavish and wholesome. Sunlight fell across Candace's face and bare arms, sharp, antiseptic, fortifying. The air tasted full of salt and restorative minerals and felt invigorating to breathe deep into her lungs. The water pleated into little toppling waves and smoothed then puckered again. Candace's long hair whipped across her face. She'd have Theo shave her head next morning, she decided. The day and the work exhausted and enthralled her.

The Lark children awoke that evening, rose from the floor, and left the shanty to begin their roaming. As they started off, they met their mother panting and bedraggled on the path, smiling, cradling a twenty-pound cod with the handline, jig, and drail piled on top of it.

TABITHA AND CHARLOTTE HONEY played with Millie Lark and sometimes helped her to loosely shepherd her sister and brothers around so they would not get hurt or into serious trouble. (Most of the islanders had been and remained indulgent of the Lark children, but one or two would swat a child with a wooden spoon or cuff her on the ear and drive her off if they found her poking her head through the window or inside sitting on the only stool, licking a dirty dish.) Millie was the second Lark child but her younger brothers and older sister did not really talk and could not see very well and could not take very good care of themselves, so Millie kept half an eye on them through their wakeful nights. Mostly that meant either making sure her brothers, Camper and Duke, did not wade deep into the frigid ocean because, although they loved the sea so much that Theophilus said they'd been mackerels in their previous lives, they could not swim, and because they got hypothermia almost every time and lay arm and arm in the children's sleeping nest two days afterward blue and grinning, half delirious with joy. Or gently preventing her older sister, Rabbit, who eschewed nearly all human food and was the thinnest human being anyone had ever seen—gaunt, hollowed—from eating the bark off a spruce or peeling a starfish from a rock in a tide pool and biting its arms off one by one.

THE MCDERMOTT SISTERS, Violet and Iris, were the daughters of Ginny Black, Sarah Proverbs' sister Vidalia's daughter, and Terrence McDermott, Aaron McDermott's youngest son's youngest son. Ginny and Terrence had both been dark—both Congolese, they claimed—but with the island's usual mingled background of darker and lighter, African and European forbears, the full range of their ancestors' features were expressed in Violet and Iris as if through a prism. Violet had milky skin and tightly curled burnished-copper red hair that flared red beneath the sun and fuller moons, and had her parents' broad nose, across which dry dark freckles were speckled. Her mouth was full, like her parents' as well, her lips pale. Her eyes were the color of greening copper. Iris had her parents' acorn dark skin, but the narrow nose and thin lips of her Irish ancestors persisted in her face, as did their hair, which she inherited straight and black. She had one brown eye the color of loam and the other eye winter morning sky blue, it being the watchful eye of their great-aunt Sarah Proverbs herself that came back in an island daughter every now and then to see for herself that her kin were making do and behaving Christianly, according to Ginny, who told the twins that Iris was the third girl on the island since the Honeys had settled it to have one brown and one blue eye.

Violet and Iris lived together in the cabin of an old schooner their grandfather, Ainsley McDermott, had fitted down into a stone foundation. The cabin stood three feet high and had to be entered and exited through its original scuttle. Because it was mostly underground, it was the warmest home on the island in the cold and the coolest in the heat.

The sisters lived by taking in washing from Foxden. They boiled people's clothes and sheets in a huge old hog scalding pot set over a banked fire in the middle of the dirt yard and kept two washtubs on the roof of the cabin, one for scrubbing the stewed clothes over a washboard, the other full of cold water for rinsing. One sister tended the fire and shaved chips of lye soap into the simmering water and rowed the dirty laundry around the cauldron with a forked hardwood stick the size of a canoe paddle. The other sister worked at the washtubs standing in the open scuttle of the cabin. The sisters drank four kettles a day of tea so black that light could not pass through it, and like Esther Honey they smoked mugwort in clay pipes. The women's teeth were stained from the tea and smoke but otherwise strong and straight except for an impressive gap between Violet's top front teeth, through which she could launch a jet of tea and hit a dog in the ear from ten feet, to the glee of the island children. The sisters were forty years old. They looked sixty but for the fact that they were both especially physically strong even for islanders and unlike almost everyone else neither had ever had whooping cough, mumps, measles, scarlet fever, croup, pneumonia, asthma, or any other of the illnesses that beset their fellows and commonly sent them to the burial plot in the clearing in the trees in the middle of the island. Both women had lye burns on their hands and forearms. They were poor as church mice, but they liked to remind everyone that they still made more money than any man ever had on Apple Island.

Neither Iris nor Violet married or courted, to the extent that such a word described how young people on the island took up with one another and started families. At the age they'd have longed and looked for partners there were no boys or men of right age. Violet complained about the poverty of men while she did the washing or stacked wood or plucked weeds from the garden. Once, some man who must have seen one or the other sister picking up or returning a load of washing on the mainland rowed over one night and squirmed through the grass, as if every Lark child and Eha, up with the tide, could not see him clear as a snake on open sand, thinking he'd sneak into the cabin to get at whichever sister he'd seen. He writhed down the dark scuttle into the cabin, where Iris was waiting for him with a flatiron. She split his forehead open and that wicked little serpent twisted and writhed all the way back to his boat, blinded by its own blood pouring over its eyes. From the shadows, Rabbit Lark watched the brained man slither past. She held a robin's nest to her mouth, eating the pale blue eggs from it one by one.

Men held no interest for Iris. She preferred talking with and about the island women—sisters, aunts, cousins, and grannies—about what they knew and only told one another when no men or boys were around, and reciting what she and Violet learned from them like a psalter.

Iris and Violet cared for three children—two sisters and a brother, named Norma, Emily, and Scotty Sockalexis. The children were the orphans of a Penobscot woman named Cheryl who had shown up on the island with them five years earlier, in 1906, out of nowhere. She claimed her husband had died on a log drive down the Penobscot River and that she was the sister of Louis and Andrew Sockalexis, from Old Town. Louis had played professional baseball for the Cleveland Spiders, she said, and Andrew—Drew (only she could call him that, she said)—was going to run in the 1908 Olympic Marathon in London. They were going to come for her and the children when they got their money. Meantime, could they stay here. She didn't like it in town and she didn't have any money otherwise. She and the children looked like they'd been living in the woods.

Iris and Violet conferred.

She's nobody's sister.

She is not.

Nobody's bride.

Without doubt.

I guess she's worse off than us.

I'd say so.

Violet resisted taking Cheryl and the kids in at first because, she said, she didn't trust Indians.

Iris said, Vi, it's not Indians you can't trust, it's people. Men, mostly, if you want to know the truth. Maybe white men most of all, I'll grant—and you know what I mean; *plain white;* not the color of their skin but the state of their minds, just like being a man or a lady is a state of mind. But it's a veritable prejudice to say you don't trust Indians as a rule.

Anyway, some man, or men, white ones by the looks of the children—
or Norma and Scotty at least—Emily's skin looked like brick cooling
from red hot to brown—certainly had done wrong by this Cheryl Sockalexis, whether on purpose or by default.

Iris and Violet said Cheryl and the children could stay.

Cheryl helped with the washing and was good in the garden. The
children began to go to school. Candace Lark found some sailcloth and
gave it to Theophilus and he made simple, stiff smock dresses for the
girls that stood up on their own when they were not being worn and a
pair of pants and a shirt for Scotty that stood up on their own, too, and
gave them to Cheryl. Cheryl combed Norma and Emily and Scotty's
hair and listened to them repeat the maths and Bible verses Matthew
Diamond taught them. Norma and Scotty were adequate students, but
Emily proved to be so adept at mathematics that she finished Matthew
Diamond's modest curriculum in a month and he had to ask the society
for an algebra textbook so he could teach it to himself first then Emily.

After two months, satisfied her children were in a good way, Cheryl
Sockalexis left the island one night and was never heard from again.

ZACHARY HAND TO GOD PROVERBS lived in a hollow oak tree. At least,
he spent as much time in the tree as the weather would allow without
freezing to death. The tree stood on a rise on the lower southeast edge
of the island, with its opening in the lee of the prevailing winds. Zachary was a master carpenter and woodworker and his one-room shack
sat back from the tree, nestled in a granite hollow, sound and sealed and
square, built by Zachary himself, with the tools Benjamin Honey himself had first brought to the island. Like that of everyone else on Apple
Island, Zachary's age was a mystery, or unknown in any case—not a
mystery to himself or the other islanders because none of them followed

any calendar and keeping track of how many years old somebody was never occurred to them. It would have been a mystery to them why someone would bother doing such a thing, as a matter of fact. Whatever age he was, Zachary was old, older than Esther Honey, who was probably the next oldest islander left, old enough to have come to the island as a very young man in January of 1866 after the war ended and after the 29th Connecticut Colored Infantry Regiment he'd fought in had been decommissioned because he'd heard about the island from one of the Virginians he'd fought alongside who'd said his father had known a man named Honey a long time ago who it was said had gone north and founded an all colored town on an island. Zachary had lived his entire life on Apple Island since then.

Neither Zachary nor anyone else on the island thought of him as a hermit, though he spent his time in the tree pondering the meaning of creation, the meaning of his and his fellow islanders' mean existences, and carving scenes from the Bible into the insides of the tree. He had begun, at his own eye level, with simple subjects that he practically scratched into the wood like a child whittling graffiti with a shard of slate. But he found the labor calming, engrossing, and it lent itself to his meditations. Being a fine carpenter, he soon adapted certain of Benjamin Honey's old awls and files to his purpose and began cutting arcades of alternating capitals and apertures in which he depicted Samuel beheading Saul, Judas kissing Christ, Christ sending the devils into the swine, Isaiah naked in the street, rebuking. He carved more and more slowly, in more and more detail, with more and more expertise, integrating tricks and perplexities, deeper layers of background. He loved, in order, sculpting robes, vegetation, faces, and most of all, hands, through which he took special joy in expressing despair, support, betrayal, supplication, forgiveness, healing, benediction, blessing, revenge, comfort, and murder, hands raised high, hanging limp, clenched, slack, palms out, extended, turned in, retracted, bathing feet, supporting elbows, wiping tears, tightening nooses, drawing swords, jabbing vinegar sops, thrusting spears, caressing sleeping faces.

Zachary worked by the light of a candle. As the carvings rose higher up the tree, he made them narrower and more convoluted in order to draw out the composition of each figure and scene so he would not run out of space before he ran out of mortal time, so that he would not complete a work at which he felt more and more he should finish his days laboring, dying as he etched the most elegant possible toes for a barefoot mother weeping for her child. When he finished a ring of scenes, he removed the log upon which he stood to carve and replaced it with another, slightly taller log and began the next level. By the time he and the other islanders were evicted, anyone looking into the hollow of his tree would see a thick log and Zachary's feet and half his shins disappearing into the upper insides of the trunk. When he was not in the tree pondering and performing these devotions, the carvings visible at eye level, from the outside, looked childish and crude. Had anyone—Rabbit Lark, say—managed to set the log (which Zachary rolled behind his shack and covered in cut brush when he was not using it) and climb on it up into the dark tree, and had she brought a candle of her own, and, preferably, a large, strong magnifying glass with which to examine every detail; had she lit the candle and seen the feasts and processions and births and murders, the ascensions and descents, the riots and adoring congregations all flared before her and around her, all with such depths the flickering candle light would have made the figures and animals seem to heave and surge and dance and stagger in the backgrounds each time the flame was brought directly in front of a section to see the movement clearly everything in it freezing still and everything in its periphery stirring and rising into obscure motion, and the levels reaching upward beyond the candle's light into the dark heights of the tree, she would have felt as if she'd been transported to some dim, flickering, otherworldly cathedral, creation itself as close as the cold tip of her nose and as prehistoric as the first breath that broke upon the waters.

ON ESPECIALLY FINE Sundays, the Proverbs sisters sometimes tried to lure Zachary from his tree.

Uncle Zachary, come out of that rotten old tree and have some tea with us.

It looks like you're stood up dead in your own coffin there, Uncle Zach. Won't you come out and let us make you some supper.

It was true. The old man, hands clasped, eyes closed, looked like a contented, perfectly preserved corpse, grateful for true rest. Zachary thought on that while his neighbors tried to lure him out. Eha can cut a plank and shave it to fit the opening and seal me right up inside. The old man smiled and sighed and snuggled his shoulders deeper against the curve of the wood.

He is not coming out.

He is not.

What is it about that tree?

Well, we'll bring tea later.

And flowers. Lupine in Skunk Meadow.

Zachary liked when the sisters left a cup of their special black tea and a spray of flowers at the opening of the cleft. It made the tree feel like a shrine.

The tree opened in the lee of the prevailing southwestern winds, so when it stormed during his devotions he enjoyed the rains and the blowing in the comfort if usually cold, soaking confines of what he had come to feel was his true home. He had carved two niches inside the tree to the left and right of the opening. The right niche was lined with a patch of tin and Zachary lit a votive candle in it as often as the winds blew it out.

A small ivory crucifix stood in the left niche. During storms, he spoke to the ivory Christ and the candle flame ruffled and bowed and straightened and bowed again as the wind snuffled around and into the trunk and scuffled its way back out. The tree swayed in the wind and Zachary moved along within the tree, comforted in that snug wooden berth like he'd never otherwise been.

Some mornings Esther Honey came at sunrise for the pleasures of addressing Zachary in the old speech of their grand-grandparents and giving gratitude for past and ongoing kindnesses.

How is it with thee this morning, Zachary Hand to God? she asked, shivering and pleased.

It is well, Esther Honey, especially to start the day with you. How art thou?

Sometimes the children found Zachary meditating or dozing, it was impossible to distinguish. They stood trying to be quiet, hoping to startle him when he awoke. He let them fidget and juffle a while then opened one fierce bug-eye, slowly, and glared, which made them scream. Scotty Sockalexis threw a stone at him once and it struck the old man on the forehead. Zachary did not stir and the children ran away, sure Scotty had killed him. He went around with a fat purple goose egg over his right eye for a week and never said a word.

Rabbit Lark collected crickets and wrapped them in mint leaves and munched them and watched Zachary carving late into the summer nights.

THERE WERE THREE DOGS on the island, too—a maniacal little terrier called Fitzy that single-handedly kept the island nearly free of rats; a gigantic, imperturbable brindled mastiff named Grizzly, who had the habits of fetching the island children from the water whether they liked it or not and sometimes gently sitting on them when he thought they were being naughty or too mean toward one another; and a friendly but emotionally fragile mutt with brown body, black mask, and white socks, called Sulky, that if spoken to sharply went off in a huff and found a corner and stared at it for an hour. The dogs roamed freely, sovereign, liable to no one, loved by all. They lounged in yards and patrolled the shores. Grizzly loved lying on top of Eha Honey's feet, leaning up against his legs. Fitzy was happiest with a dead or dying rat in his jaws, which he'd parade around the island with until he was sure everyone had seen his latest trophy. Sulky especially liked being around Iris and Violet and the Sockalexis children when they did the washing. When it was cold, the dogs all slept together with the Lark children in their nest.

The islanders gave the dogs what few scraps they could spare—fish heads, apple cores, crumbs of bread too moldy for a person to eat.

SO MANY FREEZING, starving days and nights on the island. So many weeks on end in the dark, huddled together, praying, whispering for light, a little warmth, a little bread.

Winter blizzarded and blustered for another week, then deferred to spring. Spring ruled, noisy and bright, and deferred to summer.

MATTHEW DIAMOND PUNCTUALLY arrived at his summer home in Foxden, visible right across the channel, on the evening of each June 20th and signaled his coming to the islanders by raising a U.S. flag up a pole in his yard the next morning at dawn.

Mr. Diamond is back.

Yep, saw a light in the window last night. Must've got in late.

Yep, there he is.

Five minutes after the flag went up, Mr. Diamond could be seen coming across the channel in his boat, which the relief society had raised funds to buy a motor for the previous year, so he would no longer have to row his way back and forth each day, regardless of whether the tide was with or against him. At first, the boat was a white wedge on the water. Then Mr. Diamond became visible, dressed in his dark suit, hunched slightly forward, one hand reached back and guiding the new motor. The children and Eha went down to the landing where they met Iris and Violet McDermott and the Sockalexis children and waited for the boat to strike shore. The children jumped up and down and crisscrossed their arms above their heads as if the boat might miss them on the beach and pass without stopping. Mr. Diamond raised his free hand and waved it back and forth over his head. Eha bowed slightly and doffed his derby. Iris and Violet frowned and nodded. Mr. Diamond cut the motor, the boat glided the last several yards and nosed into the sand, and the old missionary arrived once again on Apple Island.

ESTHER HONEY NEITHER liked nor trusted Matthew Diamond. He was fully white and her monster of a father had been fully white or looked it, anyway. Esther's aunts had warned her when she was a girl that her father had bad blood, had thin, watery blood—simple, they called it— no vigor to it, unfortified. And that was even before her sister, who was as light-skinned as their father, left the island, on her own for good, without a word, when she was barely old enough to be called a woman, because their father'd started trying to get at her, and before her mother got sick and went to bed and died, and before her father had taken Esther herself up like a wife, had put away the Bible and the Shakespeare he'd taught her and her sister to read and put her in the part her mother had played and acted like she was his wife and not his daughter and she'd gotten pregnant because she couldn't just leave the island like her sister because she was as dark-skinned as her mother had been, and she'd had Eha.

Esther loathed her father and his memory with a steady, seething rage it had taken her years to cool to a simmer and her dislike of Mr. Diamond felt like the same sort, if not half as furious. Whenever he was around, her kidneys ached and her arthritis burned. Summers, always her favorite season, now unnerved her because of his daily presence. A decent man, well intentioned, almost certainly, she thought. Truth be told, he was as mild and gentle and apparently smart as any man she'd ever seen, and that made it hard to square with her worst feelings. But he made her think of her father every time. It was involuntary; it just befell her, like a bad dream. So it was almost as if her father had never stumbled off the bluff to his death the night after she gave birth to Eha. Or, it was like he had stumbled and fallen to his death, then haunted her ever since (and he had—Esther thought that was him standing in the sea, half-hidden behind a rock at the bottom of the bluff, or that was his shadow cast onto the water below the landing even though there wasn't anyone standing above it on the dock, or she saw a silhouette in the top of a bare tree during a winter dusk and knew it was him because he crawled all around it, spidery and silent, and even the outermost, thin-as-fingers branches did not so much as twitch under his weightless creeping) and now his ghost had deputized this otherwise kindly-seeming man to do his haunting for him.

When Matthew Diamond had first come to the island and first paid a visit to the Honeys' home, after having rowed across the channel and dodged and parried and landed a couple reluctant kicks in the ribs of the dogs as they barked and snapped and howled at the stranger, he'd stood between Esther and the ocean, backlit, face in shadow, hat in hand, a little ruffled and sweaty, a little out of breath, but mild and calm, and introduced himself and told them about the school the relief society was going to pay to have built, by him, of course, and any islanders who might be able to help, how he'd teach math and grammar and geography and some Latin and a little art, too.

I was once a bit of a painter, he'd said. Not very good, and it was a long time ago, now, but enough to teach the children a little about drawing and color. My Latin is still good and I'll teach Scripture, too, of course.

Smiling so far as Esther could see, sincere so far as she could hear, but at the news there'd be a school and this Mr. Diamond would be with them every day during summers, she'd been certain there would not be a soul left on the island within five years. She'd heard it all before, threats and promises both, threats being far more common than promises, but either way no one had ever actually set foot on the island to see out their intentions, well-meaning or otherwise. She believed, and every story she'd ever heard from any of the old islanders confirmed, that no good ever came of being noticed by mainlanders, which always meant being noticed by white people—plain white, her mother and aunts and cousins called them, to distinguish them from the lighter-skinned Apple Islanders, in whose veins ran blood from every continent but Antarctica, just like everyone else's there, no matter what shade their skin. Beware, she could hear her mother and aunts saying in those low tones to which mainlanders were deaf. Keep an open eye on this one. The more good he tries to do, the more outside attention he'll bring, and that's no good. No good at all.

Now, here the mainlanders were, on Apple Island, in the form of this courteous, plain white man who turned Esther's guts because he reminded her of her father and whose coming surely forecasted disaster. Courteous, and innocent, really, Esther thought, but innocent as in, as in—she searched for the word and it came to her from Shakespeare, from Hamlet—innocent as in artless. He was not innocent in the sense of being blameless, but in the sense of being oblivious to the greater, probably utter, catastrophe into which the, yes, artless graciousness of bringing the school and lessons would draw them all.

THEN CAME THE precious, indigo nights of August, a breathy calm ocean almost slumbering, dreaming of its own depths. The last light slaked west. The world sailed into the high caverns of night and everyone on the island came outdoors and sat together in pairs or trios or quartets, quiet, remarking now and then on the evening. Someone sang a song somewhere, maybe Violet McDermott tipping the last tub of wash water behind the schooner cabin. The children explored and wandered and called to one another, the summer constellations humming, their light pulsing in time with the revolution of the planet.

Tabitha had plucked flowers all morning. Noon, she'd braided them into bright rings of white, red, lilac, and green. At sunset, when the Lark children appeared, silent in the first long shadows, Tabby stood them in a line and crowned each one with a garland, chanting Latin proverbs as she went: *Qui pinget florem, non pinget floris odōrus; Dum Aurōra fulgit flores collĭgĭte* . . . . The chaplets had wilted since morning and settled limply on the children's glowing white heads. The blossoms released their fading scents, as if in harmony with the last light inside the clouds and sky beneath which the island lingered in an eventide of peace, and off drifted the Larks, enflowered, ordained to the night.

Eha watched the children from the yard. They were white and dim. They looked like they were floating. They seemed happy to delight him and the other adults with the secret of levitation. Eha hooted low and husky to them, like the mother owl. The mother owl hooted back from the Penobscot pine and the happy children sailed away in their different directions and dissolved into the dark.

The first international congress on eugenics is taking place this month in London, England. In his opening remarks, Major Leonard Darwin, son of the famous Charles Darwin, spoke of the dangers of interfering with Nature's ways. He said all gathered must pledge aloud that to give themselves the satisfaction of succouring their neighbor in distress—without at the same time considering the effects likely to be produced by their charity on future generations—was to say the least weakness and folly. We in Foxden and its surrounding communities would do well to weigh the wisdom of Dr. Darwin's words, considering the band of Nature's "problem children" drifting off our shore on Apple Island.

MATTHEW DIAMOND LAY awake most nights, nearly until first light, when exhaustion overtook his regrets. No matter how many worries, practical or invented, his brain scrambled over, he always circled back to what he'd written to his old friend from seminary, Thomas Hale, in a moment of dreadful, naked candor, after his first week with the Apple Islanders, four—no, five—years earlier, when he'd written out, in words, in ink, on paper, for all time, although he was neither so vain as to imagine his letters would ever find their way into posterity nor so naïve as to fool himself into thinking that what he wrote in words in ink on paper would have been any less true or known by God if they had only remained in his skewed, inexcusable heart, *that despite all the spiritual & intellectual convictions by which my God & my Scripture have fortified me since I can remember, & in which I have wholly believed if appallingly never felt—that all men are my brothers, all women my sisters, all souls my family—I nevertheless feel a visceral, involuntary repulsion whenever I am in the presence of a living Negro.*

MATTHEW DIAMOND WANTED to teach the Apple Island children about everything in the world, from the newest moon orbiting Saturn, called Phoebe, to Queen Elizabeth, *that Occidental Starre.* He wanted them to know the Declaration of Independence and to memorize the Emancipation Proclamation of 1863. He wanted to teach them how to compose sentences in Latin and recite lines of Shakespeare and Milton. So, he had. Most of the children learned as most children do—peevishly, fitfully, with modest success. Some had learned with inexplicable ease and passion. Otherwise blithe Tabitha Honey took to Latin as if she were not learning it but remembering it. Geometry elated somber Emily Sockalexis; she sopped it up so avidly that Matthew Diamond soon had had to relearn much of it himself in order to help her keep advancing. And Ethan Honey drew almost as well as any art school student.

Matthew had a room in the schoolhouse for nights when he did not go back to the mainland. He sometimes stayed so he could start a fire in the woodstove at first light if it was stormy and cold, or copy a stanza of Keats on the chalkboard before the children arrived. *Perhaps the selfsame song that found a path / Through the sad heart of Ruth, when, sick for home, / She stood in tears among the alien corn.* Sometimes, he stayed to teach himself the next math lesson for Emily Sockalexis, or prepare a passage for Tabitha Honey to compose in Latin, or an assignment that would challenge Ethan Honey's skills at drawing. Sometimes, he stayed in the hope that it might help rid him of a degree of his—there was no other word for it—disgust, which, also incomprehensible but a relief, he did not feel toward any of the children, only the adults.

Children were forbidden to enter Mr. Diamond's room, so it would not become infested like every other chamber on the island with bed bugs and lice. The children obeyed the rule with the solemnity of law. They made a show of not even looking into his room if he left the door an inch ajar when they arrived for classes in the morning. If the door was not shut and Mr. Diamond was there, they deputized someone who backed up to it, eyes shut, hand blindly waving for it until she found the knob and drew the door closed, as if even seeing what were inside the room might turn her to stone. It was like a skit or a play they performed, to show him how much they respected him and his cleanliness. If Mr. Diamond happened to be writing on the chalkboard with his back to the class or outside ringing the bell, the children strained to see what they could through the slim open space, hoping to glimpse what book he had open on the neatly made bed or a letter on the table he might be composing to another missionary friend who was teaching children their own age in China.

Matthew Diamond discovered during his first summer on Apple Island that Esther Honey herself not only could read but regularly read both the Bible and a tattered sheaf of pages from Shakespeare's plays she kept tied together with string. He asked her who'd taught her to read the Bible, and who'd introduced her to Shakespeare. A dreadful kind of palsy seemed to overtake the woman's whole body.

Father, she said and sat, silent, furious it seemed, even, waiting to move on or end the conversation, and possibly any further conversations, right then should he ask about that any further. So he didn't ask any more questions about that and once or twice each summer he'd find time to visit just with her and sit outside the Honeys' shack and talk about poor Lear and poor Job, steadfast Cordelia and wicked Lady Macbeth, brave Ruth and Hannah and Esther's mighty namesake.

Poor Lear. He had disobedient children.

I like how he ended up in rags. Imagine, a king dressed in beggar's rags.

Expose thyself to feel what wretches feel.

How Shakespeare loved to get his kings into rags.

Strip thy own back.

The King in heaven a servant; every king on earth a tyrant.

Poor, impatient Lear. His hard old heart only softened in the breaking.

EXCEPT FOR MILLIE, the Lark children did not attend school or Bible lessons. If it was a cloudy, dark day and she roused before the sun began to set, once in a while Rabbit Lark would drift into the classroom. Mr. Diamond and the children said, Hello, Rabbit, and let her be until she bit a stick of chalk or took a sip from the inkwell. Then Mr. Diamond took his own apple from the desk and held the girl's hand and led her back outside. He plucked a sprig of seaweed from Rabbit's hair, which looked like it had a scoop of wet sand worked into it.

The children will be done soon, Mr. Diamond said. Why don't you wait here for Millie? He guided the girl to sit on the back step. You may sit right here and have my apple.

Sit here and eat the apple and the others will be out soon.

Rabbit bit off the top of the apple, fruit, stem, and core and tried to swallow it whole. It corked her windpipe. She kecked it up, chewed it twice more, swallowed, and it went down. She stood and left.

Next time, Mr. Diamond thought, he'd slice up the apple first. He returned to the classroom. Who can tell me the first line of President Lincoln's Gettysburg address? he asked.

Dr. Darwin told the congress of doctors and scientists assembled from around the world that Cleopatra, who was the daughter of a brother and sister, is the perfect example against the deformed issue of incestuous marriages. That she was the crown jewel of a beautiful race may be accepted. But what doubt is there, he asked, that, were she alive today, she would be admitted to the manic-depressive floor at a hospital for the insane, with histories of paranoia and nymphomania? Another question we in Foxden should pose of our local situation, unwholesome as it is.

WISH CHALK TASTED like white snaps when I bite white sticks or unhappy man clicks white sticks on black wall and makes white bugs and white chalk clicks like a white click bug in a click white bush. Honey is bitter to the wicked, acid sweet.

THE FIRST COMMITTEE from the Governor's Council to inspect the settlement and residents of Apple Island consisted of three councillors, the council secretary, two doctors—one a general surgeon, the other a specialist in phrenology and brain physiology, with a particular interest in subjects deteriorated by inbreeding, both members of the Section on Eugenics in the American Breeders' Association—and an intern from the hospital in Bayport, along with a reporter from the *Foxden Journal* newspaper, a widow, really, who owned a majority share in the paper and commandeered column inches once a month in order to scold the town about its civic and moral shortcomings or to heap praise on some trifle of good manners or piety she'd seen in church or on the street downtown. A young photographer clattered behind the group with his heavy equipment. Behind the rest of the party, a quiet, scowling, stout block of a man in a dark suit and dark derby followed, his jacket open, a pistol handle jutting out from its leather holster under his left arm. Matthew Diamond accompanied the group from household to household.

The committee began with Iris and Violet Proverbs and the Sockalexis children. Violet was in the yard, stirring a load of overalls and dresses in the scalding pot. Iris and Emily Sockalexis stood back-to-back in the open scuttle of the pilothouse, Iris scouring a dress over a washboard at one washtub, Emily pummeling a pair of denim pants through the cold rinse water in the other. Scotty and Norma Sockalexis struggled to spread a wet bed sheet over the split-rail fence for drying.

Violet saw the group first and called out to her sister. Iris shouted to them who were they, still scrubbing the dress.

We're from the governor's office. And doctors.

Doctors, huh? Iris stopped her washing and studied the group. I didn't know doctors traveled in gangs. She wiped her hands on her apron and told Emily to finish rinsing the pants then finish with the dress. She climbed down into the pilothouse and came out the front door.

We need to see the other girl, too. And them, one of the men said, nodding toward Norma and Scotty, who stood holding either end of the sopping sheet, staring at the intruders. The other men began looking around the yard, noting the layout, the ammoniac stink of the boiling soap, the messy hopper bin full of white ash where the sisters drew the lye, the patched and worn clothes the children wore.

Iris grabbed the laundry stick from Violet and brandished it at the men.

You're not anyone we know, she said. Stay away from there. And you—get!

This is an official matter of the state, one of the councillors said.

State my eye.

Now, Iris, please, Matthew Diamond said. I don't like this any more than you, but they *are* here on the state's authority, and there's nothing we can do right now to change that.

One of the doctors had brought a pair of metal calipers from his medical kit and without having asked was fitting them on either side of Scotty's head even as the boy still held one end of the wet sheet. Violet dashed over and batted the bizarre tool out of the doctor's hands. Scotty dropped the sheet and tears spilled from his eyes.

Get that damned ice picker away from his head. Violet gathered Scotty close and cradled his head against her bosom.

The doctor stooped and picked the calipers up and wiped them clean with the forearm of his coat.

It's not an ice—It is a scientific instrument. It—It won't hurt. This is necessary, ma'am. Please just—

Necessary my teeth, Violet said. Go near him with that thing again and I'll— She feinted at the doctor as if to punch him.

Matthew Diamond said, Violet, no! Just. Just *stop* and I'll help sort this out. I can write to the—

Mr. Diamond, Violet said without taking her eyes off the alarmed doctor, you're a good man as far as it goes, but your letters ain't worth balls on a ewe, pardon me, and I'm going to write a busted jaw right on this cute flatlander's face, and she feigned another lunge at the doctor.

The doctor jumped back and Matthew Diamond tried to get in between him and Violet, who launched herself at the man full bore. Iris was about to charge the head councillor and run him through with the laundry stick. But then the stout man in the dark derby and dark suit with the pistol sticking out from under his arm coughed, *Ahem!* loud as a giant, once, from where he stood on the path just outside the yard. He looked up from his shoes and found Iris's gaze and stared straight at her and frowned even more deeply and shook his head back and forth. Then without moving his head so much as half an inch he raised a brow and turned his eyes to Violet.

The sisters and Matthew Diamond stopped and took in the man with his dark derby and dark suit and that pistol under his arm. Iris tossed the stick on the ground at the head councillor's feet and Violet slackened from her boxer's stance.

Well, Violet said. So it's like that.

Just like that, Iris said. She turned her head to the side, keeping eye contact with the man, and spat. Exactly just like that.

The man nodded and tipped his hat and resumed frowning at his shoes.

Good Christ, ladies, Matthew Diamond hissed under his breath. Please, just keep your wits. And think of the children—

The doctors measured the women and children's skulls and foreheads and cheekbones and noses and ears and mouths. They checked their arms and hands and legs and feet and checked their teeth with wooden tongue depressors, all the while dictating numbers and mysterious comments to the intern, who repeated the numbers and comments out loud.

Four and seven eighths.

Four and seven eighths.

Sixteen and a quarter.

Sixteen and a quarter.

Brachycephalic.

Brachycephalic.

THE COMMITTEE EXAMINED the Honeys and it was all Esther could do to stop herself from screaming as she watched a doctor measure Charlotte's and Tabitha's heads with the calipers. Something about those grown men pushing and pawing at them, at all of them, but especially the girls. The doctor manipulated her head this way and that while she sat in her rocking chair glaring at Matthew Diamond. The doctor ran a tape measure front to back and side to side and pressed a metal ruler on the middle of her forehead. He called out numbers, too, and muttered, Huh, and, Mm-hmm. He took her chin in his hand and she startled and groaned out loud.

Be still, he said. This is just like a normal checkup.

Neither Esther nor any of the other islanders had ever had a checkup or been within ten miles of a hospital.

The doctor thumbed Esther's gums up and down in order to see her teeth and jawline.

Matthew Diamond said, Doctor, really—is all this—

Yes, it is all necessary, the doctor said, feeling along Esther's jawline. His fingers were soft and smelled like turpentine.

Matthew Diamond imagined the doctor's mother sitting in a parlor with tall, bright windows, in a dark velvet dress with lace at the cuffs and neck, the doctor with his arm resting on the mantel as he prodded at the fire with a poker. He would never dream of saying, Mother, there are some measurements I need to take. . . .

The other doctor adjusted a micrometer around one of Eha's nostrils.

Livestock, Matthew Diamond thought. No. Lower than that. He wanted to say, This woman can recite *Hamlet*, you know.

The doctor continued measuring Eha, murmuring to the intern, Mulatto; high-grade imbecile, or moron; insanity; probable eroticism.

The intern from the hospital showed Tabitha and Charlotte and Ethan images, of a telephone, a steam engine, President Taft, and asked them what and who they were and recorded in a notebook that the subjects could not identify any of the objects or persons depicted. Matthew Diamond wanted to say, this girl could answer your questions in Latin.

The photographer, a man named Bernard Richardson, set up his elaborate wood and brass tripod and mounted the wood and brass boxed camera on top of it and took portraits of the islanders, singly, in couples, and in whole families. He composed a class picture of the children and Matthew Diamond at the school.

The widow, whose name was Norma Clearland, interviewed Matthew for the paper and asked questions meant to demonstrate her own scriptural mastery. When Matthew gave answers Norma did not like, about religious instruction or the mixed-race students, she drew her chin back and primmed her mouth, as if refraining from correcting the naïve older man only because of the dire circumstances in which he toiled.

The committee finished its investigation and left.

A WEEK LATER, an article by Norma Clearland appeared in the *Foxden Journal* newspaper, surrounded by advertisements for fig syrup, fresh mined coal, small trousers at smaller prices, and Harvard cigars.

HOMELESS APPLE ISLAND RESIDENTS MADE
WARDS OF STATE: QUEER SQUATTERS DEEMED
DEGENERATE, IN NEED OF ASSISTANCE

A reporter recently accompanied a Governor's Council to notorious Apple Island, to investigate that little rock's queer brood of paupers and the squalor in which they live. The formation of the Council no doubt was inspired in large part by the meeting of the first international congress on eugenics, held this summer in London—a most welcome gathering of the greatest minds from North America and Europe to bring the authority and clarity of science to bear on the matter of the races. There is no disputing scientific fact, and the decision by the Council to make the islanders wards of the state has been made on that very basis.

The typical Apple Island family traditionally has had a turncoat white for a father, a scrawny frau black as coal for a mother, or vice versa, and a litter of tan children their issue. What a blood inheritance for the little ones. The settlement is more like a shantytown than a village. All souls cohabitate this way and that, black, white, mulatto indifferent. All are related by blood, and many or most are clinically idiotic as well as lazy.

The only encouraging sign in the midst of the blight is a neat, well-swept, single-room schoolhouse. This unlikely institution of learning continues to be presided over by Matthew Diamond, a retired schoolteacher from Massachusetts who has been trying to redeem the lost souls on Apple Island for five summers now.

Mr. Diamond has instructed the island children in subjects such as mathematics, reading, writing, basic hygiene, and Christian morals. A reporter found a schoolroom full of clean, neatly dressed children who two years ago could not write nor do sums nor recite a passage of Scripture, never mind properly wash their hands or comb their hair. Today, most of them can read short sentences, count, cite the Lord's Prayer, and compose thank you letters to the Relief Society. One student, a handsome, fair-skinned boy, is even a bud-

ding artist. Mr. Diamond showed several of his sketches—birds, seashells, the other island residents—to a reporter, who declares him the mulatto Rembrandt of Apple Island.

This glimpse of light in the middle of so much poverty and low intelligence will certainly not be enough to turn the settlement around, however; the respectable people of this town do not want such degrading things near their front door. Such regrettable circumstances do nothing to impugn what a reporter is pleased to pronounce the modest good works of Mr. Diamond.

TWO WEEKS LATER, a packet for Matthew Diamond arrived at the Foxden general store's mail window. It contained a print of the class photograph, framed for hanging, and smaller prints of the picture for each of the students. A handwritten note was included:

Dear Mr. Diamond, I thought you and the students of "Apple Island Academy" might like to have these. With regards, Bernie Richardson.

FOUR WEEKS LATER, postcards of "Negro Island, Foxden Township" somehow appeared in the Foxden general store, made from Bernard Richardson's photographs. Art Dunlop somehow had had twenty-five copies each made of six different photographs, each with a caption he wrote himself. A photograph of Grammy Honey sitting in her rocking chair in the side yard with Tabitha in her lap read, "A Deuce of Spades." One of Eha leaning against the house with his derby pushed forward low on his forehead read, "The King of Spades (What a Threadbare Crown!)." The seven children in line in front of the schoolhouse, with Matthew Diamond cropped out, was labeled, "A Flush of Spades." A photograph of Zachary Hand to God Proverbs standing in his tree, hands crossed over his chest, eyes closed, looking positively Egyptian, had the caption, "Queer of Spades." Art Dunlop thought the captions were clever—funny and creative—but that the cards should not be in with the rest of the postcards of hotels and pretty bends in local rivers, so he put them in the back, near the guns and ammunition, next to copies of a mildly lewd hunting memoir by a local character named Richard Pibb, who went by the pen name Deadeye Dickie Wags, and a pamphlet of stag jokes he'd also compiled that he thought hunters and fishermen might like for telling at camp.

Bernard Richardson happened to be in the store one day and saw the postcards made from his photographs. He demanded Art Dunlop remove them.

Those are *my* pictures, they're *portraits* of those people—and official documents, he said. They're not for you to turn into a bunch of dirty jokes.

Art Dunlop stood behind the sales counter adding figures on a pad. He looked up and said, I guess you're free to buy the lot if you care to. At retail.

Well, you don't have my permission to—

Otherwise, you're just about trespassing if you say anything more about it.

Bernard had very little money but he took the coins he'd meant for cigarettes and a bag of licorice drops and bought all the copies of the picture of the children at the school, thinking, At least I can get most of the kids' pictures off the damn shelves.

Art Dunlop counted the pile of twenty cards (five had already sold) slowly and deliberately, twice, added the sum total, twice, and said, Fourteen.

Something about Art Dunlop not even having the courtesy to say, Cents, after fourteen infuriated Bernard, never mind how in the world he figured fourteen cents for twenty cards. He slapped a dime and a nickel on the counter. Art Dunlop picked up the dime and looked at one side of it then the other, tapped it against the metal cash box, as if to test what it sounded like, then pitched it into the dime compartment. He did the same with the nickel then put a penny for Bernard's change on the counter. Bernard tore the stack of photographs in half then into quarters then into eighths and dropped the pieces on the counter.

Would you be so kind as to throw this out for me, Bernard said. He turned, and as he went out the door he called back, And keep the penny.

The remaining postcards sold modestly well the rest of the summer.

MATTHEW DIAMOND NOTICED the little chalk drawings Ethan Honey made on his tablet. Ethan drew crickets and crabs and starfish, the apple on the bench, and the biscuit on top of his tin. Whatever was in view from his seat in the schoolroom during lessons. The drawings were very lifelike and Matthew believed that Ethan had real talent. Matthew had been to New York once and Boston three times, he told Ethan, and he had seen galleries hung from floor to ceiling with the great paintings of Europe and America, and Ethan's drawings reminded him of many of the paintings he had seen that were called still lifes.

Still lifes are paintings of things you find around the house or outside, usually arranged on a table in a pleasing way, in light that makes them seem, well, numinous, as we discussed last month during Bible, Matthew told Ethan. Sometimes they are a bouquet of flowers in a coffee pot on a stool outside the front door. Sometimes a cluster of grapes with a pear and four ripe strawberries on a board next to a window in mid-afternoon. Sometimes they are water in a green jelly glass, a pewter spoon, and a bowl of chestnuts on the bench next to the fire late in the evening. Sometimes they are seashells, a starfish, and a piece of blue glass at sunrise. Anything at all that catches your eye and you find beautiful. And you have to think about how the light strikes them, what shadows the objects cast, what of the light passes through them and illuminates them from inside, what of the light is held inside the glass or translucent berry.

Ethan liked to listen to Mr. Diamond make up those ideas for paintings. He could see them in his mind, could see their light moving through glass and water and reflecting off the blade of a knife. Ethan thought he could probably find all the things Mr. Diamond said on the island except grapes, which he knew were fruit but had never seen or tasted for himself.

ETHAN SPLIT WOOD and fetched water and went to school lessons and afterward he took the pencil and sheet of white paper Mr. Diamond had given him and a flat board his father had found for him and walked to the little bluff facing the mainland. He reached into one of his shirt's breast pockets and took out a small, dull spoon and a medicine bottle made of blue glass. He arranged the spoon and bottle on a rounded step of the bare granite at the top of the bluff, worn and pitted by glaciers. From the other shirt pocket he gently scooped a dead chickadee he had found by the schoolhouse that morning. The bird was sleek and unruffled, its claws curled and retracted against its body. It was impossible to tell how it had died. Ethan could not believe one of the island cats had not found it first and eaten it. The body had begun to smell in his pocket during school, faintly at first but more it seemed as the morning went along. He laid the bird in front of the medicine bottle and spoon. The noon sun was brighter, more glaring and direct than he'd have liked. He found a stick from a scrub oak and wedged it into a seam in the granite and removed his shirt and draped it across the stick's branches, making an awning over the bottle, bird, and spoon. He sat on the granite and hunched over and began to draw, starting with the bird. At first the outline of the bird floated curled and dead in absolute white space. Then came the bottle and spoon and the three objects rested on a common invisible plane. Ethan sweated and became hot and distractedly wiped his face and the salty drops that ran down his forehead and hung suspended from the tip of his nose. Wind and surf reverberating against the rocks and through the trees, the noon sun, unclouded and reigning straight above, afternoon chores, his father and grammy and sisters and the island itself all dissolved into a single uninterrupted buzz as Ethan drew and found the lines and their weight with the pencil, pushing its tip or easing up, observing the lines darken or lighten, lend depths or define surfaces, render light bending through the bottle or a shiny little sun pooled in the bottom of the spoon's bowl, or still being collected in death inside the fine feathers of the chickadee's black hooded head, stored within them until the flesh they were fastened to perished and they swirled away over the rocks and off the bluff into the air, leaving only a frail little machine of bones. Ethan drew and imagined the earth after the flood and Noah's sons and wives ranging across plains and cragged hills and wondered whether at first they found the bodies of the drowned everywhere they went, jammed under boulders, slung in the tops of dead trees, splayed on the plains, and what it must have smelled like and the two vultures and two turkey buzzards from the ark taking up their given thrones on the jutting hipbones of the nearest corpses and whether those first months after disembarking were spent piling the dead large and small into heaps and burning them in pyres that consumed families and villages, the people intermingled in the thick braided columns of black, pungent, fleshy smoke that drifted up into the sky and across the land and settled back across it in a fine layer of ash in which all the seeds of the renewed world were sown and by which they were all quickened. Ethan leaned closer and worked on the details of the little bird's mask and imagined dark Ham at dusk, exhausted from dragging bodies by their ankles and heaping them in piles to burn, angered at not having been able to resist looking at the faces of the dead and trying to guess what children belonged to what mothers, what husbands belonged to what wives, what beloved servants to what kind masters, loyal to and in love with every corpse despite what his somber sober god-struck father had told him about their wickedness, and which he had and still wholly believed, as much as he missed the former world, standing by the radius of embers and bones left from the day's cremations, looking east across the plains and seeing the faint glow of fair Shem's blaze at the base of the foothills in the distance, then looking west and seeing the plaited columns of smoke from coppery Japheth's fires rising near the sea, and missing both his brothers more sharply than he thought he'd ever have been able to imagine after having been shut up with them in that boat for so many weeks.

Ethan wondered, Had God spared those brothers the grim work of clearing the dead from the world? Had He made sure to rinse the lands of that first race of people, every one of them drained away with the receding waters into the bottoms of the oceans where their myriad bones turned and settled in the profoundest depths, sifted and collected around the pilings of the earth?

The island the Honey's own ark, then, except that Noah's ark had come to rest on a mountain and he and his family had scrambled down from the deck and dispersed across the world, across the Hellespont and Arabia, Egypt and through all Africa, across the Mongolian plains and the American west, while the Honeys kept to their own island ark and left it as seldom as possible. When Noah and Japheth and Shem and Ham and their wives paraded down the gangplank onto dry land, herding moose and black bears and setting loons and wood ducks free from their cages, there was not another single soul alive on the planet. It may as well have been another planet.

Ethan drew and daydreamed about the Bible stories Mr. Diamond read to him and the other school children and the afternoon passed and the sun burned his back and shoulders and neck. That evening he had to lie shirtless on his stomach in the grass while Grammy Honey spooned cold tea onto his inflamed back. Charlotte and Tabitha sat on either side of him and fanned him with leafy maple branches they'd stripped from a sapling. Later during sweat-soaked bouts of sleep, a nightmare tormented him that he was suffocating within a pile of burning bodies, struggling to turn face up so he could cry out over the clamor of the flaming pyre and booming surf to frowning Japheth that he was not drowned, that spared or forgotten he was not one of the drowned.

Ethan took a fever in the night and Grammy cooled him with a rag soaked in cold weak tea. He muttered about Noah and dead families buried in common graves and Grammy whispered to him, Hush, think of what a glorious month in heaven it must have been while it rained down here, all those people arriving, freed from all the evil their hearts had been set on since every one of them'd been little kids.

EARLY THE NEXT MORNING, Eha rose from his sleep and looked at his sun-poisoned son sleeping on a pallet on the floor with his sisters. Ethan was awake and heard his father shifting himself and rising off his bed, the floorboards taking his weight, the one-room shack distributing his weight throughout its joints and beams. He opened his eyes and the burns on his back seemed to flare afresh, like a bed of banked coals poked in the dark dawn. Chills swept over his back and shoulders and up his neck. Sweat popped from the pores of his face and brow and felt freezing for breaking over the hot skillet of his skin. Heat pulsed from his back. It felt as if his stomach might be sick and he let out a quiet little sob. Eha made his way over and around the bodies of his youngest daughters, snoozing on their pallets, and knelt by his son. He placed a hand on Ethan's head and stroked the boy's hair with his thumb. Such a big strong head. Such thick hair. His mother's. Such a beautiful child, just this past week an infant in my arms, a babe I could hold whole in this cupped hand. Ethan whimpered, as if the effort of enduring the night were letting go beneath his father's touch. Eha felt the sun's heat radiating back out of his son's skin.

Burned forearms, singed noses, sun-branded necks were nothing new to anyone on the island. Men, women, children were all well used to such scorchings from the sun directly above and from its reflection off the mirror of the Atlantic in which their tiny pebble of a home sloshed. Grammy had a repertoire of cures. Cold tea. Mint compress. Macerated plantain weed. She munched leaves and spat the paste into her fingers and smeared it across the boy's back. Grammy's remedies had none of the salubrious comforts of the medicine on the mainland—no baths of cold fresh milk or poultices of oatmeal mixed with spring water, no slab of raw beefsteak plastered over a black eye. Her compounds were spare and vaporous, essences distilled, brewed, steeped, reduced, concentrated into drops and small thimblefuls, by a medicine woman who herself mostly survived on pipe smoke, black tea, ocean air, and the Word of God. She concocted salves salutary to lean lives lived on shallow soil and bare rock.

An Act concerning operations for the prevention of Procreation. —Be it enacted:

The wardens of the State prisons and the directors of State hospitals and schools for the insane are hereby sanctioned and ordered to appoint for each said institution, two proficient surgeons, who, in conjunction with the physician in charge at each said institution, shall constitute a board to examine such inmates as are reported to them by the warden or director to be persons by whom procreation would be injudicious.

Such boards shall assess the physical and mental condition of such inmates, and their records and family histories so far as such can be verified, and if in the verdict of the majority of said boards, procreation by any such persons would produce progeny with predispositions to moronism, mongolism, lunacy, feeble-mindedness, idiocy, or imbecility, without possibility that any such condition of any such person so judged will improve to such a degree as to make procreation by such a person advantageous, then said board shall designate one of its members to effectuate one or the other of the operations of vasectomy or oophorectomy, such as any given such case may be, upon such person.

Such procedure shall be executed in a harmless and humanitarian manner, and the boards making such examinations, and the surgeons performing such procedures, shall acquire from the State such remuneration, for rendered ministrations, as the warden or director of either of such prison or hospital shall reckon suitable.

COMPARED WITH HIS clear, organized school lessons, Matthew Diamond's Sunday sermons in the schoolroom were impressionistic and incoherent to the islanders as they tried to sit still and quietly, respectfully listen to his metaphysical improvisations.

I remember the story of the flood in Gilgamesh from my studies at the seminary and I watch the Israelites revise it, populating the ark not with a royal court but a single family, of which every soul born since is a member, every saint and drunkard, every hermit, cutpurse, prostitute, factory owner, railroad baron. Every deadbeat mule driver is your father, your brother, every wayward milkmaid your aunt, your sister. Not a hero and his entourage aloft on the waters. Not a king and his court. But a family, a wife and her husband, two parents and their children and their children's beloveds. I have studied the math and Noah's father, Lamech, knew old Adam, his seventh-generation grandsire, personally. Lamech would have told his son, Noah, stories he heard directly from Adam, about awaking to the virgin world with God's breath still in his new lungs, shaped from the very soil, a tongue laid into his mouth made for making words, the very first ever, each an act of worship, each powerful enough to cooperate with or contradict creation itself. Father Adam naming the animals, falling asleep one quiet evening and awaking to find Eve, mother of us all, by his side, perhaps also just rousing, not from sleep but from whatever it is that precedes birth, whatever came even before birth itself, because she was the first of any woman to give birth, her sons the first to come from a mother instead of God. I imagine those shepherd priests around the fires at night changing the Babylonian stories they knew so well to bear witness to humanity as a single family, and I am nourished by the feast that is the Word of God.

The children fidgeted and scratched and made of Mr. Diamond's sermons what they might. Ethan listened and let the words make strange pictures in his mind. He strained to understand the missionary's remarks because he sensed meaning in them and because he wanted to be able to talk about them with his grandmother and with Mr. Diamond, too.

You know, there were stories people made up later about all the wives of the Fathers of Israel converting to Judaism from their pagan religions, Matthew Diamond continued. But the Bible, true Scripture itself, has never been changed. Moses and Joseph married wives brought up in other faiths and not a word is ever spoken of them converting, at least until the later midrash, the inferior pseudepigrapha.

The bored younger children giggled when they heard the word "pig" in the middle of all Mr. Diamond's foreign-sounding talk. I believe that that silence on the subject is meaningful, deliberate, profound, that it comes from the deepest heart of God's creative grace, he continued. The Honeys and the McDermott sisters, Zachary Hand to God, and even Annie Parker, who sat perched at the end of a bench near the door, as if ready to flee should someone look her in the eye or say her name, all the Apple Islanders politely listening to him improvise a homily, all of them, himself included, maybe even especially, seemed to him for a moment so lowly, of such marginal worth, that an awkward inspiration to convince them of their own value, as priceless human souls, struck him.

And we know, too, by their very names, he said, that the sons of Noah ranged in skin color from black Ham to coppery Japheth to fair Shem. Yet they were brothers, all their father's and their mother's sons.

None of the islanders moved or changed their expression but the hairs on Matthew Diamond's neck stood up, as if in response to a charge of electricity in the schoolroom. He could not tell whether his words inspired or upset. Best to continue. Best to continue instead of fearing the worst.

A thought struck Mr. Diamond and he said, And, although there is nothing about it in Scripture, I have come to believe that those men's wives were a mixture of dark and paler complexions as well. Perhaps black Ham's wife had skin like bronze; perhaps fair Shem's wife was dark as a moonless night; it may be that coppery Japheth's betrothed was as white as pure mountain snow.

Charlotte scratched at a scab on her knee.

Tabitha slapped Charlotte's hand away from the scab and Charlotte cried, Quit that, Tabby!

Tabitha said, Then quit scratching at your cut, my darling sister! and the girls started to tussle.

Matthew Diamond looked at the tiny congregation. No reaction. Esther Honey didn't even shush the girls. Well, then, he said, maybe that's enough for the day, friends. Forgive me. My thoughts are not as prepared as they might be. I am no systematic theologian, he said and tried to add a little self-deprecating laugh, by way of discreet apology, he hoped, but what came out was halfway between a cough and a groan. Yes, yes, he said. He put his clenched hand to his lips and mimed clearing his throat, as if in conclusion. You may go. God bless you all.

The children left the schoolhouse and scattered off to their cabins and their afternoon chores. The adults lingered and thanked Mr. Diamond for his reflections. Esther Honey still disliked him and felt more than ever as if he signaled doom, but something about what he was trying to make out of Scripture fascinated her, despite herself. His ideas chased their own tails and he was a confirmed, chronic hand-wringer, and he seemed to be letting every mayor, doctor, minister, and judge hear about Apple Island, but the man was well read and thoughtful and had a strong vocabulary that he used fittingly if confusedly, and if she could not always follow his gist, she knew he wrestled with something exact and well-intended in mind. Like, if he ever settled his thoughts and untied his tongue, he just might write something as good as one of Shakespeare's worst couplets. Terrible, though, she thought, making her way home as Charlotte and Tabitha and the Sockalexis children crisscrossed in front of and behind and between the line of adults walking away from the schoolhouse along the path. Terrible how terribly good intentions turn out almost every time.

The Honey family turned off the path, followed by the brown mutt with white socks and a black mask called Sulky. Esther had Ethan help with the washing.

Ethan cranked a pair of sopping overalls through the wringer. They belonged to Mr. Cornwell, a widower potato farmer with a few acres on the main. Ethan said to Esther, I like what Mr. Diamond said about Noah and Lamech and the family of man today, Gram. How everyone is all from one family, so we're all cousins and brothers and sisters and such. Just like all us on the island. He hung the overalls over the line, cold, heavy with wet, dull to handle, and imagined walking down the ark's long, springy gangway with his family and all the animals after the flood had receded.

Esther kneaded a skirt in the wash bucket and said, Decked in purple or draped in rags, it's all mischief. She looked at Sulky, who watched the washing and sat as if waiting to be fed. She flung a blotch of suds toward him. His ears pricked and he scrambled to the whipped fluff of soap and sniffed it. His tail and ears dropped and he gave Esther a crestfallen look.

I know, poor Sulks. I'm sorry, she said. It's a lousy sauce, ain't it.

MATTHEW DIAMOND WAS distracted the rest of the day by the strange effect his words about Noah's sons had had in the small schoolroom.

Like the hair on his neck, the Apple Islanders had distinctly if invisibly bristled, he thought. Spirit, but not the good spirit, not the Holy Spirit he'd meant to inspire. He was agitated that all the islanders knew he meant them the very best and that his words, well, yes, they'd come out wrong—wrong in how he'd said them—yes, that was true, but obviously not wrong in spirit, and still they'd been offended.

After going to bed and wrestling with his worries until his thoughts made even less sense than they had that afternoon, then giving up any hope of sleep, a clear idea appeared out of the confusion—a plan, really—and, agitated and relieved, Matthew rose from his bed, lit a lantern, and wrote a letter to his friend. Thomas Hale.

Dear Friend, An idea presented itself to me during late Sunday night, which I am not sure how to articulate in a way that will not seem deceptive or opportunistic, although the greater good which I hope underlies it is dependent on a bit of, frankly, cunning. It also depends on an imposition on you. As you know better than I, the State is now certain to break up the settlement on Apple Island & evict the islanders sometime in the summer. As I try to think of ways to help find places for the people to go, it occurs to me that Ethan Honey, the young man whose artistic talents I've mentioned several times over the last two years, might benefit from a visit to your home in Enon. I mean, perhaps he might be spared the worst of the eviction by being given a kind of residency, where he, for instance, might stay on your property with the view to painting the landscapes it offers & possibly being given lessons by a more experienced painter, even possibly taking classes at an art college, eventually, if his skills improve apace. I know the complications this would bring about in terms of separating him from his family, but the fact of the matter is this: more than anyone else in his family, he looks purely white. That is, to look at him, you would not be able to tell he has mixed blood. His hair is light brown &

straight, almost blond during the summer. His eyes are greenish blue. It seems to me that, as no one in Enon would know his family history, if he perhaps were to appear there as your guest, he might be freed from the terrible prejudices he suffers here with his family. I do not know; perhaps you might have an opinion about this. I am conflicted over it—because it would be so much to ask of you (& even as I ask, I am asking you about the propriety even of asking such a thing), and because while it is true that he can paint beautifully, Ethan Honey is not the only island child with notable talent—his younger sister, Tabitha, is nearly fluent in Latin at barely eleven years (I guess; no islander knows the date of their own birth; indeed, the adults do not know how to use a calendar), and there is another girl, Emily Sockalexis—half or more Indian—Penobscot—also perhaps ten or so years old, who will be able to do algebra beyond my ability to understand let alone teach within a year. But, Tabitha Honey could never be mistaken for white. And Emily has negroid and Indian features intermixed and, frankly, a waywardness about her that suggests she has inherited her missing mother and unknown father's depravity.

I worry most that my idea may lead everyone involved into several sorts of temptation—that it does not exactly follow the line and plummet of the Word. Would such temptations be lesser than the possible good I sense in freeing this one boy, anyway, from bonds of prejudice, from that mystical body of iniquity, so called, he will otherwise inevitably suffer, even as other remarkable island children are not similarly chosen? Would he eventually see the act as a lie—which it is—but one that spared him worse affliction? His sisters and his father and grandmother would agonize over separating a family, but is there one of Martin Luther's deep and spiritual Yeses at the heart of the idea? Or am I tempting him to sell his birthright for a bowl of pottage? I would be grateful for your thoughts. Meantime, I pray, of course, and search my heart.

In any event, I remain your devoted,

P.S. I wonder whether you might be able to arrange for the boy to receive *some better artist's materials. I believe he would make rapid progress with paints & canvas. Perhaps there are books that might instruct him in the basics of color & so forth.*

EHA HONEY FOUND making words for some of his thoughts difficult. Instructing Ethan how to split cedar shingles was easy. One, two, three. Froe, split, turn, froe, flip. Like a song. Like how Zachary had taught him a long time ago. Pleasing and comfortable. Those kinds of words he savored the chance to say. Other ideas that came to him were easy and rich but when he tried to find the right words and put them in order and say them out loud his tongue seemed like a board on a hinge swinging in the wind. So he spoke little. He nodded or frowned. He growled or chuckled. He whistled. Sometimes he made animal sounds. He mimicked every bird song. He made sounds like the ocean and thunder and wind, too. Some afternoons he and Lotte sat in the yard surveying the Atlantic clucking and growling back and forth, having a fine talk.

Other ideas still, though, were darker, underwater, or he underwater and they above the surface, clear and sharp and focused. He could hear them in his head, feel their weight in his chest and their shapes in his throat, but he was slow of tongue and they went unworded. He knew everyone had the same kind of ideas, but that his thoughts outdistanced his words sooner than with other people—even the words for what he meant when he thought about this hovered above the water—dark, familiar circling birds he could not name.

ETHAN AND HIS sisters dug for clams at dawn in the dark sand while Esther oversaw them from her rocking chair, which she'd had Ethan carry and place on the shimmering tidal flat. She smoked her pipe and sipped tea from a chipped cup decorated with blue windmills and

THIS OTHER EDEN   71

watched their bent silhouettes move against the pale gradient of early light on the horizon. The smells of the tidal mud and salt water mingled with those of the grass and wildflowers and small pines that clung to the granite edges of the island. The siblings drifted away from and back toward one another, leaving trails from their rakes and craters of turned-up sand until the flat looked like a clay tablet impressed with the kind of writing Mr. Diamond had shown the schoolchildren in their history book. Cuneiform. Hieroglyphics. A record of the day's bread erased by the next tide.

Within an hour Esther reckoned they'd dug close to half a peck and called, Okay, that's plenty. By then the tide had turned and water swirled around her rocking chair and the runners had started sifting down into the sand. The girls carried the wire baskets of clams and Ethan pried the rocking chair out of the sand and the four Honeys made their way home, where they sat in the yard and shucked the clams, chucking the meat into a big tin bowl and the shells back into the baskets. They finished and Tabby took the empty shells around back of the house and pitched them onto the old Penobscot midden. The midden would be good for a drawing or painting, too, Ethan thought, even though it was only a mess of old shells. A section of the midden had sheared off last year, revealing layers of shells from centuries past. There was nearly a perfect line where the lighter, newer shells from the Honeys had begun to build on top of the Penobscot shells, which were darker and compressed under the weight of the pile, denser, almost turned back into earth, minerals. Some brighter new shells had sprinkled down across the inclined face of the darker old shells. That would be something to sit in front of and try to see and capture with the colors, with the green grass growing around it and the different shade of green brush behind it, although Ethan imagined his sisters teasing him about it, too, like they did when he drew insects and dead birds and dead fish with their eyes pecked out and their spines stripped bare by gulls.

Why you drawing that old heap of trash, Ethan? Why do you always draw bugs and junk and dead stuff on the beach? Tabitha asked.

I draw *you*, too, he said.

Tabitha and Charlotte crinkled their faces and Charlotte yelled, He's going to paint what's under the outhouse next!

ESTHER HONEY WAS too old, her arthritis too acute to cross to the main and gather berries and hunt for mushrooms and herbs anymore, but she knew where the heal-all grew in the shade along the lanes. Its flower heads looked like bee skeps and she called it bumblebee weed. She knew where the tansy grew, just above the high-tide line, and taught the girls how to rub it on the meat on the rare occasions there was some to keep the flies off when it started to rot. She knew when the coltsfoot first came out in the spring and every fall she sent the girls to collect as much bone-set as they could carry. She simmered it in the big kettle and made tea. She designated a day each for the family members to drink the rank brew in measured doses. Eha on a Monday, Ethan on Tuesday, Tabitha Wednesday, Charlotte Thursday, and finally she on Friday spent sunup to sundown in the privy having their digestions cleansed. Like a cat chasing a rat through a church organ's pipes, she'd say. She knew where the mugwort grew and she preferred to smoke that in her pipe because she said that was the true old sailor's tobacco and it cleared her asthmas better than the finest Virginian shag.

Esther waited in her rocking chair at the top of the bluff on the evenings when the women and girls had gone gathering on the main— Iris and Violet McDermott, Emily and Norma Sockalexis, Charlotte and Tabitha, Theophilus and Millie Lark (Theo an honorary member, the women teased, in his mother's dress and all, at which Theo beamed with pleasure and pride—yes the very same dress in which his mother had once gathered with them a long time ago), and even Annie Parker, too, maybe once a year, when the weather and tides were in perfect harmony, and the world too beautiful for even her to resist going out into it a little. Esther watched them return across the channel at low tide in the lowering light with baskets of mushrooms and raspberries and wildflowers and herbs above their heads, holding up their skirts, the women softly singing *Sally Brown was a Creole lady*, or *On Saturday night the wind blew west*, or one of the sorrowful lullabies Patience Honey herself had brought over from Ireland, *Seoithín seothó*, the older girls singing along, the younger ones singing the words they knew and humming the rest. If the women were in a particularly high mood, Annie Parker sang a song her grandmother, Borrowed Moment Parker, said *her* father, who she said had joined the Union Army and fought his way from Virginia to Apple Island, had taught her, called, "Hang Jeff Davis from the Old Sour Apple Tree." Esther could not always hear the songs from where she was, but sometimes she hummed one to herself, singing a word or two now and then, as she watched the McDermott sisters and Norma and Emily and Annie Parker and Tabby and Lotte in the spacious dusk, remembering crossing back herself, through the cold water, tired, enchanted, and dilated by the perfumes of the herbs and flowers and fruit in the woods and clearings.

If any of the gatherers passed close enough, Esther called out softly, as if in secret, as if not to break a spell.

Saltbush?

Scads.

High up?

All the way to the ridge.

Early winter, then.

Early winter, late snow.

Cold.

Cold.

How deeply she had loved rising before the sun as a girl, with her mother and sister, before her sister left the island forever, without a word to anyone, rising early, getting dressed in the dark, trying not to waken her father, but every sound in the new day clear and full and distinct. Although no cow had ever set foot on the island, sometimes her mother had a miraculous pint of fresh milk in a tin mug, which she had not exactly hidden from Esther's father, but just inexplicably had there for the girls on two or three of those mornings, not exactly a secret but just as a small, *ladies' only* luxury that after taking a small sip of for herself, she passed to Esther's sister, who held the mug in both hands with the tips of her fingers and tilted to her lips while Esther watched and already could smell the metal inside the cool tin mug mingling with the smell of the grassy milk and already as much as taste the sweet cool fresh rich milk itself. When her sister, whose name Esther sometimes forgot as she got older, or more, whose name she remembered less and less, passed her the mug it was all she could do not to laugh out loud for joy and wake her father at the prospect of that milk, so cool she didn't know how her mother kept it, so sumptuous and thick and fresh it was blue in the tin mug and her joy at the sweet rich grassy taste tempered a little but not after all too, too much by having to sip it into her mouth quietly and not smack and gulp it down the way she'd have liked but which, after all, too, upon reflection years later rocking in her chair on the bluff watching the women and girls return from gathering, would have ruined much of the nearly unbearable bliss of anticipation and the relish of the milk's creamy weight, its musky sweetness, so wonderful she could have sighed out loud, especially when she thought of the savorless lumps they got by on the rest of the time with that sweet taste still in her mouth.

The women and girls reached the island and crossed through the tall grass, their silhouettes dark against the dark sky, their skirts brushing the grass that bowed into the path, singing quietly, *Seoithín seothó*, as if the darkness hushed their voices, leaving the group singly or in pairs as they turned toward their homes.

Abby, Esther thought, watching night unfold and reveal the stars. My sister's name was Abby and she looked just like our father and left us without a word when she was practically still a child.

ETHAN STUDIED THE painting book that the society had sent along with a wooden box that opened at the top and was miraculously full of paints and oils and brushes. He read that there are paintbrushes made of fitch hair and weasel hair, hog's bristle, and mink, which is the best and has the finest snap to it of all. He read that colors painted over a ground lighter than themselves give a warm tint and those painted over a darker ground tend toward coldness. He found that just as the book said of certain paints, people's skin changed when exposed to the sunlight. Not only did skin change as the sun seared it and the air cured it, but the light of the sun changed the colors of everything, people, water, stones, and air, by the minute.

The book said a painter of people should never flatter his subjects. He neither should make women younger than they really are nor men handsomer. Do not lend affability to a scowler or grace to a lout. Such practices contradict the conscience of art.

Light is caused by the vibrations of the particles of which all matter consists. The eye perceives color with nerves attuned to its various waves. There are red-seeing nerves and violet-seeing nerves, for instance. Of landscapes, sunnier vistas consist of reds, evening scenes of blue and violets. Plentiful sleep is essential for the daily recovery of the artist's eye, which is dulled and tired by light.

Colors to be used for flesh when painting portraits are: flake white, yellow ochre, raw sienna, burnt sienna, light red, vermillion, raw umber, burnt umber, blue black, terra verte, cobalt.

Ethan watched and saw that this islander was now olive-green, now yellow, now purple cascading into blue. In the evening, this sister darkened nearly black. At noon, she shone copper-bright in the sunlight. Mr. Diamond was in fact now coral, now orange, now empurpled into indigo, now emulsified into milky gray. In the evening, the Lark children shone pale under the moon. On the rare occasion one of them was up and around at noon he flared away into near transparency, his dark arteries bundled and pulsing, capillaries bright, buzzing, pink, nearly audible. Every face streaked and marbled, speckled and dotted and brindled with perpetually shifting repertoires of colors.

The book said that madders should be locked up in copal or amber so as not to change. Pigments that revise after application are called fugitive. Ethan used colors different from those recommended by the book sometimes, just to see how they made people's faces look different—eye sockets shallower or deeper, fissured and dark, cheeks prominent and shining, hachured, faces tight, glowing and full of bones or toothless and like an empty leather bag.

A HEN HAWK CAUGHT a rabbit chancing the open meadow. Eha saw it grab the rabbit by the saddle and lift it from the ground to sink its talons deeper. The hawk lowered to the ground and pushed its beak into the rabbit's neck. The rabbit's free hind leg thumped at the ground. The hawk held the rabbit and looked across the meadow, fastening its grip deeper into the thrashing animal. The hawk began to pull strips of fur and bright strings of muscle from the rabbit's back. The hawk's chick, a tierce large and strong enough to hunt for itself but still relying on its mother for food, flew across the meadow and perched at the top of a hickory tree. The rabbit stopped kicking and lay limp in the mother hawk's claws. The mother hawk tore and swallowed a morsel from the rabbit's flank then flew up and perched in the hickory tree next to her chick, which, side by side, Eha saw was larger than her. The carcass sat in the open meadow and the birds watched it. Eha watched the birds for an hour. It was afternoon and he had nothing to do and looking at the beautiful birds gave him pleasure. He wondered whether one of the dogs might try to steal the rabbit—Fitzy, the little terrier, might be foolhardy enough—but none did. Eha dozed. He roused a moment later and the birds and carcass were gone.

FROM A LEDGE halfway up the bluff, Ethan watched his sisters return from picking berries and mushrooms on the mainland, late for the neap tide. The three paintings he was working on were drying in the sun back at the house, so he went to the ledge where he could draw in peace, away from everyone else, for a while at least, so he could sketch and let his mind go where it wanted without interruption. The ledge could only be reached by climbing down the face of the bluff along a series of shallow sills—as Ethan thought of them—that were loose and crumbly. The climb was not without its perils and that made the place feel precious, secret. True, Grammy often sat in her rocking chair on the peak of the bluff, above him to his right, no more than forty or fifty feet away, and he could smell the smoke from her pipe and occasionally hear her humming one of the songs the women sang, but he could not see her nor she him so, everything considered, he had a place all his own.

Tabitha and Charlotte came out from the trees on the opposite side of the channel with their baskets and waded into the water. Ethan drew the channel and the patterned flowing water and his sisters breasting against it, making offset patterns, with a stick of charcoal. They were both strong swimmers and he was not worried about their safety. They knew the pull of the tide through the channel, how to lean against it, float with it if they needed.

THE WATER IN the middle of the channel was waist high on Tabitha and came nearly up to Charlotte's armpits. Both girls held their full baskets above their heads. Tabitha slogged through the water in front of Charlotte. Charlotte began to half swim, stroking at the seawater with her free arm. Dark, yellow-brown drifts of wrack swirled around her.

I'm afraid of a big eel in the seaweed, Charlotte said. The huge, brindled mastiff called Grizzly saw the girls from where it lay in the sand on the island side of the channel.

Tabitha stopped and turned to her sister. Gimme your basket, Honey. There's no eels in this part. Grizzly rose and ambled into the water and paddled toward the girls.

Okay, give me your basket, Tabitha said. Charlotte held the basket out for Tabitha to take but slipped on the submerged rock. A handful of strawberries jumped from the basket and plinked into the water and sank among the waving bands of seaweed.

Careful. Here, now you can swim back. What's that Grizzly coming out here for?

I can't swim in my smocks, Charlotte said. She dunked herself underwater and her thin arms and the cloth of her dress flailed and splashed, then she surfaced bare-shouldered holding her sodden dress balled up in her hands.

Now I can swim.

Well hurry it *up*, Miss Honey, Tabitha said. I'm freezing. I got a arm cramp. Let's get a move on. Go on, now, Grizzly; get outta the way; we got to get to shore. Grizzly reached the girls and took Charlotte in his mouth by the scruff and dabbled back to shore while Charlotte screamed and thrashed and yelled to let her go, she was stark naked. Tabitha swam ahead with the baskets and dress. Grizzly followed and gently deposited Charlotte on the sand. Charlotte got up and felt at the back of her neck for punctures.

Quick, get your dress back on before anyone sees, Tabitha said and chucked the wet dress to her sister.

Grizzly stood next to Charlotte while she wrangled herself into her soaked clothes, facing the island, looking back sidelong at her, waiting. She yanked her smock straight and slapped Grizzly on the muzzle, then boxed his ears, then kicked his rump and yelled, You about broke my neck, you great big stupid bear.

The dog lazed back over to where he'd been lounging before and lay down and began to snore.

LOTTE AND TABBY, Ethan thought, gatherers traversing a plane of bright corrugated water. Sit, the water looks like a steel washboard. Could be a mile deep, ankle high, a bare film, a plating. Stand and the sunlight vanishes. The plating vanishes. Proves light not water. Colors in the water resolve. Dark rocks and the rows of waving wrack and the water-green sun-bright sand. A school of huge fish hovering headfirst into the current not twenty yards from Lot and Tab. Lot and Tab traversing that old channel through the even older water. A dinosaur might as well walk out from the pine trees on the mainland, step into the channel, dunk its head in the water, and chomp away at the soggy seaweed.

Ethan's sisters crossed the channel and a pair of charcoal sisters resolved onto the paper. Those sisters, lesser, shadows, but actual and on the paper—now and now and now still—and would exist until the paper was crumpled and thrown into a stove for tinder, or disintegrated from the wall in a drowned house. His blood-and-bones sisters. These charcoal sisters. Mr. Diamond had told him some charcoal was made from bones.

Ethan's sisters and Grizzly reached the rocky shore. Tabby waited for Lotte, who wrung her dress as best she could, put it on, then pummeled the dog.

Ethan thought, These carbon sisters on my drawing will always be in the carbon water, crossing the carbon channel, beneath a carbon sun, watched from above by people of bones and blood and muscle and mind.

He rubbed the hatched water behind the two figures in the drawing and two carbon shadows appeared projected behind them on the carbon water, of carbon girls and the carbon baskets filled with the carbon berries they held above her heads. What kind of world would that be, in which a shadow was composed of the same stuff as the girl who cast it, and the blueberries she ate the same stuff as she? What if when I stood, my shadow was flesh and blood? What if berries were flesh and they grew on branches of arteries pulsing with blood and decked with leaves of skin?

Ethan rolled up his sketch and put it in his shirt. He faced the face of the bluff and scaled his way back to the top, diagonally away from where his Grammy sat, so that when he reached the top he was behind her and she didn't even know he'd been right under her, drawing away. He jogged down the path to the beach and met his sisters.

You watching us, Ethan? Charlotte said.

About to come save you, he said. Before Grizzly beat me to it.

Naw, Ethan. I was fine. We were both fine, 'cept now my neck feels half broke from that stupid dog.

Good berries?

Little ones. Tart, Tabitha said.

Charlotte held her basket to Ethan. He took a berry and put it in his mouth. He slowly pressed it between his teeth until it split open, acidy and sweet and salty from Charlotte's wet hands. He was almost surprised it did not taste like soot or blood.

What'd you draw? Charlotte said. Ethan showed his sisters the drawing.

Us in the water, Tabitha said. Where's Grizzly?

He'd a ruined the picture, Ethan said. He wanted to wink at Charlotte but she was intent on the drawing.

Is that one me? Charlotte said.

That's you, Ethan said.

Charlotte looked like she might cry. Ethan held the drawing away from himself to get a fuller look at it.

The water looks big, don't it? he said

It does, Charlotte said.

Same old channel, Tabitha said. Always been like that. You just never seen it like that when you in it.

I know, Charlotte said, and switched the berries to her other hand. I know. Just, it's a fright looking down on us from the sky.

ESTHER SAT IN her chair, smoking, watching her granddaughters come across the channel and the dog take one of them by the scruff and her grandson run down to the beach and meet them and help them with their baskets and, probably, tease them about getting caught behind the tide. He was so good to them. And they were good to him. Love, pure and simple. None of them gave a thought yet to what people beyond the island saw as their polluted blood. Even after that shameful visit from those doctors. Soon enough, she thought. Soon enough, Pharaoh will come after us, like he always does. She thought of the Hebrews leaving Egypt, Pharaoh's army at their heels. She thought of Patience Honey's vision in the middle of that hurricane, of Moses parting the sea, and she thought about the Hebrews moving from place to place through the wilderness, forty times, over rivers and wastelands and mountains and deserts, which was what she felt more and more the Apple Islanders were on the brink of having to do themselves. She tried to name for herself in order the places where the Israelites had camped, a list she'd been able to recite as a girl, *Succoth, Ethan, Migdol, Marah, Elim*—with *twelve fountains and seventy date trees*, she remembered—but she got muddled after *Rephedim—where there was no water.* As permanent as Apple Island had seemed, if you sat back and thought about it, it really was just another encampment, made then struck in endless flight from the Egyptians, the

Assyrians, Babylon and the rest—the kings and marching armies and poking and prodding doctors of the world.

Ethan carried the girls' baskets of berries and flowers and mushrooms and the three children trudged up the beach toward the house. Esther followed their progress and as they got closer she found herself overjoyed by them, each her own little modest person, each unself-consciously taking care of one another, even as they teased and screeched and laughed and complained. And she recalled the fact that the first thing she had wanted to do the minute their father had been born and cut loose from his cord was to take him by the ankles and drown him in the first puddle, spring, tide pool, or bucket of water deep enough that she could find, and flee.

And she had. Tried to drown him. She'd sent her father for water and when he'd gotten out of the house and headed for the spring she'd taken Eha naked, wet, and weltering down to the water. The landing was too public. Someone would see, she'd thought. The bluff would have been too brutal, tossing the child hard enough to clear the rocks below, flinging him out into the waves. She meant to drown her child, her son and her brother, but properly, with due seriousness and humility, but she was bare-legged, bleeding, and staggered. She didn't even have a sack to put the child in. He was just naked in her bare arms, bawling, sticky. She made it to the south shore where there were tide pools and spits of sand and barnacled rocks. She managed to reach the end of a tract of rock at the edge of the incoming tide, now covered in an inch of fizzling water, now exposed, now in water again. The baby stopped bawling. He lay still and quiet in her arms. For a baby it must be cold, she thought. Cold for me. She shivered. Cold, and slathered in bloody gunk. Dirty, unclean. Is he asleep or fainted? Blemished dove, blemished lamb. Moses's mother kneeling at the river, pushing him in his little ark into the bulrushes—flags, they're called in the story. Poor Moses. Orphan, immigrant, stranger. Cast away because your mother couldn't keep you and wouldn't kill you. Esther shivered again, fainty, exhausted. Murderer, too. Moses murdered a man. His mother took him to the river to save him, not drown him. Esther sobbed; she didn't know what to do. She could not keep the child, got on her by her father, but she could not put it in the water. She knelt on the rock, now submerged in the tide. The water swelled and flooded up her thighs and pulled back. The baby turned its head and stuck its little pink tongue out and kept it there, like it didn't know how to pull it back into its own mouth. It straightened and balled its fingers.

My fingers. They look like my fingers.

She put him down on the rock in front of her. He lay on the rock and the water rose and swirled over his face. The water swelled and took him up. He turned in the pull of the backwash and the water drew him past the edge of the rock.

She grabbed him up. She hugged him to her breast, trying to cover as much of him with her skin as she could, while she gathered the nerve to put him back in the water again and leave him.

Keeping your son warm before you drown him? Just open your arms and let him roll into the sea.

He might float.

You going to sit and watch till he sinks or floats off? Do it; stand up; turn and walk away.

How else?

That's the only way. How else do you drown your child? But the tide's coming in, foolish girl. *In*. He's going to get sucked right back between the rocks and when the tide goes out he'll be stuck there in the sun and the gulls will peck at him. Where will you be? Sitting in the yard? Smoking your pipe? Fixing supper for Papa? His father. Your husband. Your father. Washing a shirt and your baby dead, crabs and flies and birds eating him? Papa won't even ask where it is.

Yes, he will. He'll ask.

No, dear Esther Honey; he won't say word one.

Esther's imagination reached the end of what she could think up for her life with the baby or without it and she wished herself back to when her father had done with her mother what he'd done to her and wished her mother had foreseen what her husband would do to their child, and their child, someday, naked and seething on a sinking rock with her child and fended her husband off howsoever she might have, even sacrificing her own life to save her child-to-be and her child-to-be's child-to-be from ending up on that sinking rock bleeding and ravaged and at the end of what she could imagine for herself.

Esther watched Tabby and Lotte and Ethan come up the path. The memory of curling up on her side, still-unnamed Eha in her arms, the water by then alternately pulling and pushing them both toward the depths and back onto the rocks, and her thinking that was cruel—Just drown us now, quick—as ever overwhelmed her, not because it was vague and dim and made her feel like she'd suffered some awful half-recollected disfigurement while practically still a child herself, but because she remembered every single detail of it all and because she did it all on purpose. She shuddered, at the shame of almost having murdered her son and therefore her three grandchildren, but also in gratitude for God having taken all their fates out of her selfish hands.

Or Zachary, she corrected herself. Gratitude for Zachary—or God through Zachary—having taken all their fates out of her selfish young hands.

ZACHARY HAND TO GOD came back from a small job he'd taken on the mainland helping fix the front steps of an old widower he'd known since the war. He tossed his bag of tools onto the beach and dragged his rowboat up past the high-tide line, just onto the dune grass, and flipped it upside down so it wouldn't fill with rainwater. He fetched his tools and strode up the path, eager to eat a mouthful of this or that then get back into his tree. The prophet Micah was on his mind and he meant to carve him pleading God's case to the mountains and hills because there were no just people left on earth to hear his argument. He overtook Charlotte and Tabitha and Ethan on the path, Ethan carrying two baskets—filled with fruit and flowers and mushrooms: morels, chanterelles, and his favorite, chicken of the woods—and the girls trudging behind him, their clothes soaking wet.

You Honey girls look like you're about half drowned, he said. The girls and Ethan stopped.

Naw, Mr. Zachary, we're fine, Charlotte said.

Nah, we're fine, Mr. Zachary, Tabitha said, imitating her sister.

Grizzly had to rescue Charlotte, Ethan said, teasing his sister and trying to sound like the grown men did when they joked with one another.

Charlotte touched the back of her neck as if feeling for teeth marks. That damn dog! she said.

Zachary opened his mouth wide and widened his eyes in mock amazement. Now, Lotte, he said. Grizzly ain't damned; he's a blessing to you, to all you kids. He loves you and thinks he's saving you from drowning. Anyway, what treasures did you bring back from your hunt? he said, looking in the baskets, eyeing the mushrooms.

We got berries, and these flowers, and these mushrooms, too, Tabitha said.

Chicken of the woods, Mr. Zach, Ethan said. Your favorite.

Want one? Charlotte asked. We got plenty. She took a bracket of the golden-yellow fungus from one of the baskets, broke off three of the fan-shaped gills, and offered them to Zachary.

Now *I'm* blessed, he said. He took the mushrooms from Charlotte. Always heavier than they look, he thought. Feel like suede to the touch. He put the mushrooms to his nose. Their mild, earthy smell comforted him. Once or twice he'd had to practically live off them during the war.

Ah, wonderful! Zachary said. I'm going to go fry them up right now!

The children and the old man walked together, then the children turned off toward their house. Zachary paused and saw Esther watching them from her rocking chair. He waved his hand back and forth over his head to her then continued on, calling back to the children, Thank you, lovely Honeys! Give my love to your Gram, and to your father, too. And don't go half-drowning anymore—you don't want damn Grizzly fishing you out of the sea again.

ALL THOSE YEARS AGO Zachary Hand to God had watched Esther with her newborn baby on the tide-swashed rock until she'd rolled over and lain with her face down in the water, the child still tucked in her arms, in the water, too, and he'd set down his heavy clanking bag of tools and strode out over the rocks and knelt and turned her and the baby toward him so that the baby had lain on her breast. He gathered them in his arms and took them back to the Howdens' shack, where he found his neighbor and longtime friend, Grant Howden, standing dumb and damned and stupid.

Look at you, Grant, standing there, dumb, damned, and stupid as anyone has ever been.

Grant stood, still holding the pot of water he'd fetched, blank of face and brain, like he didn't even know or care that he was the maker of all this misery. Zachary didn't know how many no-good full-grown sons he'd watched steal their old mothers' money and food and blankets, and drink every jug, bottle, ladle, skinful of wine, whiskey, beer, moonshine, or worse they could snatch away in their shaking hands, until they lay in their mothers' beds vomiting their pickled insides all over the counterpane and dying right there and their mothers having had to have lived seventy years in order to get their hearts broken like that. And he couldn't count all the atrocious old men who'd mauled and molested and

murdered their own sons and daughters with their bare hands and practically skewered their young dead bodies and roasted them on spits and
eaten them headfirst, like backwoods Saturns, and tossed the bones into
the dirt for the dogs to gnaw, licking their own children's grease from
their fingers, glutted and serene, then lain down and fallen into the gen-
tlest, most peaceful of sleeps. Looking at his old friend Grant Howden
stand there like he had nothing to do with the devastation of his own
daughter was nearly enough to make Zachary resort to murder again
himself, except that his memories of fields covered in the butchered bodies of men and horses, their guts unspooled and tangled together, and of
trudging through the broth of earth and blood all the bodies stewed in
and the stench of it all broiling beneath an August sun and dogs feasting
on it all had cured him of killing.

Get that water heated, Zachary had said to Grant. They're both near
dead. She's bleeding and he's near frozen blue. Give me the sheet from
your bed and your shirt and get that water heated and bring it back to
me, then get out.

IT IS NEARLY MIDNIGHT. Esther wakens in her bed. Her baby is beside
her, safe, sleeping. Someone has cleaned him and swaddled him in a
wool blanket. She lies on her back staring up into the darkness. Her
body aches all over. She checks herself where the baby came out. She
cannot tell if she is hurt there but she is not bleeding and nothing feels
worse than the rest of her. She is hungry and parched. There is no food
or water on the stand next to the bed. Her father is not in the shack.

Esther gets out of bed. Her arms and legs and back hurt. Her neck
and head hurt, too. She rises to her feet and stands for a moment to get
her balance and wait for her head to stop spinning. Her child does not
stir. When she looks at him she becomes aware that her milk is coming,
already there, in fact. Part of her ache is her quickened milk.

Since her child sleeps, she goes to the door of the shack and opens it slowly onto the night, as if she is trying not to be heard or seen by anyone. The island is dark before her. The ocean is dark beyond the island. The sky is overflowing with clusters of stars that rise from the dark horizon of the ocean and reach overhead and descend into the trees on the mainland behind her, where the setting half-moon blazes. Her eyes adjust and the island glows and the moon swathes the dark ocean in its reflected light. For the first time, she realizes that looking at the moonlight on the ocean is like looking at the sun through two mirrors.

Esther steps into the dark yard. The hard soil in front of the door is cool and soothes her bare feet. The sound of the ocean is like deep, planetary breathing, strong, abiding. The air is cool and mild, scented as always with pine and salt and grass and flowers. Esther can smell herself, too. She smells different. There's blood. She can smell her milk, which has soaked through her shift. Her sweat smells richer, riper. Like a woman, she feels. Not a girl. She'd still felt a girl even throughout carrying the child.

Esther walks out of the yard and reaches the path that leads to the bluff. The stars and moonlight illuminate the path but she does not need to look where she steps, she knows the way so well. As she approaches the top of the bluff, the silhouette of her father rises into view against the starry background. He stands at the summit, at the edge of the bluff, in his usual place, his arms folded, rubbing his pipe between his fingers, letting smoke bubble from the corner of his mouth. As always, he looks calm, contemplative, to her, like he is taking stock of the day and fitting it into its place in the world. As if he is meditating or praying, but also arranging things.

The air is mild. The tide is heavy and thuds into the rocks below the bluff and withdraws from them hissing and gulping. Esther is silent in her bare feet. She reaches her father without him noticing. She stands behind him and looks at his broad back, his thick head of hair, deep red in the light, black now. He exhales a cloud of smoke from his mouth. It curls, arabesques, floats past the bluff, over the rocks and water, hovers for a moment, then scatters.

Esther steps forward and pushes her father off the bluff. She is surprised how easy it is—a good shove and there he goes into the dark. Any harder and she might have gone over with him.

The Governor's Council Committee on State Beneficiaries and Pensions. The Standing Committee submit the following report *To His Excellency the Governor and the Most Honorable Members of the Executive Council*, concerning State Paupers and the Overseers of the Poor, and in particular the pauper colony on so-called Apple Island, for years a disgrace to the adjacent communities and a blot upon the State.

In the summer of 1912 the committee of the Governor's Council visited the island, with additional friends invited as guests of the Honorable A. B. Cranmoor, President of the Council. After viewing the conditions, it was decided that the cause of humanity and public health necessitated the colony be broken up and the inhabitants segregated. Thoughtful objections to such a course were voiced by Matthew Diamond, M.Div., retired schoolteacher, who works closely with the colony residents. Mr. Diamond's objections were overridden. It was resolved that to clear the Island of its people the State should hold a title to the property. Subsequent to the visit, Judge Lambert convened his court and committed seven of the islanders to the State School for the Feebleminded.

A YEAR TO THE DAY after the Governor's Council first visited Apple Island, Matthew Diamond sits across from Eha Honey at the single table in the Honeys' shack, waiting for an answer. Eha made the stools the men sit on and the table between them. Esther Honey sits in her rocking chair a few feet away. Eha wears his usual loose overalls, which are covered in sawdust, stiff with pine sap and patterned with white crystalline blossoms of salt from the soaking and drying and soaking again of his sweat and ocean water and the long, coarse, colorless shirt he sleeps in every night. He wears boots tied together with twine and patched with tar. His derby hat sits in front of him on the table. Eha is small but in the tiny kitchen nook, crammed with the washbasin and woodstove, piles of drift and scrap wood, tackle broken or whole he cannot perceive, Matthew Diamond feels the strength coiled in his compact body, vibrating from it. Matthew Diamond has cut down many trees and dug many ditches and diverted many streams and built many lean-tos, cottages, and bunkhouses, and he can tell when a man has labored for his life.

The cold spring sun cuts through the window in front of Esther at a sharp angle and gilts half her weathered face in gold and casts the rest in shadow. Eha sits on the stool, silent, eyes directed to the tabletop but seeing what who can tell and he suddenly seems so dense of matter to Matthew Diamond as to be monumental, the stool beneath him about to explode as if a block of marble has just been lowered onto it and it only remains to be seen along which exact grains in the wood it will explode and collapse beneath the monolithic man. The sharp sun cuts behind Eha, across the raw-planked floor, and lights the back of his head and makes a bright halo of his braided and corkscrewed silver hair decorated with the trinkets his daughters weave into it. The sunlight shines off the bald crown of his head. Diamond scolds himself for not having noticed right away that this is the first time he's ever seen Eha without his hat on, up close, that even when he has noticed Eha without his derby on from afar, Eha has always put it on the moment he's seen Diamond; and Diamond knows he should have noticed that Eha has taken it off now in preparation for the decision he intends to announce, and that Diamond hadn't noticed because he was so intent on succeeding at his scheme to get Eha's son Ethan to Massachusetts, to save him, as he now clearly and shamefully but without a change of opinion sees it. Jews married Egyptians and Moabites Jews. The patriarchs took wives from far and wide. There was that on the one hand, and on the other there was the fact that

Noah's family peopled the world after the flood and therefore, like it nor not, Scripture unquestionably told that every man and woman with whomever you are confronted is a member of your family, so Matthew Diamond sits across from Eha Honey, and what he would call the indelible worst of him feels pity for the mixed-blooded man sitting across from him, whose son is light enough skinned and blue enough eyed and straight enough haired and artistically enough gifted that Diamond could call on one of the very few favors he thought he had to ask from his old friend and fellow seminarian Thomas Hale in order to take the boy away before the inevitable upcoming eviction from the island of its inhabitants, all combinations of colored and white, interbred within the same family, although the half dozen households go by different last names, half off to the asylum, the rest off to nowhere, to anywhere, to wherever they might singly or as a whole contrive to survive or perish, it makes no difference to the state. With what Matthew Diamond would call in hope but in his heart not quite believe the indelible best of him he has, as best as possible, put aside his doubts and fears about deceiving— there is no other word for it, although sometimes he calls it veiling, in the holy sense of the word, he hopes, but does not quite believe, in the spirit, anyway, of a veil protecting from view truths that might shatter a person—a father as to his motives for sending his son away.

Eha sits with his hands clasped in front of him on the table, mute. Esther sits in her rocking chair, mute, still. Son and mother still and mute and modeled by the light, framed in the bare wood of the shanty the son built which, for the first time, Matthew Diamond realizes, is, for its rawness and, he might call it, pungent, seasoned insides, beautifully and soundly constructed, not a shanty, but a sturdy, solid, square-jointed house. He suddenly wants to put a stop to it. He has an urge to tell Eha, who he forbears calling his friend because of the at least— what, tenth, half, totally?—false pretenses under which he is urging this man to have his son, Ethan, leave the island and travel south to Enon,

Massachusetts, to further his art and live on the estate of his friend—
friend friend, fellow, almost peer, if it not for Thomas Hale's family's
heritage and wealth, the sort of heritage Matthew Diamond spends his
days preaching against in favor of the common heritage of all souls; he
suddenly has the urge to tell Eha—mute, composed, dignified as a king,
as a true deputy of—what? grace?—and about to, Matthew Diamond
abruptly realizes because Eha has taken his hat off for the first time since
he has known him, about to consent to sending his son to Enon to study
painting without suspecting the motives behind his being persuaded into
doing so; he suddenly has the urge to tell Eha, Never mind; keep the boy
here; hold on to your son; keep your family together no matter where
God takes you.

But Matthew Diamond says nothing. The spring breezes rise and fall
outside the open window. The stool he sits on is spare and hard. The
shack smells of bodies and shellfish and animals and tobacco smoke. He
is thirsty. He is exhausted from his insomnia and he is sickened by his
incurable aversion to these people he truly believes he has been ordained
to help.

Eha looks at his clasped hands and wrings them once, and again.
They are rough and dark and thick-veined. The knuckles of his fingers
are white. They look as if they have been sanded.

Esther Honey stares at the space in front of her, composed, expres-
sionless, unblinking. Furious, Matthew Diamond thinks. She's letting
her son decide what he wants for his son. He doesn't think there's anything more to this than giving his son a chance to do what he loves. And
she hasn't said a word to him otherwise. And she is furious.

Because she knows.

Dear Jesus, Matthew Diamond thinks. Of *course* she knows. He is
so startled by the force of the revelation that he almost cries out loud.
Of course: how many other fairer-skinned Apple Islanders over the last
hundred years have realized that if they just slipped away from their

mothers and fathers and brothers and sisters and cousins and go somewhere no one knows them, no one will ever know about the blood that
flows in their veins, no one will ever be able to tell from their skin or
their eyes or their hair that their great-auntie was from Kamerun, that
their father's father came from Nubia by way of Mississippi, that their
mother was a full-blooded Indian? At least a few. At least two, three,
four? Maybe—maybe even one of her own brothers, one of her own
sisters.

Sweet Christ, Matthew thinks, I don't even know if she had a brother
or a sister. Or *has* one. I don't know anything about her mother or her
father. Matthew looks away from Esther. He feels like time has stopped.
He feels like he and Eha and Esther Honey and the room have all turned
to marble and he will spend eternity suspended in this dreadful irrevo-
cable moment.

Lawyers are filing documents. Judges are signing orders. Scientists
and doctors are collating data. Pharaoh's heart is as hard as ever.

Eha Honey unclasps his hands and puts them flat side-by-side on the
table. He leans backward and nods at Matthew Diamond. He smiles and
says, Ethan can go paint.

THE ISLANDERS PREPARED a send-off banquet for Ethan three days before he left for Massachusetts.

That morning, Iris and Violet McDermott took their pay for the week and went to the mainland and bought cream and milk from a bachelor farmer whose laundry they did and instead of heating water for washing, they rinsed their metal tub out and started a vat of chowder with a cod Candace Lark caught and a bucket of clams from Eha. Esther gave the girls directions to the far back corner of a field whose certainly by now long dead farmer had decades earlier stopped harvesting each year so that she and her mother and the other women could have some corn or potatoes for the island and whose subsequent owner had continued to leave untouched for the gleaners without a word or interruption. Tabitha and Charlotte returned with sacks of corn and they spent the afternoon shucking the ears and picking the silk from the rows of niblets. Annie Parker snuck off to the main with Rabbit Lark and they picked strawberries and raspberries and blackberries and Rabbit found nearly a handkerchief full of truffles. Eha gathered oysters from their beds and lobsters from his traps, and, how no one ever knew, a dozen brown bottles of ale brewed in Portland. Matthew Diamond asked for and received loaves of fresh bread from a baker in town and a block of new butter from a dairy. Theophilus Lark went about the island and borrowed every cup and plate and cleaned them all with his rag. He found two old doors and laid them end to end on sawhorses in the meadow to make a trestle table and brought four benches from the schoolhouse. Eha prepared a fire downwind near the tables and set a huge, ancient metal pot of water on it.

At seven o'clock, the islanders congregated at the tables. Matthew Diamond made a brief speech congratulating Ethan on his talent and encouraging him in his upcoming journey, which was no doubt frightening but also a blessing. Eha Honey presented Ethan with the rigging knife he'd inherited from Esther, who'd inherited it from her mother, who'd inherited it from her father, and so on, all the way back to Benjamin Honey, who'd carved the outline of Africa and the leviathans and mermaids into the whalebone handle himself.

Everyone cried, Three cheers for our Ethan! Then Mr. Diamond said a brief thanksgiving prayer for the meal and for everyone on the island. Everyone said, Amen, and Eha dumped all the wriggling lobsters into the boiling water.

The islanders feasted on lobsters, the tenderest they'd ever had, they all agreed, drenched in the melted fresh butter, bowls and bowls of the chowder, the creamiest and richest they'd ever had they all said, fresh bread, with the crustiest crust and softest insides anyone had ever eaten, broken in chunks from the loaves, slathered, too, in the fresh butter, oysters, the coldest and briniest and most succulent ever, everyone shouted in between sucking them from their shells, corn that everyone agreed was the sweetest they'd ever tasted as they munched their way along and around ear after buttered ear, the darkest, muskiest, most mysterious and beguiling truffles ever to have sprouted, and the sweetest, plumpest, freshest berries anyone had ever tasted, they said popping one after another down, or cramming handfuls at a time into their mouths, as the children and Annie Parker did. And the beer. Glorious, they all said. Rich, dark, creamy, fortifying. Everyone had a small glass, or two, including the children and Mr. Diamond. Even Rabbit Lark sipped some from a teacup painted with roses. The dogs galloped around the table, laughing and catching all the scraps the islanders threw at them in their mouths. The women sang their songs and Eha and Zachary Hand to God growled some old sea shanties and Matthew Diamond sang a lovely hymn in a clear, beautiful voice. Ethan was so overwhelmed and abashed that he wept even as he spooned more chowder into his mouth and cracked another lobster claw and sang along with the women's desolate, joyous songs.

The islanders were so used to diets of wind and fog, to meals of slow-roasted sunshine and poached storm clouds, so used to devouring sautéed shadows and broiled echoes; they found themselves stupefied by such an abundance of food and drink. For that evening it seemed to them as if they were sending Ethan off on all their behalves. And it seemed as if by sending him off to paint his beautiful pictures they all might somehow unhouse homelessness, might somehow bankrupt poverty. It seemed to all of them that evening as if they somehow might even starve hunger itself.

THE MORNING AFTER the feast, Ethan woke with bleary eyes and a slight headache from the beer. He took the small circle of mirror that had been his mother's from its shelf near his father's bed and sat on the rocks on the west side of the island and drew four self-portraits.

He had never drawn himself before and the picture of himself that emerged on the first piece of paper startled him. Rather than the face of the man he thought of himself as, the portrait looked startlingly boyish. Even though he had smoked tobacco for three years already and smelled like a grown-up and thought of himself as a man, he realized as he saw himself for the first time as others must see him, that that thought of himself as a man was the sort a child has. Suddenly, he panicked at leaving the island. For the next drawing, he studied himself in the mirror, scowling, almost, with concentration, and composed a portrait of what he thought he must have looked like, say, when he had had his first vertiginous, dizzying smokes at twelve years old, more boyish. That drawing, he realized, was technically better than the first, but a lie of a kind, not what he saw in the mirror but something he made up in his mind. The wind toppled the mirror. Ethan lifted it like the lid of a music box. The sun flared in the glass and his face appeared, backlit, ringed in its light, darker for the contrast than it really was, and for an instant he saw his father's side of the family pull forward to the front of his features. The image arose and disappeared in an instant but made an afterimage that Ethan superimposed onto the third portrait. He drew an oval within the square of paper and darkened the four corners around it so it looked like a cameo. He meant to make the portrait look like that of a Jacobin or Founding Father, an African commodore or king, Benjamin Honey, really, as he imagined his father's father's father's father's looks refracting down through the generations into his own, lighter and far more like his mother to outward appearance as he really was, and he deliberately drew the picture in three-quarter profile, which he knew by the portraits in Diamond's history book was more formal, more momentous. Gulls lifted from the water below the rocks and cried. Ethan stopped short of giving himself a high white collar like the ones he imagined old-time navy admirals wore, and a thick earring, like the ones he imagined pirates wore. He put deeper shadows in his face to make himself look more serious. The face now looked commemorative, as if copied from a statue. More like an African made to look European, he thought.

Eha bellowed from the house.

Coming! Ethan yelled back. He drew the fourth and last portrait in ten minutes flat. It was sparely drawn and without affectation.

His father bellowed again.

Yes! Ethan yelled. He placed the four drawings side by side. Something about each of the first three seemed false, forced. Too old, too sorrowful, worried-looking as it stared back at him. Lonesomeness swept over him. He didn't want to disappear from his family's life, their memories, their pictures of him in their heads, didn't want them to forget him, look at these old portraits decades on, his sisters showing them to their grandkids, saying, This is my brother; he gave this to me the last time I saw him; I never knew what happened to him, if he's still alive somewhere or died in a war or had a family or lived alone. Ethan squared up the four drawings and tucked them into his shirt so no one would see them and hurried back to the house.

ESTHER DELOUSED ETHAN the day before he left for Massachusetts. Everyone on the island was infested with vermin, every dog and cat with fleas, every bed and blanket with bugs. Esther sat Ethan on Eha's nail keg in the yard.

Got to do it before dark, she said. So I can see the bugs. She wrapped her own hair in a dishrag. So mine don't defect and become yourn.

She stood behind the boy and tipped his head back and trickled kerosene from a tin can onto his head.

It stings, Ethan said. And stinks. The fumes whirled behind his eyes and inside his thoughts.

Means it's working, Esther said.

When she'd used all but a few last drops of the kerosene she put the can on the ground and raked her fingers through his hair. Eha sat in the rocking chair, watching. Esther massaged at Ethan's head. She puffed her pipe.

Kerosene'll kill 'em, she said.

Eha said, Kerosene'll kill 'em.

Ethan, hoarse and teary, said, Kerosene'll kill 'em.

Esther worked Ethan's hair and puffed her pipe and the three of them were quiet in the bright salted light.

After a minute, Eha said, Maybe you'd better lend me your pipe, Mother.

Esther froze, Ethan's hair clutched up in her hands. She stood for a moment and gently sucked at the pipe stem. A puff of smoke came from her mouth. Then another.

Maybe it'd better, she said. Maybe you'd better come get it.

It'd be best, Eha said, rising. He crossed the dirt and leaned down and delicately enclosed the pipe bowl in his large, calloused hand, covering the mugwort embers smoldering inside, and took it from his mother's mouth. When he was a few feet away from his kerosene-soaked kin, he plugged the pipe between his teeth and puffed at it.

Not bad, he said, and sat back down.

Esther began picking away at Ethan's head again, drawing a nit at a time from his hair and placing them in the kerosene she'd saved in the can.

Easier with my razor, Eha said.

Esther said, Can't go over there looking like a convict.

True enough. Eha drew on the pipe and held the smoke in his lungs for half a moment and exhaled. He stabbed deep into his hair and scratched at his scalp. Maybe you can do mine after.

Not enough tobacco in Virginia to get me to dig into that mess, she said, crunching a nit between her nails.

Nor birdlime or squirrel bait, neither, Ethan said. How does it get so knotted up, anyway?

Eha patted his braided and bunched hair as if feeling for sparrows or mice. Elves tie it. When I sleep.

Esther thumbed her grandson's hair from nape to crown, the thick sheafs riffling behind like pages. Her fingers ached, joints swollen, the pain in her knuckles running in lines up her fingers into her palms, up her wrists, deeper into her arms. She saw a nit and held the hair up and reeved it through the lock. Kerosene fumed from his soaked head. Ethan sat quiet and submissive though she pushed and yanked and grabbed and plucked. Lovely child. She leaned closer, squinted, and drew another bug.

She murmured to him, Make pictures beautiful as you can.

Yes, Gram. I will.

Pictures of what you really see.

I will, Grammy.

His head bowed, listening, heeding, mindful. She thought, He doesn't even think of it, of me, him, of us. He loves me. I love him. Despite everything. Despite all you or I or any of us ever will be. She pressed the sides of his head with her thin, aching hands as if to settle him, although he was still.

She wanted to kiss him on the head but couldn't because of the kerosene, so instead she whispered, I'm going to miss you very much.

ESTHER GLEANED THE last nit from her grandson's hair and the bottom of the lowering sun punctured on the pine treetops and its light splintered across the yard. She rinsed her hands in a bucket of seawater and took her pipe back from Eha and struck a match and kindled it alight and dropped the match into the can of kerosene-soaked nits and a flame *whupped* from the can's mouth then burned wobbly and dim like a brazier at an improvised altar in a nomads' camp. Ethan went down to the shore and walked into the water up to his thighs and bent and bathed his hair.

The salt water burned his scalp even worse but it felt clean and efficacious and he thought, So at least I know I'm still my grandma's grandson and my father's child.

Ethan slept outdoors that night, just beyond the gateless gate, in a grassy clearing so he would not catch any lice or bedbugs back from his family. Crickets chirped in chorus, the Atlantic winds blew over the island, the surf boomed in the hollows below the bluff. Ethan lay wrapped in a century-old wool blanket, freshly washed by Iris and Violet and bug-free, looking into the reaches of stars. His head stung and felt perforated. As he lowered into sleep the salty pined breeze and cricket songs and schools of stars poured into and birled around his brains so the night became his mind and his mind the night and the mother owl watching over him swooped down from her tree and through his dreams.

2

BRIDGET CARNEY HAD an afternoon alone to herself so she spent it in the library. Mr. Hale had left for Concord that morning and once she finished cleaning up after breakfast she was free. A spring storm blew across the yard beyond the high windows. The trees at the borders bowed in the gusts of wind and straightened in the pauses and rain swept in sheets across the greening grass. Water poured from the corners of the roof and braided and tailed away from the windows and seemed to be drawn spinning back up into the sky then dashed back against the house and sounded like buckets of nails tossed against the shingles and glass. The white sky filled the room with a bright silvery-white gray light and Bridget did not light any lamps. She sat in one of the deep upholstered chairs arranged in front of the dark fireplace and listened soundless and still to spring blustering and whisking up new flowers and greening the grass, blowing across the open mouth of the chimney three floors above, and sounding wide hoarse intermittent notes through the firebox she imagined was a song of promise and upheaval played by the presiding spirits of April—the same spirits, she thought, as she thought of her mother and father, as those that tumbled and crashed over her cottage back home, just beyond the southwestern tip of the Dingle Peninsula in Ireland, on Great Blasket Island.

The winds calmed at intervals and the room descended and settled into deep silence, deeper than no sound, into deeper denser depths of the season, and stray, fat dollops of rain spattered singly or in pairs or quartets in sequence against the wet wood or wet glass, against the perfect silence of the stilled outside air. The silence sharpened the bright

silvery-white gray light and the light sharpened the colors in the room
and the outlines of the gold mirrored clock on the wall and the black and
white etchings of the tulips and anemones and their black frames, and
the black and white rubbings of the knights in their armor from the Ital-
ian gravestones, and the red and black and brown spines of the books on
the shelves, and the gold lettering embossed into them, and the leather
on the chairs, and the upholstery on the couch and the wooden tables
and brass and porcelain and pewter lamps on them, and the livid crim-
son of the Persian rug and the mossy green and gray-blue flowers and
rust-colored vines woven across it. Overnight, the storm would almost
surely make sleeping uncertain for her, the noise and roaring in the dark
unsettling, and she'd possibly even end up provoked, tired, grouchy the
next morning when she came to the kitchen, and after she ate her toast
the racket with the crockery and china would make her want to com-
plain out loud although no one would be there to hear her, the only other
person in the house old Mr. Hale, Thomas Hale, up in his rooms, looking out the windows or at a copy of Milton or Ovid. But for the hour,
nothing could have quieted her more, hushed her heart, soothed her into
perfect melancholy peace more than the mild violent rejuvenating tigers
of spring charging the length and breadth of Enon.

That night she slept deeply and without interruption. The fitfulness
she had worried about during the afternoon never came to pass and as
soon as she closed her eyes she dropped like a diver in a bell into the
depths of sleep. She woke the next morning with no recollection of having dreamed, but she did have a sense of recently having been traveling
with thrilling speed, and underwater, she realized, as well, of perhaps
being shuttled to waking clinging to the knobbed back of a torpedoing
whale, perhaps returning her from a secret visit back to her home, where
she'd stood on the dark familiar beach and looked at the dim silhouette
of her cottage on the slope, sorrowful, but comforted knowing her parents were asleep inside, perhaps themselves dreaming of her standing on

the beach in the dark, asking her, Why have you come home, Bridget? Why have you come back to us from the water?

SOME MORNINGS BRIDGET woke early, when the huge house was silent and still except for the clocks and hulking radiators clanging in remote rooms. She navigated the stairs so that they creaked as little as possible, the quiet a smooth fragile shell she did not want to crack. She often found old Mr. Hale standing at a window in the library, watching the light rise from behind the hickory trees across the meadow. He said good morning to her quietly, as if he, too, did not want to break the spell of silence, the latency of the house in fledgling day, as if like her he took pleasure in watching the world rouse into the light and the light flood into and fill the house with waking and bustle, even though it was only the two of them for the time being, except for Alan Dodge, the caretaker, and the boys from town who occasionally helped him with larger jobs.

It is nice when the sun rises this early, Mr. Hale would say on a spring morning. I don't feel like I'm up all night, like I'm so much a ghost.

Bridget had an abashed affection for the man but he seemed like a living memorial, or like a guardian spirit, or quite what she could not say, but that an inner decorum and formality and modesty of manner were required when she was with him, which she loved and which she felt with no one else. He alone made her feel as if her work, her life, in America, the awful trip over the ocean, being away from her mother and father—so far away it barely felt real anymore, felt as if her sorrow and longing were for people and places her imagination had invented—Mr. Hale alone could make her feel as if her job were important enough to bear being an orphan. There was something rarefied and ancient about him. She did not know how old he actually was—she imagined he must be at least eighty. Older even. Maybe much older. To talk with him was to talk with someone who had spoken with men who personally remembered the American Revolution. He spoke with her in a gentle, mildly surprised way, as if she might be a premonition rather than a girl. They treated one another with the solicitude and tenderness of beings from different planets meeting for the first time, even though he left the run of the house to her so long as she attended his few and moderate needs.

Have you been up all night, sir?

Much. Not all. I slept from midnight to half past three. In the chair, of course, but. Are you cold?

No, sir. A little. But I like it.

I used to like that, too.

Were you reading?

Some Ovid.

The ones you told me about the flowers and animals and girls?

No. Ones after he was deported from his home. Poems about exile. A little glum, but they fit being up late at night alone. They seem noble after midnight. *To embrace hope is good; not so hope's endless disappointments*, and so forth.

Bridget placed the tray with his black coffee and toast on the desk.

They always turn maudlin when the sun comes up, though, he said. And I'm always a little embarrassed to have been enchanted by them again.

Bridget saw Mr. Hale's young self in the thin, esoteric old man standing at the window. His posture was straight and his white hair short and neat. His blue eyes were lucid and luminescent. They saw, still saw, what was before them but also what they had seen years before, and it seemed, too, a little of what lay in store. He seemed to carry within him his own father and grandfather, even his great-grandfather. She had accompanied him on his walk through the woods twice—rare, special occasions, solemn and hushed, not because the old man was sanctimonious, but because Bridget was so reverent of him, and bewildered, too.

He sometimes paused and surveyed the lay of the land and whether it confirmed to him his sense of where he thought he stood, according not to how things were then but how they had been at some time that seemed to her prehistoric.

On the second walk he had stopped for a moment and looked around, then pointed to a spot on the ground and said to her, Dig just there a little, perhaps, yes, there. She knelt and swiped away the orange pine needles and scooped up a wedge of earth. She squeezed the soil in her fist and it crumbled away. She opened her hand and there in her palm lay a Penobscot arrowhead.

We have a guest coming, Bridget.

Yes, Mr. Hale.

Mr. Hale stood at the window in his study, looking at the high grass in the meadows.

A young man, Mr. Hale said. He's an artist, or he means to be. He is a kind of refugee, I suppose. I've arranged a place for him at the art college in Barnton in the fall. If he does well there, I suppose he could eventually study at the Museum School, in Boston. My friend, Mr. Abbott, is the president of the Copley Society; I am sure he could find a place for the boy if he has talent. That would be something . . .

Mr. Hale broke off speaking and looked from the window to Bridget, standing dutifully and without any idea who Mr. Abbott was or what the Copley Society was.

Yes, well, Mr. Hale said, none of that is important. In any case, I have agreed to let him sleep in the barn for the rest of the summer in the meantime and to paint pictures of whatever he likes around the property. I thought he might find some good subjects during the hay mowing. A friend of mine who is helping him and his family sent some of his drawings; he is quite good. I had art supplies shipped to him a while ago.

Paints and brushes. Canvas. I don't know much about paintings beyond looking at them and liking them or not. There was a book about technique, how not to make mud of the colors, I imagine—but there I go again; you are most tactful with all my wondering aloud about things.

Yes, Mr. Hale. That was very kind of you. To help the young man. Is very kind of you.

If it wouldn't be too much trouble, would you mind preparing extra servings for his meals. And see that he has bedding and a lantern for the barn? He may sleep in the old caretaker's room. There's a bed there that should still be tolerable to sleep on.

Yes, Mr. Hale, certainly.

A YOUNG MAN. Bridget did not like that. Not that she did not like young men. But she liked being alone at the Hale estate, just her and Mr. Hale, without his son, Robert, and his son's wife, Amelia, and their ten-year-old daughter, Phoebe. They had left two months ago and were not due back for almost a year. Mr. Hale's son was an astronomy professor at Harvard University in Cambridge and he had taken his wife and Phoebe to Peru, where Harvard had a new telescope observatory, in order to map the stars. Mr. Hale told Bridget that his son had discovered a new moon orbiting the planet Saturn fifteen years earlier and had named it Phoebe. When his daughter had been born five years later, he'd named her Phoebe, too, after the moon. The moon was dark, Mr. Hale said, darker than all the others, and it circled around Saturn in the direction opposite all the others, too. Bridget could not help but think of those facts whenever she took care of Phoebe the girl, who was not dark of mood and who did not in any obvious way oppose the family's or village's manners, but whose behavior and personality nonetheless struck Bridget as a touch more out of humor, a shade more contrary once she knew the astrological facts.

Phoebe had developed an odd, dirty habit before she left for Peru. One morning she was playing at the edge of the pond after breakfast, Bridget minding her in the distracted way she sometimes did, still wearing her kitchen apron, her hands in the front pockets, fiddling with the house keys on the big steel ring, humming to herself, smiling but not at any particular happy thought. Bridget looked at the clouds and looked at the pond and looked at the broad meadows beyond the pond as if she were seeing them for the first time or realizing for the first time that this was not Great Blasket, although she'd been in Enon then for more than two years. Phoebe kneeled in the clean white and gold gravel that the groundskeepers had raked evenly over the little beach area no one used, except on occasion her grandfather when he stood at the water at dawn and smoked a pipe after a sleepless night of reading Milton or Ovid and looked at the still, misted surface of the water for a giant pike that presided over—tyrannized—the pond, a miniature sea monster for a miniature ocean.

There had been rain the night before and the gravel was still wet and looked like precious stones.

Now your smock will be wet down the front, Bridget said.

It's not too bad, Bridge. It's not that wet, Phoebe said, raking through the gravel with her fingers, picking up a pebble, putting it up close to her eyes, turning it between her forefinger and thumb, trying to get it to catch the sun, seeing if it might capture a little light, and tossing it aside when it remained dull.

It'll dry off by the time we get back to the house. Are you thinking about that boy from the harrier, Freddy? That snapped Bridget from her reverie, which had included in a vague, atmospheric way the young apprentice at the stable in the village. She frowned at Phoebe.

What's wrong with your mouth? Why are you talking funny?

I think I bit my tongue.

You don't think you bit your tongue, Phoebe Hale. You bit it or you did not.

Maybe I did it asleep. Were you thinking about Freddy?

Then you'd have woken yourself from it. And talked funny at breakfast. And eaten your oatmeal funny. And Freddy nothing; I've got plenty other on my mind today.

Well, maybe I just did it now, looking for treasure, and didn't even feel it. Do you like him?

Bea, you've not put more stones in your mouth, have you? As she asked, she knew. You have! You've got those dirty rocks in your mouth again!

No I don't. It's a sore coming on. Is he going to be there when the men take the horses for shoes on Friday?

I haven't the slightest idea where in the whole of dear, green Enon that boy will be on Friday. And sore my hat. If I'd done such a thing at home, my mother'd have clapped my mouth shut and pinched my nose till I swallowed the lot, then fed me another mouthful to make sure I'd sooner jump from a tower into the sea than put a dirty rock in my mouth again. Out, she said, out! and held her hand open under Phoebe's mouth.

Phoebe frowned and spat four slick, glowing pebbles into Bridget's hand.

Is that why you moved here? Phoebe said. To get away from your awful mother?

Two gunshots sounded from the woods beyond the Hales' meadow, flat, dry, small. Freddy and another boy from the village emerged from the trees two minutes later. They crossed the field and passed in front of the firs, headed for the road. Both slouched and walked slowly, leisurely, as if young princes, Bridget thought. They held their guns by the stocks, barrels down, casually, as if the rifles were pitchforks or rakes.

Phoebe yelled to them, You're trespassing on my family's property, but that's alright with me! Both boys looked up at the girls.

Shush, Phoebe! Bridget said. The boys continued across the field.

What were you shooting at? Phoebe called.

Nothin', Freddy grunted.

Did you hit it? she asked.

A COMPANY OF itinerant Dutch farm workers from the Hudson Valley appeared at the Hale estate every summer sometime in the middle of July to mow and hay its thirty acres of meadow. They usually arrived one evening at dusk from wherever their last job had been, a small caravan of two or three wagons driven and accompanied by quiet men wearing wide-brimmed field laborers' hats turning off the road at twilight, the men setting up camp in the barnyard. The men made a small fire and ate a simple meal in silence and went to sleep soon after. An hour before sunrise, the men rose and ate a simple breakfast and drank black coffee and smoked pipes, silent except for the ringing scrape of their scythes being sharpened by the crew captain's son, a boy of twelve who was deaf and sometimes sang out notes as he ran his whetstone along a blade, and if it was too early in the morning and his singing too loud his father gently touched him on the shoulder and he knew he was singing out loud and stopped.

Sunup, the men spaced themselves abreast along the edge of the east meadow and at the captain's word began to mow, raising and sweeping their scythes in unison, the high summer grass collapsing in front of them as they advanced.

THE YOUNG MAN that Mr. Hale had invited for the summer—Ethan was his name, Ethan Honey—showed up at the house late in the afternoon during the first day of haying. Mr. Hale had told Bridget that Ethan Honey would take the horse trolley from the train station in Barnton to the center of Enon and walk the mile from there. Bridget was in the barn preparing the bed for him and when she came out she saw him across the meadow where the men were mowing, standing as if paralyzed at the entrance of the drive. She felt shy to meet him and wished she could pretend she hadn't seen him and go back to the house and wait to be introduced to him by Mr. Hale, when she could get a good look at him, say, Nice to meet you, and leave as if she had other, pressing chores she had to get to right away. Now, she was dusty and sweaty and knew her face must be bright red the way it got when she worked in this kind of summer heat.

But Bridget waved anyway and yelled, Hello! Are you the painter? This is Mr. Hale's place!

The young man took a couple steps toward Bridget and hesitated.

She called out, Yes, yes, it's alright! This is the place.

The young man walked up the long drive and as he came closer Bridget saw that he was a boy, really, no more than a year older than her, maybe fifteen, maybe sixteen, even, but not any older than that. And she saw that he was from poor folk, like her. His clothes were old hand-me-downs—worn but well patched and mended— now rumpled from his long trip. Bridget imagined the sack he carried had one extra shirt in it, at most, and probably not another pair of pants. His face and arms were deeply sunbaked. He obviously spent his time outdoors. But he looked pale somehow, too—like he might have had a bad dose of something.

Or all this is a shock, Bridget thought. That was it; he was a culchie—a bumpkin—terrible names that came to her for the boy—not hers; they were the words she'd heard her cousins tell they'd been called when they'd once gone to Tralee.

I'm Bridget, she said. I set up the room for you in the barn. There's a bed there. All your painting supplies arrived for you a couple days ago. Come along. I'll show you.

The boy—Ethan, Bridget reminded herself—did not speak but followed her to the barn and into the room, looking first up into the reaches of the rafters, then sticking only his head through the doorway to the room, looking around in it before he entered, not knowing what to think or what to say or do, the way she thought a dumbfounded child might act first being shown his bed at an orphanage. Dust still hung in the air from Bridget's sweeping. The room was hot and still and had that stale smell of dryness and thick long-settled dust recently disturbed.

You can sit down on the bed. It's okay. I just finished getting it ready, although it may not seem like it. You must be tired. It's so hot in here; I'm sorry; they're mowing the meadow and I thought it might be bad if I opened the window; the grass and the stubble and everything that gets kicked up gets into and onto everything—but I can open it for you if you'd like. Bridget made a step toward the window, wishing she could disappear, but also more and more interested in this boy. She saw his fingers were smudged with black soot. He smelled like sweat, and tobacco, so he smoked, too. She wondered what he painted, what his paintings looked like. Mr. Hale's house was full of paintings, some very beautiful, but many just boring portraits of well-dressed, stern-looking people. Ethan might like to see them sometime, she thought. I could give him a museum tour.

Before Bridget could unlatch and open the window, the boy (*Ethan*, she reminded herself again) spoke his first words.

It's alright, he said.

Bridget turned from the window. Ethan was sitting on the bed, holding his sack on his lap. He did; he looked like a child, so shocked by where he found himself that there was nothing he could do beside sit on the edge of the bed and hold his sack and wait for whatever came next to befall him.

The window is alright, he said.

You might like to open it later tonight, when the mowing's over and the air settled, Bridget said. You must be hungry. I'll go get you something from lunch.

Bridget practically ran from the barn. She felt awful for doing so, but other than when she minded young Phoebe Hale, she was mostly used to taking instructions and saying please and thank you and not much more and she did not know what to say to the boy. She brought three slices of bread and a cold chicken leg and a pitcher filled with cold spring water and ice back to the barn but Ethan was asleep, looking as if he'd simply fallen over sideways from where he'd sat, his legs still hanging half off the bed.

Bridget put the food on the stand next to the bed and put the pitcher under the stand on the floor. She thought, Even if he sleeps until tomorrow and all the ice melts, it will still be cool for him when he wakes up, parched and wondering where in the world he is.

Do you mind if I watch you draw? Bridget asked Ethan when, after a day spent mostly watching the mowers from just inside the opened barn doors (and stepping back out of view whenever Bridget came out to bring him food or to hang the laundry), he first ventured to the meadow and began sketching. She normally would not have dared to ask, but Ethan seemed both so strange and familiar—seemed like he was someone she knew very well, even, possibly—but so displaced from where and when she knew him that he also seemed a total stranger. And when she saw him from the windows over the kitchen sink, carrying his easel and big sheets of paper and a wooden box that turned out to contain the charcoal sticks he sketched with, she found herself so curious about what he'd draw and how it would look and wanted so much to watch how it was done that she could not resist asking.

I'm done with my morning chores and don't have anything to do until before lunch. I've never met an artist before.

Ethan Honey had always drawn with his sisters and the other island kids scrabbling around him, and in front of his grammy and his father.

In front of Mr. Diamond, too. But he was mortified at the thought of this girl—this girl he found very lovely, he realized, too—his own age, watching him while he worked (that he was *working*, struck him suddenly, as well) and began stuttering out an excuse why he'd prefer her not to but every reason that came to mind sounded feeble or offensive or mean-spirited as he struggled for the words so he stopped hemming and hawing and said, No, I don't mind at all.

So Bridget spread a picnic blanket she'd brought with her over the stubbled grass, behind where he was working, and sat down and saluted her hand against her forehead to shade the sunlight and watched in silence.

I forgot to bring a hat for the sun, she said.

Well, you remembered to bring a blanket to sit on, he said.

ETHAN SKETCHED THE windrows of hay and the meadow took shape in the blank space around them. He sketched the tedder and the men raking behind and it may as well have been haying an invisible meadow on an invisible planet. Or an afternoon cutting grooves around a planetary cylinder, Bridget thought. The light in the real meadow before her was full of suspended pollen and dust and chaff from the mowing. She could almost see the pollen powdering the hair on Ethan's bare forearms and his head.

The hot bright afternoon and the gleaning birds and the mowing men and this beautiful boy, paused in front of his sketch, rolling a cigarette, his charcoal-covered fingertips blackening the paper, and he licked across the edge of the cigarette paper with his bright tongue and put the cigarette between what Bridget noticed with a slight rush of breath were his full lips and took a kitchen match from the back pocket of his pants and struck it against the little wooden box he kept his charcoal sticks in and touched it to the end of the cigarette and deeply inhaled smoke into his lungs and held it and crossed his arms and stood back from the drawing and contemplated it and let the smoke from his lungs in a sustained relaxed torrent that made a matted blue cloud in the sunlight and smelled sweet and made her want to smoke. This boy before her, smoking his cigarette and looking at the sketch deciding it was done, seemed like a ghost, not because he was otherworldly or like a hallucination but because Bridget knew that she would remember this moment for however long she lived in its perfect entirety—the grass, the sunlight, the blue cloud of smoke, the tedder and the windrows and the mowing men, this boy she found more and more beautiful—and she could already feel what it was going to be like to look back on it and remember the young girl she'd once been and the young boy who'd stood right in front of her and whisked a stick of charcoal around and nearly miraculously rendered the grass, the light, the mowers, the windrows, the huge, heavy, volumed, shadowed, sunny, swarming, monolithic stacks of hay—everything she saw and anticipated remembering—onto a white pane of paper exactly as it looked to her own eyes.

THE TEDDER WUFFLED the hay and the men followed behind, raking the hay into windrows that followed the contours of the meadow. Bridget thought of the phonograph in the library and how the stylus traced the grooves cut in the wax cylinders and sent electric vibrations to the box and one of Verdi's arias poured from the horn, as if someone were singing from the past to a lost lover today through an enormous lacquered black and gold lily. Many of the artifacts and conveniences of the Hales' home astonished Bridget when she first saw or used them, but not the phonograph. Her neighbors on the island back home had been nearly the first in all Ireland to have one, poor as they were, and her father had somehow managed to buy the second one. Her mother and father sang along with "Never Mind the Why and Wherefore" on summer evenings after supper. Winter nights, her mother sang "Sweet Spirit, Hear My Prayer" along with Marie Narelle. She imagined a sunbeam swinging down from behind a cloud and tracing the windrows of hay like a stylus. She thought of asking Ethan what music he thought would sound from a phonograph made from light and gyres of cut grass, and would a picnic party on the moon hear the music.

ETHAN HONEY SMOKED and looked at his drawing and it reminded him of the island. From the rise where he had watched his sisters cross the channel, when the sun was out and the tide high and the waterway between the island and the mainland illuminated and undulating, the currents inside its liquid jade body had sifted the dark ragged seaweed into long slowly rotating cylinders like the windrows of hay he gazed at now. He suddenly again wanted to be home. He was hot, probably sunburned, again, on his arms and nose and face and his neck, too. The hot sweet hay perfume mingled with the cigarette smoke and he wanted to sit down but there was no natural place to do so in the middle of the field. Ethan wanted to turn around and look at the girl again—Bridget? Yes, Bridget—but he could not think of a good reason to give her if he did. He already could not quite remember how she looked and was surprised that he even wanted to. He thought, You could paint her and look at her as much as you liked. But the thought seemed rude, rough, put that way, which he didn't mean. The rows of hay rotated cylindrically in place in the vaporous heat, raspy and scratchy, clumping and dropping over themselves, rising and falling in long bands as if the contours of the meadow were swelling and hollowing on the surface of a tide. There were good places to sit and rest or watch or doze or talk or draw all around Apple Island, the exposed granite on the bluff, the rocks near the water when the tide was low, the bank next to the spring in the stand of birches on the southern end of the island, the benches everyone had outside next to their doorways, Gram's battered rocking chair, his father's keg of nails that Ethan loved to sit on and draw a bee or butterfly or Gram while she smoked her pipe with her eyes closed facing the sun, rocking slightly, or talked about the island—which she swore she'd never once stepped foot off in what Ethan imaged must have been her near hundred years; few of the islanders knew what year it was, never mind what year they'd been born, at least until Mr. Diamond began announcing the date each morning at school; and Ethan had never seen her do so, and he wanted to believe it was true, but didn't—and in his sudden dizziness in the sweltering, landlocked meadow he wished he could sit down on the keg next to her and have a drink of cool water from the spring that always seemed colder for being sipped from the tin ladle they kept hung from a nail on a nearby tree, but the ladle would not be up with Gram at her chair but in the birch stand where the spring was but Gram was at the house and not the bluff so where was the spring and there was always fresh clean sea air not full of dust and pollen and chaff that glued up in your nose and your throat and made it hard to breath and.

Are you feeling well, Ethan Honey?

Yes—he turned around, glad for the excuse to see the girl again, but hot, confused, suddenly not quite sure why he was in this field with her, painting hay.

Bridget.

Bridget, he said, embarrassed. Of course he knew her name. He hadn't forgotten it. He'd just forgotten *himself* for a second there.

I think I better maybe have some water. He was panting. He tried to stop, but he could not seem to get quite enough air into his lungs.

Bridget perked up. I'll get you some. I'm glad to, she said.

I think I'd better sit down. Ethan wiped the back of his neck with his handkerchief. Bridget led him to a swath of shade under a red pine tree growing alongside one of the stone walls that bounded the property along the dusty street, which connected the part of west Enon called Egypt to the center of the village.

Bridget told him to sit against the wall and close his eyes and breathe easy and there wasn't any poison ivy in the wall to worry about, the men took care of that every spring, and she'd just go up to the house and get some water. Ethan watched her run off and he wanted to scramble over the fence onto the bright blistering dirt road and hurry all the way home. But he didn't even know which direction to take. And he wanted to be there when the girl, Bridget, came back.

Shade cast by the pine extended over him and beyond, reaching just short of the first rows of cut hay. The branches of the tree stretched above, dark and still, holding heat inside them. The mowers raked in a bright band of light between the branches and the shade, their torsos and legs obscured behind the intervening rows of hay. Their calls to one another reached Ethan in quavering syllables warped by the inter- vening hot air. The light and the heat and the hay intervened. The men worked across a translucent sash of papyrus, bright and glowing, unroll- ing across Ethan's field of vision. The men's voices did not match with their movements.

Hear after I see them. Haven't heard a bird or insect since morning. Were there birds or insects this morning? No surf. So quiet, he thought. His eyes closed and his head nodded forward and he fell asleep. The Dutchmen worked in a meadow of waves, scything the tide, mowing breakers, reaping the hissing, carbonated grass.

ETHAN? ETHAN HONEY?

Ethan woke, his dreams of the field and the ocean evaporated and resolved into Bridget holding a wooden tray with a glass pitcher, two drinking glasses, and what looked like a dish towel wrapped around a brick. Pale yellow liquid that held the sunlight filled the pitcher.

You fell asleep. You're in the Hales' meadow, in Enon.

I know, he said. He sat up quickly and smiled at the girl, trying to appear clearheaded even though his face burned and was soaked with sweat and part of his brain still could not recall where he was. He felt like a little child. Yes, he said. Yes, I know.

Since Ethan had left the island and traveled by train through Portland and Portsmouth and more towns and cities than he'd ever have thought there could be between the island and the village of Enon—though as he thought that he also realized that he'd never really imagined how many towns there might be, itself a small revelation—a small, hinged hatch opened to reveal another small but startling dimension of his ignorance in the act of it being filled with the knowledge that dispelled it: since he'd left the island, he had not only suffered the simple sorrows of leaving home and family, but had plunged through a continuous, cascading befuddlement of new facts and sights and sounds, every one of which, in itself more or less fascinating or mundane, connecting with every other and constellating into more or less astonishing clusters of impressions he did not know in the least what to make of before they passed the train window. Shock and aftershock struck and echoed and shaped the vastness of the world across the inside of his skull, or so it felt. It was no more than seeing his first automobile idling at a train stop, and so also seeing his first driver, in a mud-spattered long coat with a pair of goggles strapped to his face. It was no more than seeing women wearing clean, new, richly colored dresses, wearing beautiful and shapely and perfectly fitted hats. It was no more than seeing brick mills that appeared to be larger than the whole island he came from, with smokestacks that appeared not just to reach the clouds but actually to be making them or possibly venting them from the insides of the earth. It was no more than seeing buildings six stories high. It was no more than seeing only people his mother and grammy and aunties called plain white and, after not being able to name it at first, realizing that every one of them with whom he came into even the briefest contact, which, certainly, had not been very many, treated him as if he were plain white, too, unlike the main-landers in Foxden, who knew his folks. It was no more than these things, but it was these things, piled up, in sequence, clotted and expanding and spiraling, making him breathless and feeling small, exposed, frag-ile, panicked, alone.

But he also felt a terrified thrill. He strained to envision how he could put all the color and forms, the sheer swarming depths of it all onto canvas or paper. How could he get all that with paint or charcoal? Ethan found himself naturally puzzling over how to shape and capture everything—and everyone—he saw, and he realized, too, that deliber-ately preoccupying himself with such matters also helped to stave off the panic threatening to overtake him.

I'm sorry I left you so long, Bridget said. I was getting you a cup of water then Mr. Hale called me for something and when I was done I thought that maybe some lemonade would be nicer.

Lemonade was new, too. In fact, lemons were new. Ethan knew what lemons were; he'd seen them in the still-life paintings in Mr. Diamond's art books. But he'd never seen a real one. He knew what lemonade was as well, or thought he did. Lemons squeezed into water. He tilted his head back, stretching the muscles in his neck. So sleepy, like a spell. Like a sleeping potion, the pine and cut grass and hot sun and still, hot air and the men's far-away voices, the spicy dry soil beneath the tree. Perfume. He wiped wetness from his cheek and chin, and pine needles that looked like cat whiskers and some dirt, twigs, and spider webs and mulchy whatnot from his hair, even more embarrassed. Drooled in my sleep.

The sun and heat can do that. Put you under a spell, Bridget said. I've fallen asleep around here and not woken up practically until sundown my afternoon off. I feel like I've woken up in another country. Some-times I even think I'm back home and that's worst of all. But it's alright; you're right here.

Bridget unwrapped the bundle as she spoke, pulling open a corner of the cloth at a time and fully laying it out until what looked to Ethan like a block of solid glass sat on the square towel.

It's ice, Bridget said.

Yes, he said.

It was as clear as glass. You could read a book through it. It was like crystal. Not cloudy. Not smoky. Not gray. Flawless. No bubbles or cracks or lines. Bridget drew an awl from her apron and gripped it in reverse and began stabbing at the block with a sturdy, steady strength that reminded Ethan of the girls and women on Apple Island. Glistening ice chips piled on the cloth. A film of water formed on top of the block and spittered with each nick of the awl. The cloth beneath the ice darkened with water.

Melts fast on days like this, Bridget said. Pardon my hands, she laughed. She scooped the ice and dropped half into one glass and half into the other. Her hands were bright pink and wet with the icy water. Her fingernails were chewed down, the skin around them livid and scarlet. As if she saw Ethan noticing, she drew her hands behind her back and dried them on her dress.

Bridget lifted the pitcher with one hand still behind her back, which made her look formal, and Ethan saw she was flustered and blushing and he felt his own cheeks heat again. Bridget poured lemonade into each glass and it sounded sharp, cold, etched, spilling over then flooding the ice. She handed a glass to Ethan and as it passed from her hand to his he had the sense that, except for the charcoal on his hand, he could mistake Bridget's hand for his own.

Bridget sat back on her heels and the fields were bright behind her beyond the shadow of the tree. A breeze took some loose strands of her red-brown hair and blew them across her face. She drew them back behind her ear and put the glass of lemonade in her lap and looked down at it.

I made it myself. Phoebe, the girl in Peru, and Mr. Hale like it very sour, but when I can I make it with lots of sugar. They don't mind. There's more than enough of everything here.

Bridget's voice soothed Ethan and her accent made whatever she said seem a little like a lullaby for the moment, fitting for this huge dream, this spell as she'd called it.

He brought the glass to his lips and sipped the lemonade. The sour and sweet and cold exploded citrusy and pale on his tongue. It tasted so good he gasped a little.

It's so. It's. How does it keep? The ice. How do you keep it— Ethan sipped at the drink again, then swallowed the rest in a gulp.

Bridget smiled and tasted her drink, although she usually quaffed the entire glass, too, when no one else was looking, even though it gave her a piercing headache that seemed like an icicle shooting through her brain afterward, which she liked, too, in its way, because the pain balanced the sweetness in a way she could never explain.

It's ice from Enon Lake, she said. It's famous. They send it to London. Mr. Hale has an interest in it. It's called the Enon Ice Company.

An interest, Ethan thought. Mr. Hale has an *interest* in ice. He chewed a shaving of ice and the lemon and sugar coating prickled at his tongue. He wanted both to drink the entire pitcher of lemonade at once and never to have so much as another sip of it again.

I can show you where they keep it. It's underground, packed in sawdust so it stays frozen. They have it all through the summer.

Lemonade, and ice through the summer, a house bigger than twenty houses, Dutchmen mowing huge, rolling meadows, this girl from over the ocean, so lovely, so kind to him, this dream, this strange dream, this huge, addled dream of a kingdom so far from Apple Island.

EVENING CAME OVER the meadows and the haystacks lowered into deep blues and purples as the sky flared and lowered, too. Ethan put his drawing supplies in the barn with his sack and sat in the broad open doorway and rolled himself a cigarette. He struck a match against the barn door and touched it to the end of the cigarette and drew his breath as if to pull the flame through the tobacco and paper into his mouth and over his tongue and down his throat, as if it were fire itself with which he meant to fill his lungs. The tobacco and paper ignited and flared and glowed and he exhaled the smoke from his lungs into the night and listened to the last settling birds. Bats zippered back and forth in the air, eating insects. Ethan had spent the day concentrating on the light and color and textures of his painting, but now he found himself thinking about Bridget, how he'd missed her that afternoon when she'd not been able to visit with him and have a talk.

The kitchen door opened and clapped shut across the yard and Ethan heard Bridget humming to herself quietly as she took down the linens she'd hung out to dry that afternoon. He meant to leave her to herself, but without being aware he recognized the song she was humming and sang a line out loud because it was one he'd heard his grammy and the other women singing coming back from their gatherings.

Seoithín seothó.

It was Irish, a lullaby, his grammy had told him one night as the women passed in the dark, singing together. It's a mother singing a lullaby to her sleeping child. She sings, Oh, you, my kin, my love, and my jewel. She sings, There are bright fairies outside on the roof, playing in the spring moonlight, hoping to call you away from my side and take you to the fairy mound, but I will never let them take you. Hushaby, hush, she says. *Seoithín seothó. Alleluia.* Hallelujah.

BRIDGET IN THE lowering light, unclipping the sheets from the lines. The lines spring back taut when she pulls the sheets from them, like the plucked strings on the homemade driftwood fiddles her father and uncles played at night. She walked along the water with her father, looking for good pieces of wood. He traced the outline of a neighbor's fiddle on a sheet of paper in charcoal, like Ethan drawing in the meadow. Her father worked on the fiddle all one winter, when there wasn't much to do and it was dark most of the time and the wind moaned and fog covered the island and the fairies moaned and wailed out in the dark and knew death, too. There is something about that Ethan, with his charcoal and sunburned face and neck, something about him she can't put a name to. The sheets are so clean and stiff they crunch when she folds them and places them in the basket. One sheet is her own and she will put it on her narrow bed in her small clean room tonight before lying down to sleep and it will feel crisp and clean and smell clean and good in the heat and she will open a window to let the fresh air in and it will feel so good and she will miss her mother and her dad and her sisters and brothers so much that the comforts of the sheets and open window and lonesomeness of missing her family will make her cry herself to a dreamless sleep. She reaches the sheet on the last line and discovers that the side facing the open meadow is covered in flecks of hay and dust from the mowing. Foolish girl, she thinks. You should've known such a thing would happen today. Scolding herself comforts her because she hears her mother's voice when she does. She hears her mother's voice and she tries to see if she can shake out the sheet by taking it from the bottom and stepping back and drawing it out and snapping it so the hay will come off. She begins to sing.

Seoithín seothó.

She sings and snaps the sheet although she knows that that will not do and smiles, pleased to hear another voice quietly singing along with her from a distance before she realizes that there is another voice singing along. It is Ethan, who by the smell of his cigarette in the evening air she knows is sitting in the barn door around the other side of the house. And he is singing the lullaby along with her. And that is it. She realizes that is the familiar thing about him. He is an islander—an islander, like she is, and he knows her island lullaby.

BRIDGET STOPPED SINGING to hear Ethan singing better, but he stopped when she did. Ethan sat in the barn door and Bridget stood among the bare clotheslines, in the last light, silent, listening to one another's suddenly meaningful silence, the house separating them, each so suddenly aware of and concentrated on the other that they may as well have been standing face to face, the distance, the yard, the house, the overhanging dark, the first stars plinking on above, everything between and beyond them as if it were removed and each the only body or soul the other knew in the world. So long as she stood still and silent, Bridget thought she may as well be standing face to face with Ethan Honey and not only that but holding both his hands and staring him in the eyes. But that was only for an instant, for as long as it took to realize they may as well have been standing face to face and holding hands, and Bridget broke the silence with what she hoped sounded like the innocent, practical sigh of a maid at her work and hoisted the basket of clean sheets and bustled back into the house. She'd liked to have run to Ethan and shouted, I knew it, I knew it; you're an islander! What island? Where? Who are your kin? Are they any Carneys? Any Guiheens? Hicksons? But she was so flustered from the singing and in the moment when she went silent and did nothing, the coincidence grew into something too big for her to bear over the walk around the house to the barn doorway where Ethan sat, something too intimate and more complicated and deep than just a sign of recognition between two near orphans who found themselves ornaments on the Hale estate.

Ethan in the barn doorway listened during that moment of silence for Bridget to begin singing again, but realized that she'd heard him singing along and stopped. He could not tell when she gathered the rest of the clothes from the line and returned inside, but he knew that she stood in the yard hushed and quiet for a time while he sat hushed and quiet and held his breath and his cigarette went out and love for her thrilled through him.

ETHAN.

Bridget called his name in the dark. Her voice, clear and quiet, sounded as if she were right next to him, speaking in his ear. Dozing, he startled, knowing it was Bridget, knowing she was not lying next to him but at the small door next to the large doors, just her head stuck inside the barn, but still alarmed at being called from sleep in the night by name by a ghost or an angel. This was the second time she'd caught him asleep, after the time in the meadow.

Ethan, she said again.

Uhm, yeah, what? he croaked back. He saw her face in the door pallid, blue, lit by the sharp high moonlight shimming through the cupola.

Come, she said. Come here!

What?

Come. Here.

He lifted himself from the bed and went to her, hunched over, tiptoeing, almost as if he were sneaking. She took his hand like a child's and led him across the yard to the kitchen door.

As freely as Bridget came and went in and out of the main house, Ethan had not yet been inside. He stood in the back doorway off the kitchen sometimes and smoked and talked with her while she finished her work, but he had never set even a foot across the threshold. Now, he stopped short at the entrance.

All the Dutchmen are asleep, she said. And Mr. Hale is asleep in his big chair, all the way up on the third floor. Hurry. It's the only time he sleeps except in the day. She opened the white door onto the darkness of the kitchen and tried to drag Ethan in by the hand.

I don't like to, Ethan said.

So many hallways and corridors and rooms. Ethan had glimpsed enough of the house's mysterious, confusing depths passing its lit windows at night. Should Bridget have the devil in her and mean to tease, she could step aside into a doorway behind him, into another dark room, from right next to him, whisper, Find me if you can, and he'd be as astray in that palace as if in primeval woods or a maze in a myth, all the more so for the thickets of lamps, spindly old chairs and glazed vases, alcoves with clocks shaped like little brass pagodas on narrow tottering tables or like wooden cottages atop mantels high as cliffs, a tall case clock at the end of a dim hallway like a giant dozing owl, head bowed, eyes closed, wings folded until he passed, when its eyes would open golden and honeycombed, large as numbered dials, and its wings would unfold silently and reach down the length of the hall and gather him back into their silent depths, more silent than silence because they not only would make no sound but would absorb it from the air and cancel it in their layers, and entomb him at the dark end of the forgotten hallway forever.

Bridget yanked him forward over the threshold into the kitchen as if she were his nanny. Ethan allowed her to lead him. So long as she was ahead and he could see her and so long as she kept hold of his hand so he would not get lost. Straight into the kitchen as through a gangway, he only had the seconds it took to cross the room and exit through a swinging door to sound and form an idea of its butcher-block and enameled-iron enormity as if by echo. Straight down a narrow passage that seemed longer than the meadow path from his shack to the schoolhouse on the island, rooms and hollows and side halls and holds smoothly coming into dim view, opening on the peripheries, retreating behind in the gloom. The vastness of the house lent the sense of being confined. Ethan felt like it was a huge galleon, its cargo the piled, stacked, stuffed, heaped riches, the intricate, rarefied, exquisite treasure of people who would be like gods, riding out some flood with all the riches of their court, like in the history books Mr. Diamond had taught, the boat laden, low in the water under weight of gold and precious stones and armor and boxes and baskets and chests and bureaus and vaults and iron safes crammed with jewels and rings and pendants and sacrificial silver daggers and stone altars and bills of sale for continents and oceans and nations and human beings, even the moon, and the sunlight reflecting off it, in languages he could not read and it was all to his humiliation and he needed fresh air, to be outside because it was as if Bridget led him belowdecks, as if he could hear cross timbers flexing and bracing bolts shooting into their staples behind him and the ocean squeezing the hull more tightly and feel himself heading toward the deepest, narrowest, tightest, most airless space where he would be shackled and forced to lie on his side and pant for breath and alternately roast and freeze and rub against the raw planking until his skin began to strip away and the moans of all the other souls crammed into the ship became louder than the thundering sea as the ship thudded through a portless eternity.

Ethan reared like a spooked pony led to stowage in a ship.

Bridget tugged him forward.

Silly, we're here, Bridget whispered. They stood before a closed door. Bridget turned the glass knob and pushed the door open. Beyond was a moonlit room, a parlor of some sort, with two deep, high, wing-backed chairs set side by side, toed in toward a dark fireplace, a narrow table between them piled with compact, leather-bound books and a large magnifying glass on the top book. Bridget stepped into the room.

It's over here, she said. Come a*long*.

Ethan saw Bridget smiling at him in the dim light. He saw the yards reaching away into the night beyond a line of huge windows, flooded in moonlight, bathed in cooling breezes. The sight of the yards calmed him. They were wide, spacious, opening out from the depths of the house just like an ocean calmly rolling around an enclosed, overstuffed, stifling, rank livestock pen in a ship. He could jump through a window if it came to that. He imagined the cool fresh night air filling his lungs and head as he dove through the old glass.

Bridget beckoned with her hand, as if to reel him to her. She stood next to a small framed painting hung on the wall flush with the window. The placement of the painting seemed casual, offhanded, to Ethan, the way one of his sisters might put one of his drawings of an acorn or chestnut up on a bare spot somewhere in their shack.

Come, Bridget whispered again. I think of you whenever I look at this. She struck a match and touched it to the wick of an oil lamp and the room filled with a clear, white light. She lowered the flame and most of the room contracted back into shadow.

Ethan Honey, would you *please* come here! We can't do this for very long! She glared. She stepped backward, then aside, lifting the lamp level with the painting.

THE PAINTING WAS of a small, tidy bundle of asparagus, tied together with twine, placed on a dark stone tabletop, glowing under pure white light from somewhere above, ivory except at the tips, which blushed thistle-purple and pale green, as if just quickened into color by the lamp. Deepest olive greens and blacks surrounded the vegetables and conveyed a boundless emptiness beyond, as if the sheaf lay on a table at the bottom of the hold of a vast, gutted ship, the light falling on it from a scuttle high above in the darkness solely to illuminate the spears, pale as cream, blushing into purple, quickening into green, lustrous, catalyzed by radiance that did not fall over the rest of the tabletop or cause the vegetables to cast shadows the way real light would. The light was unnatural, arbitrary, invented by the painter. It dropped through immense heights to reveal of all things this immaculate crop, impossible in the depths of such an ancient, abandoned Ararat darkness, impossibly kindling the impossible harvest into color.

It's just a bunch of asparagus, Bridget said. A little painting of some foolish vegetables, but it's the one I look at the most of all of them.

Ethan leaned closer and closer to the painting, trying to see how it was possible, to see how the painter had turned a handful of plants into an emblem for the whole world.

BRIDGET AND ETHAN lay side by side at midnight, holding hands beneath the fir trees on the rise in the front meadow. Bridget made her eyesight blur and watched the stars spin and flicker. The starlight pulsed in time with the chirping that filled the air all around them, and the hypnotic pulsing repeating chord came down to her in the meadow from the stars.

Why don't the stars make any sounds in the winter? Bridget said.

What sounds? Ethan said.

Their chirping sounds. They only make that sound in the summer.

Ethan was confused for a moment then understood.

He answered, I'm not sure. I've wondered about that. I've wondered whether they do make the same sound but their voices somehow get swallowed up in the cold on their way here, or whether they lose their voices in the winter, or whether they change their voices so that we can't hear them but other animals can, or other people on different planets. He didn't want to trick her, or make fun, but he did not want to embarrass her, either.

Bridget said, There are people on other planets?

I think so, said Ethan. He was unsure of what more to say and already sorry he could not think of a gentle way to tell Bridget the stars did not chirp but crickets did.

People like us?

I don't know. I hope there are. I hope there's a boy and a girl on that planet right there—that's Saturn; I *think* it's Saturn—I hope there're a boy and a girl looking at the fleck of light in their sky that they think is Earth, talking about how they hope there's a boy and girl there talking about them.

Bridget thought about the girl on Saturn. She imagined her in luminous, pale yellow dresses and stockings as black as space. She imagined that their sky was bright black, even during the day. She knew from talking to Phoebe and her father that Saturn had rings around it and the idea of watching them spin hugely and silently above in the sky frightened her. The thought of the rings speeding overhead dizzied her and she remembered visiting the Bunker Hill memorial in Boston with the Hales on a bright gusting afternoon the previous spring and looking up the granite obelisk from its base and how it had seemed as if it was about to fall over onto her and Phoebe and Mr. and Mrs. Hale. Despite herself, she'd begun to cry. The fact that no one else noticed the tower falling almost scared her more than the falling itself. Everyone traded bits of history and talked about how many stairs there were and Bridget was frightened mute at being the only person who foresaw the catastrophe. She broke into tears and the Hales stopped their chatter and looked at her in surprise.

What's wrong, Bridget?

Nothing.

Why are you crying, Bridge?

Confused, she couldn't say because no one else had noticed, yet the tower still seemed to fall and fall but never came any closer to the ground. She looked up again and the tower was still toppling toward them.

I think it's falling, she whispered. It's going to fall.

Oh, Bridget, Mrs. Hale said. It's just the clouds in the wind. See? Mrs. Hale pointed up to the bright blue Boston sky and the filaments of clouds streaming past the pointed stone tip of the monument.

The monument isn't moving, Mrs. Hale said. It's just the clouds flowing behind it that make it look like it's falling forward.

Bridget had been so embarrassed by her simplicity she'd barely spoken a word the rest of the trip and most of the following day.

The stars are lights hung in the heavens for us to see by at night, Ethan said.

Fireflies blinked on and off, threading among the stars, flickering through one constellation, quenching their light, rekindling it in another.

You'd almost think the fireflies were stars, too, Ethan said.

Or the stars fireflies, said Bridget. Imagine if they all began to swirl and flash.

A single chirp suddenly sang from inside the grass right by Ethan's and Bridget's heads. It pulsed in counterpoint against the chanting choir in the sky, in the same key, the same note. Bridget leaned over on her side and stuck her face near the grass. The chirp sounded again. It was small and gave her the impression of having dropped from the sky, as if it belonged to a hatchling fallen to earth from the vast luminous nest of evening. Ethan crawled toward the voice but it stopped when he neared, as if concealing itself. Bridget propped herself up on an elbow and watched Ethan crawling, pausing, waiting, listening. The voice pipped again and Ethan gently reached forward and put his fingers down into the grass and felt around in the thick turf, tender and quiet. He cupped something in his hand and drew it up through the rough blades.

Listen, he said. He held his joined hands to Bridget's ear and made a slight opening between them. Nothing. Bridget closed her eyes as if to listen more closely.

Nothing. Then the chirp, the little peep, the star song. Bridget opened her eyes and looked at Ethan, puzzled.

He smiled and whispered, Look. He opened his hand and in the moonlight a dark cricket perched in his palm. It rubbed its legs together three times, chirp, chirp, chirp, and leapt from Ethan's hand into the dark grass.

Ethan and Bridget walked back to the house through the meadow, around the quiet, hulking forms of the haystacks, which seemed like a slumbering herd of wild beasts. Instead of saying goodnight and returning to her room, Bridget went into the barn with Ethan and into his bed with him and put her arms around him.

ETHAN FINISHED THE portrait of Bridget he'd been painting, she sitting for him a half hour here, twenty minutes there.

Bridget rose to look at the painting, which Ethan had insisted she not see until it was finished, but he said, Wait. Let me have your hand.

Bridget gave him her hand, palm up, pink and bright, calloused, cupped in his broad dark paint-smeared upturned hand. His hands felt soft and rough at the same time, soft skin but like iron bolts and nuts fitted together underneath.

Don't be scared, he said.

I'm not *scared*.

The smells of his paints and the spirits on his hands and in the rough cloth of his clothes and the sweat on his skin swirled in her nose and behind her eyes and through the tight space inside her head between her brain and skull, but she was not afraid. He pulled his slipjoint knife from his back pocket and it jumped open in his hand. He took the tip of her middle finger between his thumb and forefinger and squeezed it. It firmed at the pressure and turned livid. Ethan touched the tip of the blade to her finger and a drop of blood beaded from it. She barely felt the nick.

Nothing else is that kind of red, she said.

I've seen flowers that red, he said. Strawberries. Cherries. But everything in the world changes colors every second.

He held his palette beneath her hand and guided her finger over a smudge of red paint. He squeezed her finger and the blood trembled and swelled and dropped onto the paint. He drew a drop of blood from his own finger and added it to hers.

Here. He gave her his handkerchief and mixed the blood into the paint with a small brush. Look.

She rose, stiff from sitting still on a bale of hay for so long, and stepped toward the canvas. She expected looking at the portrait would be like looking into the mirror, but she came around the easel and saw the painted girl and it was like a mallet striking her heart and like her heart was a bronze gong inside her ribs and its sounding somehow unstrung and remade her. She did not see herself. She saw how she was seen. The painted girl's face seemed stark, stripped, her skin pink here, white there, be-freckled here, be-pimpled there, porcelain here, pebbly there, her pale forehead in shadow beneath the hat she wore, her coral nose flushed by the sun. Bridget saw the girl's skull, her bones beneath her skin and muscles. The girl looked her straight in the eye and smiled slightly, but bowed her head a little, too, like she was sturdy and shy at once. The girl was placed in the left part of the canvas. Behind her on the right were the fields and haycocks and the high horizon full of light and clouds, a veil of rain sweeping past and, nearer, thick, matted bright and shadowed grass and long looped thorned vines and Queen Anne's lace and delicate fanning ferns and, almost without substance, dim at the edge of the coarse heavy dark grass directly behind the girl, a strawberry plant with a mass of shadowed green fruit.

Bridget wiped tears from her eyes and gasped a little laugh. To think how closely, with how much care, how much courtesy and gentleness he had looked at her.

Watch, Ethan said. He touched a bright pinhead of their mixed blood and paint to one of the faint green strawberries and the entire dark, massed lower part of the painting seemed suddenly to deepen and reach farther back into the plane of the canvas, deeper into the imaginary shadows of the painted meadow, and the painted girl almost to come nearer as if she had leaned almost imperceptibly, tentatively forward.

Wherever the painting ends up, wherever in the world, on whatever wall or in whatever—he laughed—whatever museum, part of you will be there, in that berry in the grass and flowers.

And no one will ever know, Bridget said. She imagined a man and a woman dressed in fine dark clothes standing side by side in front of the painting, looking at it on a wall in a small gallery with a windowed front in a city where it had just rained and the light coming through the windows was silver and gray and bright and uniform and the man and woman had brought some of the cold wetness of the rain inside the gallery.

No one but us, Ethan said. Unless you tell someone someday, like your kids.

ETHAN PAINTED EACH DAY until the light fined into dusk. Bridget tended her chores and minded Mr. Hale, but with Phoebe Hale in Peru for the summer with her parents there wasn't as much work as usual, so she went to the meadow several times a day and sat on a blanket and watched Ethan paint and told him about her home on Great Blasket Island and he told her about his home on Apple Island. Sometimes neither said a word, Ethan concentrating on the paint and colors, Bridget half watching him, half riding the updrafts of her own daydreams.

WHEN THE DAYLIGHT is no longer adequate, Ethan gathers his supplies and recites from the painting book Mr. Hale had sent him on Apple Island, Evening is the hour when different shapes begin to blend together. When he returns to the meadow the next day, he prepares his supplies and recites, Morning is the hour when shapes begin to distinguish themselves from one another again.

SOME NIGHTS BRIDGET still sleeps in her bed in the house, but most nights she sleeps with Ethan in his bed in the barn and rises before the sun and Mr. Hale and returns to the house and splashes cool water on her face and fixes her hair and begins preparing Mr. Hale's tea and breakfast.

———

Put the haystacks in the sky, bristling and sharp, rasping across the lowering blue.

Stack the clouds in piled rows across the meadow, simmering, hovering, combed fog stitched by the bottom to the short shorn grass, vegetal, green, drying in the day, dehydrating in the sun, sweet and wet then dry and sweet and perfuming the meadow, the deep gray purple morning clouds with the shorn dark green morning grass waving like tide grass in salt creeks then leaching white and straw as light sheers to high white noon and hangs from the pinnacle of the day, suspended in the heat and high white and white hay, suffocating, asphyxiating in breathless angelic light. How to get dawn, noon, and dusk all at once. How to get the heat. The forms and light and colors describe themselves to Ethan with perfect clarity and harmony, without explanation or reason, and he copies them down onto the canvas with the paints.

The youngest dutch mower, the twelve-year-old son of the haying crew boss, gently turns shoulder first and faints into the hay in front of his rake. The mower next to him lays his rake across the hay row and kneels and gathers the boy and carries him to shade and trickles water into his slack mouth.

Bridget didn't mean to snoop but she woke before Ethan one morning at dawn after spending the night with him in the barn and saw his canvas bag lying open on the floor next to the bed. The barn was still dark in the first light, but Bridget could see the ends of what looked like a sheaf of small drawings sticking out from the folds of Ethan's extra shirt. They were within reach and Bridget stretched and yawned and lay her hand near the opening of the bag. She teased the drawings from the shirt and tried to make them out from arm's length. The top piece of paper was not a drawing but a photograph, nearly split in two down the middle from having been folded and unfolded many times. Ethan slept on without stirring, his back to her, facing the wall, so Bridget brought the photograph near to her face and squinted at it, her eyes adjusting to the darkness. Several girls and what looked like it might be a single boy resolved into view. They sat side by side along a wooden bench. A schoolroom. Students. It looked as if some of the children's faces were shadowed over but then Bridget saw that their skin ranged in color. Some of the girls were colored. Most of them, even. Or that's how it looked. It was still too dim to tell. One of the girls and the student that looked like it might be a boy seemed white, or lighter than the others anyway. That was puzzling. Bridget slid the photograph aside with her thumb as best she could to get a look at the topmost drawing and see if it might help explain the photo. As best as she could tell, the drawing was of an old colored woman sitting in a rocking chair. Bridget could tell that Ethan had made the drawing. What in the world, she wondered. What in the world is this?

Bridget had to hurry. Mr. Hale would be up soon. She had to get back to the house unseen, with enough time to wash her face and straighten her appearance before taking Mr. Hale his breakfast.

Ethan stirred and coughed. Bridget stuck her hand under the bed and froze. Ethan turned toward her, so she rolled away and hopped off the bed, pressing the photograph and drawings to her chest.

Ethan sat up. What time is it? he asked.

Early, Bridget said. You sleep. I'm late. Mr. Hale might be up and I'll be done if he sees me like this. Bridget was terrified to take the photograph and drawings but there was no way she could show Ethan she'd been looking at them now, especially since they might mean something Ethan didn't want her to know. She kept her back to the bed and made a show of hurrying to get her shoes on and rushed toward the door. She'd have to get back to the house, fix her looks, make Mr. Hale's breakfast,

and take it to him, hopefully in time to get the photograph and drawings back into Ethan's bag before he got up. If not, she'd have to pray
he didn't find them missing before he went to the meadow. And somewhere in all that cat melodeon she'd try to get a better look at them, too,
because why would Ethan have a picture of children at a colored school
and be drawing an old negro woman?

Will you come out to see me today? Ethan asked.

Yes, yes—don't get up—yes, I'll come, she said. Early. Lie down
and sleep.

Usually, she'd go back and give him a kiss, but she whispered, See
you soon, as if someone might be listening, and went out the door.

Bridget stepped from the barn into the humid morning. It was already
hot. She tried to comb her free hand through her hair as she rushed up
the drive but it was lank and matted. Her mouth tasted sour. She was
already sweating, soaking under the arms of her dress. Usually, she
snuck back to the house jittery and happy, thrilled a little with being a
little disheveled, a touch wild, a little mad, a touch in love. But between
nearly being caught going through Ethan's belongings and, she was suddenly aware, a nameless but accelerating panic rising in her about the
people in those pictures, she felt dizzy, like she might get sick to her
stomach or faint before she reached the house.

MR. HALE STIRS on the couch in his study, where, more and more, he
has been spending his nights, especially this summer, especially in this
heat, alternating between rereading his favorite authors and not so much
falling asleep as drifting sideways from waking. This often happens
when he pauses over a line in a book and, after turning it around in
his thoughts, it eventually uncouples from his consideration and begins
transposing itself—*into other creatures, other things*—he's begun to think
because he has been reading Ovid lately.

The Old Nocturnal, Mr. Hale thinks, sitting up, yawning.

But then, what hath the night to do with sleep, he says aloud. He no longer sees his sleep as fitful because it is adequate even if it is intermittent and always trembles at the threshold of rousing. He never feels well rested anymore but he does not feel especially tired, either.

Mr. Hale has been reading passages of Ovid that his friend, Professor Miller, is newly translating for publication. Tonight—last night, now; the shelf clock on the mantel reads quarter to four; the sun is less than an hour from rising—he has been reading about yet another young mortal girl falling prey to the gods' whims, this one turned into stone, a statue, the natural whiteness of which her befouled soul darkens to black. He feels obligated to read and to offer his amateur opinion on the translations to Professor Miller, who is an old friend, but the luridness of so many stories, lingering limb by limb over the women's violent conversions into trees and flowers and stones and animals, almost as if savoring rather than grieving their fates, has been increasingly off-putting. No doubt this is because with the rest of his family and the house staff gone for the summer, his only company is Bridget, the servant girl, who is the age of the girls in the book. It is upsetting to think of her being subjected to any of the situations in those stories, and even more so to imagine any dreadful scenario in which she involved herself willingly.

There will be no more sleep, so Mr. Hale rises from the couch. The lines he read before drifting off, about the girl turned to a statue, seem slightly off from what he thinks he remembers in his old translation by Golding, about her soul not so much staining black the white stone into which she'd been turned but more like freckling or bespeckling it.

The copy of Golding is downstairs in the library. It is still a little too early even for Mr. Hale to call for the maid to bring him his tea and toast, so he decides he'll retrieve the Golding and compare it and Professor Miller with the Latin and see if there is anything interesting to be discovered. Then he will ring for Bridget.

There is enough predawn light coming into the house for Mr. Hale to make the familiar way to the library without a lamp. He even feels as if his eyes have become permanently accustomed to the darkness of night and dimly lit rooms.

The Golding is on a side table next to a reading chair by a window facing the front meadow and the barn. Mr. Hale lifts the old book and holds it against his chest, a strange habit, he thinks. He must have picked it up years ago at church, and at seminary, where so many thoughtful men went about hugging big black volumes of Scripture or dogmatics. He puts his face to the window. It is lighter outside now than it is inside, the dark sky purple-flowered above, on the verge of crimsoning across the tree line at the eastern edge of the meadow.

An animal Mr. Hale at first glimpse thinks must be a young doe trots into view along the drive near the servants' entrance to the kitchen. But the animal does not move like a deer and, as what Mr. Hale instinctively thinks should be the case is replaced by what he in fact sees, the animal changes into a person, the person into a girl, and the girl into the servant, Bridget. The innocent trotting when she was a doe discolors and deforms into haste and guile and indecency as she hurries, now obviously away from the mulatto's bed in the barn, to the servants' entrance, which, although still in shadow, Mr. Hale knows she unlocks, opens, passes through, and closes behind her, to quickly gather herself in order to appear a spotless lamb by the time he rings for his tea and toast.

BRIDGET LIGHTS A LAMP in the kitchen. She pokes the embers in the firebox and adds a scoop of coal. She pours water from a stone jug into the copper tea kettle and sets it on the stovetop. She lays the drawings and the photograph next to one another on the counter so she can get a better look at them while she ties her apron on and rubs her face with a wet cloth and rinses her mouth with water and baking soda. The girls in the photograph look like they are aged seven or eight to maybe Bridget's age, fifteen or so. All but one of them is black. Some are very dark, some a little less so but still unmistakably colored, except for the one, who is so pale Bridget thinks she must have a grave illness. Not only is the other figure a boy, he is Ethan Honey. Aside from the ill-looking girl, Ethan is the lightest-skinned of the group. The girls wear simple dresses and sit with their hands clasped in their laps. Each girl has her hair parted down the middle and pulled back. Ethan wears pants held halfway up his chest by suspenders. His hair is shorter than it is now, and parted down the middle, plastered against his skull. He holds his hands together in his lap like the girls.

Why would Ethan be at a school with colored girls? Was he an art teacher there?

Bridget's head aches now and her hands feel stiff and shake as she fumbles with the silverware and china. She drops a coffee spoon and a butter knife onto the floor and they clang like an alarm bell. *Damn*. If Mr. Hale hears her, he'll expect her to be up with breakfast right away, no doubt. She picks up the spoon and places it on the serving tray.

One drawing is of an old colored lady sitting in a rocking chair and a grown colored man sitting next to her in the doorway to a shack. The old lady smokes a pipe and has her eyes closed. The man seems to be puzzling over a tangle of knotted fishing line. His hair looks like a nest of snakes. A derby sits perched on the top of the pile of coils.

The water in the kettle is boiling. Bridget pours a splash of it into the teapot and swirls it around to warm it, though Mary knows it's already plenty warm in this weather. Really, hot tea, in heat like this. Ridiculous. Hurry, Bridget. Hurry. She spoons tea into the pot, adds the hot water, and places the pot on the serving tray.

The other two drawings are each of a single colored girl, who Bridget sees are also in the photograph of the schoolchildren, sitting on either side of Ethan. On the back of the drawing with the old lady and the man with the ropey hair and derby, Ethan has written *Gram and Da*. He has written *Lotte* on the back of one of the drawings of the girls, and *Tabby* on the back of the other.

Charlotte and Tabitha. Those are Ethan's sisters. He's told her all about them. And his nanna and da. How can these people be Ethan's family?

Bridget's already botched two pieces of bread, trying to slice them as thinly and evenly as Mr. Hale likes while studying the pictures. She groans and cuts a thick slice of bread to square the end of the loaf so the toast will be just so. She figures she'll have the uneven slice with butter and jam later for lunch, but her stomach clenches at the idea.

How can he be from a colored family if he is a white boy? Bridget tries to concentrate on slicing the bread correctly but saws another piece that is too thick at the top and tapers off to a narrow wedge at the end.

Just how can all this be, if he is a white boy? Bridget draws the knife across the top of the loaf without looking and cuts the tip of her pointer finger open—the one Ethan nicked for her portrait. She starts at the pain. Blood soaks into the bread.

Dear God. Dear Mary. Such a mess and what in heaven or hell is that photograph, what are those damned drawings?

Bridget manages to slice two pieces of bread the way Mr. Hale likes. She puts them in the General Electric and turns it on although she does not trust the contraption. Sweat is running down both her temples and her neck.

Sweet Jesus, please, please let me get these back into Ethan's bag before he notices. I don't care about those pictures. I'll never wonder about them again. I'll never even think about them; just don't let Ethan find them missing. Don't let him find out I spied on him. Oh, Lord, please don't—

From nowhere, a thought oddly both her mother's and her own interrupts her frantic prayers: Black ewes birth white lambs and white black and Ethan Honey is colored.

THE SPRUNG BELL for the study jumps and rings on the wall. The toast is on fire.

IN THE MORNING DARKNESS the youngest Dutch mower, the twelve-year-old boy who is deaf and who fainted in the heat yesterday, rises from sleep in the temporary camp the mowers have set up in the back meadow near the pond. He goes to the pond and kneels and splashes water on his face then drinks a ladle of cool water from the bucket near the embers of the fire and pisses behind a bush and walks to the barn to sharpen the scythes. His father is the oldest but still one of the best mowers, strong, and tall, taller than all the other men. The boy hopes he, too, will grow up and be tall and strong, like his father, but not taller, not stronger, as boys often feel when they are still quite young. His father taught the boy how to sharpen and peen the blades when the boy was seven. Peening is a skill of which the boy is proud, so he gets up earlier than the others every morning and peens and dresses their blades before they head to the fields. He enters the barn through the wicket set in one of the larger doors, which are too heavy for him to pull open by himself. The scythes are propped against the inside wall. The boy takes the first scythe and removes the blade. He wipes the blade clean of grass and plant sap and dirt. He places the blade on his field anvil and sands the blade to a matte finish. Then he hammers the blade from beard to tip, pulling the hammer toward himself with each stroke to draw and thin the dulled edge. Then he hammers the blade again, this time with straight blows to further thin and to harden the edge. Then he grabs the blade by the tang and sinks the tip into the top of a stump. He braces the hand holding the tang against his body and hones the edge with a whetstone, drawing it from beard to tip at the perfect angle, neither too shallow nor too steep. He repeats the process for all the scythes.

ETHAN HONEY PREPARES for the day's painting. He takes off the shirt he's wearing, removes his other shirt from his bag, and puts it on. He does not notice that his drawings of Gram and Da and Lotte and Tabby and the photograph are missing. Bridget seemed agitated when she left earlier and he is preoccupied with that. He hopes she is not angry with him about anything. As he's been doing each morning, Ethan goes into the main aisle where the Dutch boy is sharpening the last scythe blade. He taps the boy on the shoulder. The boy does not look up from his work but smiles. Ethan turns a bucket upside down and sits on it next to the boy and rolls his first cigarette of the day. He smokes and thinks about the work he needs to do on the painting. Since seeing the painting of the asparagus inside the house, he has felt a little worse about his abilities every day. He is becoming impatient for the summer to end and the classes at the art school to begin, so he can start learning how to be a real painter.

The boy finishes sharpening the blade. He looks at Ethan. Ethan gestures at the blade, Okay? Good? The boy nods, Yes, good. Ethan hands the nearly spent cigarette to the boy, who takes a puff from it and grinds it out on the dirt floor with his shoe. The boy exhales the smoke and pushes his chest out and thumps it with both hands, nodding to Ethan with a mock-serious frown.

Ethan nods and smiles, Yes, grown men, sharing work and tobacco, good.

Ethan hears the mowers approaching the barn. The massive barn doors draw apart on their iron rollers and the barn fills with light. The men enter, smoking their pipes. They gather their scythes and lead their horses into the wagon and wuffler harnesses. Ethan returns to his room, gathers his canvas and easel and paints. As usual, he heads to the smaller door at the back of the barn, which opens directly onto the meadow. He opens the door and there is a tall, elderly man standing right outside it. The man is dressed in beautiful clothes that fit him perfectly. It is Mr. Hale, who until this moment Ethan has not met.

You do not need your paints anymore, Mr. Hale says. Leave them there and come with me.

3

NONE OF THE islanders would have known him from Adam but there was the governor himself, with the members of the council, clambering out of Tommy Stanton's tender, coming along on the second evaluation of the Apple Island settlement for his own assessment of the colony, waddling over the bedrock and grass, leaning on a walking stick, stopping now and then to point it at a barking dog or overgrown chickenless coop or to gesture with his boater hat at Rabbit Lark, who stood by the path staring, a small snake squirming out of sight between her lips, which he saw but ignored because his eyes were bad and sometimes he saw things in the corners of them that weren't there, or to ask a question of one of the councillors who surrounded him in a huddle. This time, Matthew Diamond was with the group.

Can't a well be drilled? Can new buildings be built? What about a bridge?

Matthew answered, Yes, certainly, a well would do wonders, new, sounder cabins would help with the cold, woodstoves, too. I know two men here who are marvelous carpenters, and I am half decent myself. A bridge would help the islanders feel more connected to the town, and help people on the main come here with their washing or fishing lines that need mending. They could have horses and wagons, even, perhaps. They could even attend a proper church. Well, I, perhaps not right in town, then. There's a Negro meeting house—church—the— it's called the Abyssinian Meeting House—in Portland—they could get to more easily.

What fine ideas!

And we're doing so well with the school. Perhaps you've already heard, families on the mainland are even beginning to send their children here—for a very small fee. One of our students, an eleven-year-old girl named Emily Sockalexis, is so good at math she could teach it to most adults. And the same goes for a girl named Tabitha Honey, the same age as Emily; she can nearly compose her own Latin verses in dactylic pentameter, off the top of her head! And there's an older boy, too, who is off—well, we have exceptional children of all sorts at the school.

Matthew felt that he spoke too quickly. He was rushing, sounded desperate—like he already knew he was going to fail on the islanders' behalf, the facts being so indisputable. But the governor seemed delighted and impressed with his ideas.

Yes, yes, he said. Yes, indeed. What fine work you've done. Fine work, indeed. A well and a small bridge hardly seem unreasonable. And some good old Franklin stoves. Yes, indeed. Isn't that reasonable, gentlemen?

No, the councilmen answered. There would still be matters of hygiene, physical and mental. There would still be the polluted blood. There would still be depravity and imbecility and mixed races. Nothing could change those hard facts. Best for everyone, the islanders most of all, to vacate the settlement as a matter of public health. Tear everything down. Burn the shacks and garbage. Put the dogs down. Let the land revert. Let winter sterilize it. Come next spring, it would be back, or nearly so, to its natural beauty, ready for wholesome activities by visitors and locals alike. One councilman mentioned interest in putting a small hotel on the bluff.

Maybe with a half-scale, working lighthouse for a folly, the councilman said and chuckled.

Maybe a lighted boardwalk between the island and the mainland, another man said. Wooden. Romantic.

But where will these people go? Matthew asked. Where will they make new homes? They've been here for six generations.

THE GOVERNOR AND COUNCILMEN settled themselves back on Tommy Stanton's tender for the trip back to the mainland. As Tommy was just pushing off, a young clerk who'd come with the group suddenly stood and told Tommy to wait.

The clerk called to Matthew, who stood on the dock, waiting for the governor to leave. Mr. Diamond! I almost forgot! This is for you. He leaned forward over the bow of the boat and handed Matthew a telegram envelope.

It came for you this morning. The lady at the general store knew I was coming here today and asked me to give it to you because she said it was urgent. I'm very sorry I didn't give it to you right away!

Matthew's stomach seized up at the word *Urgent*, and he knew before his eyes read the actual words in the actual order in which Thomas Hale had recited them to the telegraph operator—*Expelled Honey. Indecent with maid. Fled prior to return train*—that it must be from Thomas Hale and it must be about Ethan Honey and it must be something bad. And as he looked from the telegraph in the direction of the Honeys' cabin, he knew he'd known something bad had been bound to come of his plan all along, not probably but certainly, even as he'd thought it all out, all while he'd made and insisted on it, and forced it to fruition. Now, he had to tell everyone on Apple Island that they had to leave their homes, and he had to tell the Honeys that the child he'd worked so hard to convince them to send away, for the child's and their own greater good, was coming back, somehow, according to his own wiles, disgraced, humiliated. An image pierced his mind as if it had been shot from a rifle, of himself an old man sitting on a chair in front of a window in his summer home on the mainland, staring across the channel at desolate Apple Island, his mouth limp, open, and wordless, everyone he ever knew gone.

He's gone for good, Matthew Diamond thought. He's not coming back. He's gone for good because Hale found out he and that maid were intimate and terrified him so much he believed the only noble things to do were to leave her at once and to not return to his family in shame.

The facts and what they meant cohered and struck the man at once, so entirely that he felt like he might pass out and, rather than run as fast as he could to give the Honeys the awful news he himself had caused, he was forced to sit on a large stone on the beach and lower his head between his knees, to steady the panic surging in him and to make a wordless, belated prayer.

EHA SAT OUTSIDE the front door of the Honeys' cabin on the keg of nails, a fresh plug of tobacco in his cheek, working at unknotting a clump of tangled trap line, thinking he might go fishing in the afternoon. He used his bare hands because he'd given his old scrimshawed rigging knife to Ethan for his trip, so he no longer had a marlin spike to help tease the knots loose. He thought about that and about his son, with the knife in his back pocket, and it made him happy, so he whistled a robin's song.

Esther sat in her rocking chair on the other side of the doorway, face to the sun, eyes half-closed. Tabitha clattered around in the kitchen, scrubbing an iron pan on the stove. Charlotte swept the kitchen floor with a straw broom, whistling, improvising stilted melodies that tripped along and concluded whenever she arrived from one corner or another at the open door, snapped the broom, and launched a burst of dirt and sand and dust and dog and cat hair between her father and grandmother into the yard. Two of the island dogs, Grizzly, the big brindle mastiff, and Fitzy, the rat terrier, lay at Eha's feet and looked up from their reveries at the swirling dirt, Fitzy with his usual alarm, Grizzly with apathy, and returned to their naps.

Eha saw Mr. Diamond coming up the path through the high grass and wildflowers. A pair of turtledoves startled up in front of the missionary and he stopped and watched them drum and flutter away in the buzzing sunlight. Eha watched Mr. Diamond stare where the birds no longer were, drop his gaze, take a breath, exhale, and continue. Eha thought, That's something funny.

Mr. Diamond has something on his mind, Esther Honey said. She sat up a little. Something bad.

Eha realized that that was just what he was trying to make into words to say to his mother. He knew Mr. Diamond had something to say by the way he stared where the birds had been, then looked down, then took that breath before walking again, but Eha couldn't put it like his mother did.

The spinning dust from Lotte's broom blast slowed and lifted a little in the breeze, then spiraled downward, a momentary, stray spirit, no sooner figured in the sweepings than scattered into the dirt without anyone seeing.

Yes, said Eha. He does.

Mr. Bland said he'd appreciate his line back by today, Tabitha said from the kitchen. Long as it isn't any trouble, he told me. Me and Lotte can take it back low tide when we go picking for Gram.

Lotte and I, Esther said.

Yes, Grammy, Lotte and I, Tabitha said. She came to the door swiping rusty soap and water from the backs of her hands onto her apron. She'd found an old cast-iron pan under the overgrown ruins of a cabin on the main the week before when she and Charlotte had been gathering mushrooms and herbs and berries. Eha smelled the rust. Goes well with the salty air, he thought. Taste it, too, right in the back corners of my tongue. He knew Tabitha would not be able to refurbish the pan; it was too corroded. But he said nothing. His daughter was happy with her treasure, and after a couple more scrubbings the next day or two, she'd say she'd come to the conclusion that the pan was hopeless. *Come to the conclusion* was a phrase that Mr. Diamond had taught the children at school. Tabitha liked to repeat it. Eha liked to hear her say it.

Eha held the tangled line in front of his face and gently rumpled the muddle together and pulled it apart. He traced a length of line with his finger, one eye closed, following the line with the other. Tabitha went back inside. Victor the cat snooped around the corner of the house and approached the door, sniffing for a lick of milk or speck of fish guts. Fitzy the terrier sat up and barked at Victor, who blinked once, slowly, as if in forbearance at having to share the world with creatures as idiotic as dogs. Victor licked a forepaw and wiped the back of his ear with it and lay down in a patch of sun. With his thick fingers Eha nipped two bits of line that looked separate and drew them out of the mass in a single loop. The snarl loosened and unfolded by half.

Mm-hmm. Done with it by when you go, Eha said.

Fishermen paid Eha one or two cents, now and then, to untangle lines so knotted that they could not undo them themselves, old salts though they were.

Eha studied the slub and whispered, Old salts though ye be.

Done with it when we go, Lotte yelled and backhanded a volley of debris out the door straight at the napping cat. The cat screeched and leapt off.

Lotte yelled at him, That's right, Vic; go catch a mouse like you ought to.

I heard Da the first time, Little Lotte, Tabitha said.

First time, Lottle Littie, Eha chirped.

By the time Matthew Diamond rounded the path to the Honeys' lot, Esther was in a silent dismay. She knew he had bad news about Ethan. It was like the prophets in the Bible. They didn't have any special powers of seeing the future. They saw where the present was at, was all. They looked at where the present was at with eyes that saw and ears that heard, so the future that would come from it was as clear and simple as adding one plus one. Something bad's happened with Ethan, she thought. Something very bad, but——it occurred to her with a certainty so abrupt that it seemed as ruthless as it did a simple fact——not as bad as if he looked like Eha or me, or any of the rest of us. Diamond may not have known exactly what he was doing when he got them to let Ethan go paint, but she had. Ethan would not be the first Apple Islander who'd left and passed away into that other world, that plain white world, whether on purpose or by turn of fate. Passed away for good, as good as dead, she thought. Dear Jesus, she wished this were already over, that she didn't have to sit there and wait for the world to catch up to what awful things she already knew but had to pretend she did not. She looked at Eha working the line, not an inkling that his son was lost. Dear Jesus. Dear Jesus, give me patience. And strength. Patience and strength to get through this, so I can get them through this. Don't give me a heart attack.

Fitzy the terrier popped up and barked and ran up the path toward Matthew Diamond. Grizzly yawned and resettled his muzzle between his forepaws, watching the humans, stoical. Matthew stopped short of walking through the gateless gateway in the post-and-rail fence that once had kept a sheep in the yard. He rested his hands on top of a post and bowed his head for a moment.

The lobster dory *Nellie* pushed through the waters behind Mr. Diamond and Eha watched it. The tide boomed in the hollow on the north point and Eha added to it in his imagination the slurp of salt water being sucked back out of it. Booming meant high tide in two hours. There were times in his dory when he sat and watched the waves somersault into the hollow and waited for the faint, reduced report to reach him afterward and wondered what might lie between seeing and hearing.

Matthew Diamond entered the yard. Eha thought how nice Mr. Diamond's coat was, though worn and mended in many places. He thought how nicely Mr. Diamond kept it. He'd done an especially fine job with the patches on the elbows. Esther scratched the cat behind its ears and it smiled.

I wonder whether I might have a word, Esther, Eha, Matthew said. He nodded at Tabitha and Charlotte, who stood beside Esther, the cat now in her lap, facing the sun, purring. Fitzy barked and scuttered after a mouse in the meadow. Grizzly bayed, deep as a barrel. Two barks answered from the inlet and the mastiff looked back at Eha, who grunted, Naw, now, and massaged the dog's haunch with his boot and the animal lowered his head and closed his eyes.

Esther said, Go get your baskets, girls. She thought her voice sounded as if she were already crying. See if Millie and Rabbit can come out and play or pick flowers.

Glad to be excused from chores, the girls ran out of the yard, between the gateposts. They slowed and said, G'day, Mr. Diamond; g'bye, Mr. Diamond, as they passed, then took off across the meadow toward the Larks' house, yelling ahead for Millie and Rabbit.

Matthew Diamond's face was stark, pale, his eyes red, with dark livid circles under them. He looked stricken. His hair was matted on one side of his head, wild and tangled on the other, as if he'd risen straight from bed. Esther saw he had sand on his trousers and they were wet at the behind. For the first time since she'd met him, the sight of him struck a sudden terror in her guts. All the usual well-meaning fluster was gone, as if it'd been seared off. Devastated, she thought. She knew the feeling. A part of her heart softened for the poor, well-meaning but hopeless man, but only a small part.

Well, what is it, Esther barked. Are they coming to poke us and grab us with those tongs again? Dip us in kerosene? Set us to work in some field or factory?

No, Esther. No they're not. She'd never heard him speak so softly.

Esther pressed, even as a part of her looked on, appalled by her own frightening turn at— Acting, that part of her looking on said. You're acting. You're pretending not to know what Diamond is about to tell you. You're playing a cartoon of yourself until he tells you.

They going to take more pictures, put 'em in the paper? She spat. Put us in chains? Steal our boats? Maroon us?

Matthew Diamond was startled by Esther's strange outburst. Frightened, Esther thought. He looks like *he's* about to burst into tears.

No, he said, even more softly than before.

What was that? Speak *up*, Diamond! Speak up, you . . . you . . . . What? Esther thought. Coward? Hypocrite? Schemer? Devil? No good shit-kicking excuse for a—No. *No*, she thought. Stop. Here's that old fury, that old fury my father always tormented me with. Esther nearly turned to see whether her father's ghost might be standing behind her, smiling, goading her again, guiding Matthew Diamond, his deputy, tempting her again into the humiliations of anger. And of fear. Like Hamlet, she thought. He never acted, never pretended, never did any *seeming* until that devil of a ghost bewitched him, poisoned him with anger and fear.

No, Esther, no. None of that, Matthew Diamond practically whispered.

Then Esther saw that it was at least partly with him as it had been with her when she'd pushed her father off the bluff. Her punishment for murdering her father had been the crime of murdering her father itself. Diamond's punishment for taking Ethan away from them was that he took a son from a father, a child from its family.

Look at you, that part of her standing apart said. You're not even thinking about poor *Ethan*. You're not even thinking about your own poor *son*, fiddling with that damn knot, without any idea of what he's about to hear. You're not even thinking of those two little *girls*, about to lose their *brother*. Shame on you, Esther Honey. Shame on you.

Esther closed her eyes for a moment. It looked to Matthew Diamond as if she might be praying and he understood that she already knew, because she'd known from the start why or at least part of the reason—the main reason—why he'd picked out Ethan from all the other Apple Islanders to send off into the world, so naturally she'd have known the inevitable outcome, just as he had known what the telegram said before he'd read it.

Esther opened her eyes and looked at Matthew Diamond and asked him very quietly, What is it, then, Mr. Diamond?

Ethan left where he was painting in Massachusetts.

Eha looked up from his knot, squinting. Esther stared at Matthew Diamond but would not say a word to him.

And, Matthew Diamond said and paused, as if hoping Esther would speak, would utter words that would at least relieve some of the burden of his dreadful news. But she did not. So he sighed and nodded and spoke.

You have to leave the island.

Hereditary card checklist for father, father's father, father's mother, mother, mother's father, mother's mother, siblings: epileptic; feeble-minded; insane; interbred; gonorrhea; syphilis; alcoholic; tubercular; blind; deaf; paralysis; migraine; neurotic; criminalistic; sexually immoral; self-abusive; incestuous; wanderer; shiftless; vagrant; soft-brained; migrainous; unchaste; fear of soap; scoliosis; varicose veins; vertigo; apoplectic; cripple; deformed; dwarf; dropsical; eccentric; obesity; delirium tremens; eccentric; goiter; general paralysis of the insane; paranoiac; stillborn; suicidal; normal.

A MAN FROM THE town hall arrived on the island to serve the islanders their eviction notices two days later. His name was Timothy Whitcomb and he was furious at having been ordered to deliver the documents to those degenerate squatters on Apple Island. He thought the island was like the rocks out in the bay, covered with dirty gulls nesting in their own spattered waste, but this one was covered with filthy people. As he bobbed in the bow of Tommy Stanton's skiff—he hated boats and could not swim a stroke—clutching the portfolio full of notices, he felt like his shoes were already covered in runny excrement, his clothes teeming with lice and fleas. The boat slid onto the beach. Its forefoot split into the sand and the boat tilted and grounded. Timothy Whitcomb rose and tried to step to the front of the boat so he could hop onto dry land but he lost his footing on the pitched bottom boards and stumbled off the stern into water up to his knees. He only barely managed not to drop all the papers into the shallows. It was summer but the water was still freezing and his feet numbed in an instant.

Damn! Witcomb said. Wait here for me.

Tommy Stanton nodded.

Where's the houses? Whitcomb asked, suddenly aware that he did not know where the notices needed exactly to be delivered. No one had told him. He had the names of the families on the notices, but no idea how these people lived—all together in a bunch or separately, mixed up and moving from house to house by whim, or what, exactly. Tommy pointed his face toward the clearly visible shacks above the beach and along the shore.

'Long there, he said. Three shacks.

Which is what? Timothy said, looking at his soaked shoes and pants, now coated in wet sand.

Tommy pointed and listed the names, Honeys, Larks, McDermotts. Annie—Parker, that is—and Zach Proverbs are at the south end, down there past the rise. Zachary Proverbs maybe'll be in his tree. Timothy Whitcomb growled out loud at the thought of serving notice to a man up in a tree.

Will he come down out of his tree for the papers? he asked, already marching away, double time, to get the job done as quickly as possible and get off this blasted island. Or do I have to *climb* up to meet him? Whitcomb thought of his young wife at home, and their new daughter, and their modest but at least scrupulously clean kitchen, and the pie she'd have made for his supper because it was Friday.

Not up the tree, Tommy called. In it. Whitcomb stopped mid-step, brought up short, then growled again and shook his head at his lot and continued. Find out soon enough, he thought.

ALL MORNING THE MAN from the government went about the island and the dogs hounded him—Fitzy the terrier clamped to his wet trouser cuffs, writhing and dragging along the ground behind him, Sulky trotting alongside and barking up at him, Grizzly following behind, stopping now and then and baying once as if to keep the island informed of the intruder's location. The man cursed the dogs and swatted at them with the portfolio full of the eviction papers, calling out, Someone get these mutts off me!

None of the islanders or their ancestors had ever paid taxes or had a bank account or a loan, gotten a birth certificate, marriage license, or fishing permit. They'd just lived on the island for more than a century, neither much helped nor hindered by the people on the main. While they knew the man from the town hall had to do with being kicked off the island, they were not quite sure what the papers he forced on them had to do with it.

The McDermott sisters harassed Timothy Whitcomb with questions.

What are we supposed to do with these?

Nothing; they're legal documents.

What do they document?

You have to vacate the premises.

Vacate them of what?

You have to leave the island.

For how long? The sisters knew exactly what was what. They'd raged and cried and struggled with Esther and Eha, and Matthew Diamond, even, to figure out how to prevent being run off their home. But they despised this runt of a man, with his wet and dog-torn trousers and foolish wire spectacles. He was so scrawny he probably couldn't lift a wet bedsheet out of a washtub or haul a lobster trap into a boat.

How long? Well, forever. Look, read them for yourself. I'm just delivering them, like the post.

We don't get any post here. You got the wrong place.

That may be, but you have to take the papers. Timothy Whitcomb thrust the papers toward Violet. Iris grabbed them and smacked Timothy Whitcomb across the cheek with her open hand.

Get off our place before I go get my gun, Iris said. She raised her hand to slap him again but Timothy Whitcomb turned and fled back down the path where the three dogs sat waiting for him.

ANNIE PARKER NODDED and nodded when Whitcomb got to her place, just her head poking from behind the door of her lopsided, soggy shed, muttering. Finally, she stuck her withered hand out and took the papers and shut the door on him.

Nervous as a witch, Annie said. Looks like Iris gave him a good sock-ing, though. She bunched the papers and stuffed them into a sun-shot hole in the wall.

THE LARK FAMILY stood together in a huddle behind Candace, who took the papers from Timothy Whitcomb while looking the exasperated man in the eye for some sign of what it was all about.

There's extra papers in there for you people, Timothy Whitcomb said. From the courts. Medical documents from doctors and a special school. You'll have to read them for yourselves; I don't know anything at all about them.

Candace did not understand the man's explanations, about the evic-tion or the medical paper, although she already knew they were going to have to leave the island. She couldn't discern anything from the man's eyes, because he would not look at her directly. The man hurried off and the Larks watched him until he disappeared beneath a dip in the meadow heading towards the Honeys'. There was nowhere in the Larks' hovel to put the papers where they'd keep together until Mr. Diamond or Esther could help explain what they meant, so Candace gave them to Millie, who neatly folded them in half then in quarters and placed them under a large flat rock in the grass, where she also kept a moldy copy of a Sears,

Roebuck catalog from 1894 and a religious pamphlet titled *King Whiskey* that had a drawing on the front of a skeleton wearing a fur-trimmed robe and a crown, hoisting a bottle with a label on it that had a skeleton wearing a fur-trimmed robe and a crown, hoisting a bottle that had a label with a picture too small to make out.

Physicians' Certificate of Feeblemindedness. We the undersigned, graduates of a legally organized medical college, and having practiced three years within the State, hereby certify that we have made due inquiry and examination of **Theophilus and Candace Lark, and the children thereof**, *of the* **Squatter's Settlement** *of* **Apple Island** *in said State, and find that* **they** *is more than six years of age, that* **they** *is* **not** *a proper subject for commitment to an insane hospital and that* **they** *is a proper subject for the State School for the Feebleminded.*

THE MAN FROM the court left and after his mother and Mr. Diamond had told Eha what the papers meant he hefted the nail keg on which he had been sitting and carried it to the middle of the dirt yard. He set the keg down and sat on it, facing the cabin. Esther took it as a sign of her son's sorrow at the loss of their home and meant to leave him to his mute grief, once he did her the favor of taking her rocking chair up to the crown of the bluff, so she could look out over the land and water and think and lament it for herself.

Of course, Mama, he said. He bent and took the old chair by its arms and swung it upside down over his head. He lowered the chair so that its seat rested on top of his derby hat and he adjusted the chair's balance. The rockers stuck up in the air and curved back from Eha's head like antlers. The chair's spindles and rails covered Eha's back like ribs. It looked as if he were wearing an elaborate headdress made from the bones of a ritualized kill. There was a solemnity with which the grown son carefully carried the chair up the path to the bluff, his silent mother following, head bowed, several paces back in case the chair should topple from his head, a misfortune which, had it ever occurred, would have upset Eha as much as if he had botched a liturgy. At the top of the bluff, Eha placed the chair in the grooves its rockers had made in the earth over time and Esther sat in it. He draped the old patch of Hudson's Bay wool around his mother's shoulders, even though the day was warm and sunlit, and kissed her on top of her head.

She gave his forearm an affectionate little shake and said, Thank you, child. Eha smiled at his mother calling him—gray and creaky-kneed—*child*.

Eha returned to the yard and sat on the keg and studied the cabin. Grizzly rose and sat at his feet with his brindled back to him. Eha scratched the dog behind the ear and the dog lifted his face to the sunlight and smiled and Eha surveyed his home, plank by frame by shingle.

This section of the State University's exhibit commemorating the 100th Anniversary of the eviction of the settlers on Apple Island is devoted to the artwork of Ethan Honey. Honey was one of the last generation of native-born islanders (ca. 1897). He left behind dozens of competent—and informative—drawings of the people on the island and of daily life there at the end of its settlement. On loan from the estate of Ms. Phoebe Hale, of Enon, Massachusetts, where Honey briefly resided and practiced, are drawings of the summer hay mowing in July of 1913, the workers, the landscape, and the only three surviving paintings Honey made in oil: a large landscape depicting haystacks at sunset; a small, whimsically colored piece depicting a sop of green hay in an otherwise dry bale; and a portrait of a teenaged girl identified by Ms. Hale as Bridget Carney, an Irish immigrant who worked for the family as a domestic servant and Ms. Hale's nanny for two years.

ZACHARY HAND TO GOD PROVERBS burned his eviction notice in a little pile on the dirt then entered his tree, where he fell into a spacious, troubled, waking sleep where daydreams of and hymns for old lovers and lost family unspooled and interwove through his mind.

Queer Squatters of Apple Island! Queer of Spades! he thought. (His friend the old widower he'd known since the war had told him about the article in the paper and the postcards in the general store.) That's right; I *am* queer, from queer folk, queer stock. The very queerest. Here we are, stuck on an island, a hollow, a swamp, the desert, no sooner settled than banished again. You bet I'm queer. I'm no landlord nor lawyer, no duke nor lord of the looms. I'm no cap doffer, no knee bender, no flattering stooge. I draw no writs; I pass no judgments. I set no seals. I tip no scales. No, not me; I'm *queer*. I'm queer for my self, for my self*hood*, queer for this queer self I find myself to be, queer with strange appetites, and a heart that throbs most queerly. I'm queer for other queers, queer for their shapes and colors and sizes, queer for their tastes. I'm queer for the ruthless sea. I'm queer for all the little queer creatures in the tide pools. I'm queer for the light when it breaks the horizon and queer for it when it sinks behind the trees. I'm plain queer for these people and queer for this world. I'm downright queer in love with this wreck of a world, queer in love with love itself—love's always queer, always arriving in our hearts from queer nowheres, queering everything—and there we are; wide awake all night, queer as queer can be; queer orphans, queer widows, queer boys, and queer girls; sorrel girls queer for ivory boys, daffodil boys queer for lilac girls; carmine girls queer for sable girls, cinnamon boys so very queer for boys of bluest milk.

Wicked shepherds! Burn me at the stake and hang me from a tree. Clap me in the stocks; send me down the mine; set me in the burning fields. But I am queer. And I say, Here is water, bread, a dull penny. Here're my old shirt, my plane and hammer, a roof I'll help you raise above your head. Here is my queer old body, in a barn, behind a hedge, beneath a shadow, on a bare pallet—quick—while the murderous king still sleeps. Here is a song, a painting, a jig and a reel. Here is an island for an apple, an orchard for an eye. Here is a single, perfect apple for an island.

EHA STUDIES THE home he built. It is set facing north. It has a door and a window on the north side and one window on the east side, facing the mainland. Both windows have twelve panes of glass in them. They are the only split-sash windows on the island. The windows stick slightly because the frames have relaxed out of square, but still they work. The door is made of pine and held from inside by a latch. Eha hung it perfectly and unlike the windows its frame is still square. If left open it will gently swing shut on its own. The sides of the house and the roof are sheathed in cedar shingles Eha made. Every year he splits a pile of new shingles and changes them for those that need replacing. They are true and snug. A slender brick chimney rises from the center of the roof. Eha had to rebuild it once after lightning toppled it. The house has one room. Eha is a fine carpenter, like most men on the island are, or once were. Besides Eha, now there is only Zachary Hand to God left, not counting Mr. Diamond, who could help build a cabin or replace a roof or repair a set of stairs. It was Eha and Zachary who made it possible for the schoolhouse to be built on the eastern promontory because they knew how to construct the double-landed staircase up the granite cliff.

Eha studies the house that he and Zachary built next to the site of the home he'd grown up in, which, by the time he was twelve—his father dead before he was born from a drunken midnight stumble off the bluff where his mother now sat in her rocking chair surveying the Atlantic— was a sodden, sunken heap of scraps, barely fit for a nest of snakes to live under.

Zachary showed up one Saturday morning at dawn with a rusty, but to Eha magnificent, crosscut saw folded end to end, handle to handle, balanced on his shoulder and a carpetbag that clanked with mysterious tools.

Zachary said to Esther and Eha, It's time for me to teach the boy how to fell a tree and plane a board and split a shingle and make a place fit for you and him.

Esther said she wasn't sure, that maybe Eha's lack of words might stop him from taking to the work.

Nonsense, Zachary said. The boy is blessed with a natural patience of tongue. He's a close watcher and listener. He'll make a fine carpenter.

That was twenty-five years before Zachary took to his hollow tree.

Eha's life and the lives of everyone on the island and everything they've done and enjoyed and suffered and nearly starved from and all the full moons and bright suns and green grass and blue skies and rain and snow and wind and clouds, tin cups, lead sinkers, cod and lobsters and clams and whelks and driftwood all begin to erupt in slow motion from the infinitely dense black point in Eha's thought that is the meaning of this eviction, which at first his brain could not divulge to his understanding but is splitting open and disgorging as he sits looking at his house remembering so many things. Now he looks at his house and can feel Zachary's sorrow, as if from inside, instead of just knowing that he's a sad man from the outside, and can feel the comfort of his tree and as he understands that, looking at the house he and Zachary built together, that Zachary taught him how to make, he realizes not the fact but the meaning of the fact that this house before him, from which he and his mother and daughters are to be evicted and which once empty will be set afire and burn from home to square of ash, is made of the tree that he and Zachary felled on the main, deep in a part of the woods Zachary knew about from the old uncles and grandpas and Penobscots who lived by themselves away from any town or settlement. He realizes, too, that he was once a son missing a father but Zachary has been his real father all these years since, and he realizes that he now is a father missing a son.

In the late summer of 1868, Zachary Hand to God and Eha felled, sawed, removed from the woods, and assembled into the Honeys' home a single white pine tree they poached from land owned by the Maddox Paper Company of New Brunswick. The tree stood four miles northwest on the mainland, through dense and wild timberlands. Zachary had reconnoitered the tree before he showed up that morning to take Eha with him, to make sure that there were no crews working cuts nearby and that the tree was not in an area marked for a cut itself. Once he had chosen the tree, he had marked a path to it through the woods by chipping small blazes low on the trunks of trees with his hatchet. A > meant turn right, a < left, and | meant go straight. The path was blind, Zachary said, which meant that he did not chip the opposite sides of the trunks.

Trappers and prospectors always make blind trails, Zachary said. They want the trails to run only one way so nobody can follow them on their backtracks.

Eha had been bewildered by the woods. He was used to the openness of the island and the ocean and the sky. The huge quiet still trees seemed alive and as if they were conferring, about lofty old secrets a hundred feet above, secrets they'd been discussing for ages before he intruded and would continue to ponder for ages after he'd long been gone. Like the sea, the woods felt older than he could possibly imagine. Whereas he knew the sea, though, he knew nothing about the woods and felt his presence register with them as that of a stranger, trespassing.

Don't mind that eerie feeling, Zachary said, unprompted. He squatted in front of a silver maple and nicked a sliver of bark from its trunk an inch from where its trunk sank into the earth. It won't go away, but you'll get used to it. Sort of. All this'll be gone in fifty or sixty years if they keep at it like this.

Zachary offered the slip of bark to Eha. To a Penobscot, these marks I'm making may as well be bonfires, they're so blatant, Zachary said. I knew fellas could tell each other where to go by leaving scratches smaller than deer ticks, or by pinching a twig toward the right direction, or even twisting up little tufts of grass and bending them at the tops to point the way.

Eha remembers dropping the old white pine, pushing and pulling the thwart saw back and forth between himself and Zachary, the silence of the woods huge and looming and spooky against the racket of the blade cutting through the trunk, bright strings of wood curling from the kerf like lumber but like rinds from a giant living creature, too, and the to him, at twelve years old, nearly gut-splitting thrill, and grief, too, at the deep, thundering crack inside the heart of the tree detonating up and down its entire length, the timber giving way, the living creature convulsing in a single death flurry, when Zachary's eyes had widened and lit and he had smiled, thrilled, serious, profound, too, and from the opposite end of that magnificent saw said, Get back, and the huge tree had begun its fall through the other trees around it, like one of the pillars that hold up the earth and like one of the giants that live above the clouds and under the oceans, too, that had seemed so fast it blurred in relief as it carved through the rest of the forest but at the same time had seemed to drop through the surrounding canopy over the course of so many ages that it appeared impassive, static, a still, stone carving, with the rest of the forest bursting and splintering and roaring by, the seasons themselves streaming by, freezing and thawing and darkening and flaring around it and at the end of which Eha had been sure that he would be split open forehead to trunk himself from the shock of the concussion of tree striking earth. That tree they'd cut and that had concussed the earth with such tectonic force when it hit the ground that it had felt as if it had wrenched him from the very day in which he and Zachary had been socketed was now the house at which Eha stared and in which he and his family had now lived for decades and so he lived inside a tree, too, even if it was now the cut, shaped, strapped, nailed, joined, planed planks, logs, beams of wood that had once been the tree.

Eha sits on the nail keg looking at the house he and Zachary Hand to God had made from the trees they'd cut down in the woods and remembers his and Zachary's silence and stillness in the wake of the pine tree crashing through the other trees around it, the space where it had stood now a monolith of sunlight filled with the pollen and insects and humus and leaves and birds and nests the old giant had sucked from the surrounding trees as it plunged down curling and fluttering and wreathing and turning inside its solid brightness.

Zachary had whistled low and said, It's a beauty.

There'd been no real need to get onto the tree, but Zachary had said to Eha, Well, get up onto it and see if it's sound. It's going to be your house.

Zachary interlocked his hands into a stirrup and Eha put a foot in it and Zachary launched him up onto the trunk. Zachary clambered up like he was a bear scrambling for a beehive full of honey. There was no need for the man and the boy to stand on top of the tree other than for the man to take pleasure in the work and the boy to thrill at the work and his part in it and for the view, for the simple novelty of standing eight feet up on top of the tree they'd just felled with the old saw. Zachary looked at the tree, smiling with transparent pleasure, thinking maybe about the first time he himself had cut down a tree with his father, and he seemed to Eha from that moment on like his own father, his real, blood father.

Eha thinks now how Zachary had looked like one of the men he once saw climb onto the carcass of a beached humpback whale, as if doing so were only natural, were the proper thing to do when the sea disgorged such a creature on the sand, to stand on the monster's flank, hands on hips, with other men and wonder out loud about how it had died and where it had come from and if the next tide'd take it out or if they'd have to butcher it and did Abner Ourfather maybe still have any of his family's old whale spades and didn't it already smell like perdition's bilge water and the things that open dead eye must have seen and what bottomless valleys it must have sounded, and just stand there because how many times does a person get to do such a thing, get to look out at the world from the top of a sea monster or toppled wooden colossus?

Zachary and Eha had eaten a small lunch of leftover biscuits and spring water sitting on the trunk of the tree, and afterward Eha had lain along the trunk, instantly dropping off to sleep, and almost falling off the tree ten minutes later when Zachary clapped his hands and barked, Back to it, men!

Zachary leapt off the tree and opened his carpetbag and took out dark worn heavy tools and laid them out. He picked one of the tools up and showed it to Eha. It had a rounded wooden haft, worn by use, attached at a right angle to the top of which extended a long, narrow rectangular blade, angled and sharpened at the end.

There's this, first, Zachary said, and he picked up a heavy, blunt wooden mallet in his other hand. And there's this. He held up the wood-hafted, metal-bladed tool. This is a froe. He held up the wooden mallet. And this is a mallet. And these are how a body splits a tree into planks for a house.

Sitting on the keg listening to the ocean breeze thump behind the house and thinking in turn about each board and joist and shingle and how he and Zachary had brought it all out of the woods and put the house up together, Eha feels the house shiver as if from the inside then slightly buckle, as if drawing into itself. Then, as if the drawing in were a breath gathered and held, the house converges in an instant of perfect stillness, as if filling with energy. The world goes silent, not as if Eha has lost his hearing but the universe has retracted all sound. The house soundlessly rises and hovers above the ground. As if from a small, controlled detonation at its center, the house soundlessly explodes and radiates into every separate board, post, shingle, hinge, and nail and every element soundlessly stops as if conforming to an invisible boundary, every part still in perfect relation to every other, soundlessly suspended in the air in front of him, arrested, transfixed, and Eha sits on the keg inside a sphere of retracted sound and time, contemplating every piece of the house he and Zachary Hand to God fashioned and put together, comprehending its whole anatomy as it hangs before him, plosive, cubic, dissembled, perfectly projected.

And, as if finding himself suddenly walking across thin air inside the formerly intact house—the victim of a crass joke—Victor the cat yowls from within. Sound, motion, and gravity reincorporate and the house stands whole and anchored in front of Eha, buffeting the wind and sunlight and salt. Eha spits and heads for the house to make a pot of tea for his mother. He steps onto the threshold and grabs one of the doorframe's side jambs. He holds it in his hand for a moment then squeezes it tight as he can and shakes it hard as he can. The cat scoots past, indignant and disgusted. Eha observes how the side and head jambs are joined and remembers Zachary teaching him how to build the doorway, how to make it square and stout.

Square, he thinks. Framed. In joint. Our own little castle, little kingdom.

Eha nods and passes inside.

Still Life with Ice, Lemon, Glass. July 1913. Charcoal and chalk.

Perhaps the most remarkable quality of this drawing is how Honey managed to capture not only the glossy wetness of the block of ice, but the light inside it. It seems as if there is a small sun or star locked within the transparent brick, like a heart. Ice from Enon Lake was prized for its purity and clarity. It was exported to London for sale there in the nineteenth century. Merchants put three-foot-square blocks of it in their windows with the front page of the London Times *underneath, which could be read through the unblemished ice. The Hale family held majority stakes in several ice companies.*

Honey's largely intuitive grasp of light and texture is also seen in the closely juxtaposed layers of the lemon slice's skin, rind, and pulp. The drinking glass is luminous, catching light from above and the left, out of frame, and seeming to pull volume and depth from the page.

TIMOTHY WHITCOMB SAT at the kitchen table, in front of the dinner his young wife, Beth, had warmed for him when he had returned home late from the island. Their baby daughter slept in her makeshift crib at the foot of the young couple's bed in the far corner of the room. Timothy's pants were wet and frayed at the cuffs from the terrier tearing at them, his hair clawed straight back from his having raked through it over and over as the summer sun set and he bobbed in the dory, against the tide, back home. He had not eaten since breakfast and was famished. But he sat on the edge of his chair, braced at the table, fork and knife clenched in his hands, and did not take any food. His muscles ached and the thump of his heart pounded a spike of pain from the base of his skull through his head and into the back of his left eye. His teeth ached from clamping them together all day and his voice came out hoarse and thin.

It's some kind of hell, he said. It's some kind of trick. Like a devil making fun. He almost sobbed from confusion and anger. They had the whole island but there they were all huddled together like rats in a nest. Filthy, ragged, animals. Worse. Just looking at you, stupid, imbecile. I couldn't get a one of them to say a word. And the smell. Dear Christ, it was like a filthy old bear den in those hovels. Their gray old filthy clothes and stupid, staring, dumb, blank faces. And all those cruddy dogs. I bet I got rabies. I bet everyone on the island got rabies. *They* probably gave it to the *dogs*! I had to keep shutting my eyes and opening them again because I kept thinking I was seeing things, it was all such a filthy mess.

The baby shifted in her sleep.

There was white Negroes and colored white people. Some of them were gray. Some of them pink, like they were raw or something. And some of them were yellow, like waxy cracked old piano keys. And that preacher. Acting like everything was normal as can be. Talking about teaching everyone Latin and the Bible. *Latin?* They couldn't even talk English, half of them, I'd bet.

Timothy's wife came around the table and put her hand on his shoulder. At her touch, the young man burst into tears, the last of his will finally snapping from the day's madness.

This is such a terrible job, Timothy sobbed. It's just terrible. He bowed his head and rested it on the backs of his hands, the fork and knife he held pointing downward, crossed over one another, clinking together quiet, tinny. He collected himself and drew a deep breath and let it out.

It's all done now, his wife said. It's all over. And you don't have to go out there ever again. They'll go get them all off there and I'll sew up your pants and it'll be all done and you did your part.

Timothy's outburst woke his daughter, Frances. She turned her head left then right and tried to roll from her back onto her stomach. She got stuck on her shoulder, three fourths over, her face pressed into the patch of quilt she slept on. Her eyes opened. She looked at the dim room and her parents, alarmed—still so strange every time, rousing from sleep—and cried out for her mother.

Irish Servant Girl, Enon, Massachusetts. July 1913. Oil and blood on canvas.

This is believed to be a portrait of Bridget Carney, a servant in the Hale household from sometime in 1911 until the summer of 1913. Carney came from Great Blasket Island, off the Dingle Peninsula on the southwestern coast of Ireland. Here she wears a slanted brim bucket cloche hat with a spray of chicory pinned to the crown. A festoon necklace with five diamond floret pendants is partially visible at the opening of her button-up work shirt. Before she passed, Phoebe Hale confirmed that Carney must have borrowed (not stolen, she insisted in her note to the curators) the necklace from Ms. Hale's mother's collection for the portrait. Although the July weather would have been too hot for it, Carney wears a jacket over her work shirt which, from the cut of the collar and drape, must have been the best piece of clothing she owned, although of modest quality. Honey paints her with a charming slight tilt of the head, a wistful half-smile, and a band of freckles across her nose and cheekbones. He balances the romanticism of her pose and expression by including pockmarks or acne scars in the hollows of her cheeks and a cold sore on her bottom lip.

Ellen Schmidt, an art conservation doctoral student, noticed an oddly colored flower in the field behind Carney and confirmed that it was colored with human blood—presumably Carney's or Honey's or a mixture of both. Since neither of their DNA could be traced, no sample was collected for testing.

Coincidentally, in 1953, four decades after the eviction of the settlers from Apple Island, the inhabitants of Great Blasket were evacuated by the Irish government. Most of those refugees, including members of Carney's extended family, made their way to Springfield, Massachusetts, one hundred miles west of Enon, where their descendants live to this day.

ESTHER HONEY KNEW the girl was pregnant the moment she appeared on the path coming toward the house. She'd been half dozing when the girl came into view and at first she had thought she was her sister, Abby, coming back to the island after all those years, but somehow still a young woman. The girl wasn't far along, but Esther could tell. Esther also knew that this thin, sturdy, pockmarked girl had something to do with Ethan's being missing. Everything to do with it, she saw as the girl came closer. The girl wore a coarse, well-made smock and simple, sturdy black leather shoes not made for the outdoors. A servant. A maid. In a grand house. She wore a dark, bell-shaped hat with a bluebird's feather stuck in its band and a white kerchief tied around her neck. In one hand, she carried a carpetbag too nice to have been her own. Probably stolen. From the people who owned the place Ethan went to paint at, Esther realized. Tucked under her other arm was a thin, rectangular panel it looked like, wrapped in a pillowcase, also too nice to be hers, tied up with twine. A painting. One of Ethan's. That was it.

What other painting would she possibly have gone to so much trouble to steal and carry with her all this way? So, this girl carried one of Ethan's paintings and she had everything to do with Ethan, including being pregnant. And, Ethan not being with her, Esther realized, means this girl is here because she's looking for him, too, so he is now nobody knows where, whether waylaid coming home or wandering the wilds.

Esther sat still as could be but it felt like she and her rocking chair were spinning and lurching.

You're Ethan's nanna? the girl asked, sounding like she already knew the answer, looking at Esther like she already recognized her.

The pictures, Esther thought, from that man who'd photographed them for that, that obscene, so-called study. And the drawings of us he took with him.

Who are *you*? Esther said. She's barely a woman, she thought, not even. Only just. And pregnant.

Pardon, ma'am. I forgot my manners. I'm a little tired and I don't feel very well. I'm Bridget. Bridget Carney. The girl staggered half a step sideways. She'd sweated through her dress and what of her hair that showed beneath the hat dripped with it, too.

Tabby! Lotte! Esther called. There was a tumult from within the cabin and her granddaughters appeared in the open doorway.

Yes, Grammy.

What is it, Gram—

Both girls went still at the sight of the strange older girl standing at the gateless gateway, exotic and astonishing in her beautiful hat, with such a beautiful bag and beautiful snow-white scarf around her neck. They stared at her, rapt.

Girls.

Yes, Gram.

Please get Miss—

Carney. Bridget.

Please get Miss Carney some water.

Yes, Gram. Charlotte and Tabitha tripped over one another backing into the doorway, looking at Bridget. Bridget put her bag on the ground and wiped her face with the sleeve of her dress.

Forgive me, ma'am. I'm just feeling a little—I may have a bit of a bad dose.

Esther nodded toward Eha's keg of nails. You'd better give yourself a seat, she said.

Thank you, ma'am. I'll be fine after I sit for a moment. She entered the dooryard and leaned the painting against the carpetbag and lowered herself onto the keg.

Tabitha and Charlotte came from the cabin, each with a teacup they held in front of themselves and carried toward the visitor as quickly as they could without spilling any water from it.

Here you go, Miss Bridget.

Here, Miss Bridget.

Bridget gulped the teacup of water from Tabitha then the second cup from Charlotte. She wiped her mouth then her forehead with the back of her hand and sighed deeply.

Thank you, girls. Thank you, indeed—she paused and concentrated on each girl for a moment and wiped sweat from her forehead again and what Esther thought may have been tears from her eyes and despite her exhaustion she smiled and said, almost as if she were quietly singing to the three islanders—Charlotte, thank you, indeed. And Tabitha, thank you as well.

Hearing their names spoken by the strange girl disturbed the sisters. She might be a fairy, magically knowing their names, but she might be a witch in disguise, too, so now she was a little frightening as well as enchanting.

Bridget held a hand out toward the girls, as if to calm them. Oh, no, she said. Don't be afeared. I mean, afraid. She opened her bag and pulled Ethan's drawings and the two crumpled halves of the photograph of the children at the Apple Island School from it. She held the halves up, next to one another, and said, See? I've seen your picture. And the drawings of you. I'm a friend of your brother, Ethan. That reassured Charlotte and Tabitha somewhat, but they still stayed put. Both liked how she said the word, Ethan—*Ee-tun*.

Esther said, Now, Miss Bridget Carney, who are you?

I'm from the Hale house, in Enon, in Massachusetts. I mean, I work—
I worked for them. I know your boy Ethan. We—knew each other at
the Hales'. I'm looking for him. It's. It's very important. I'm looking for
him. The girl was still panting and clearly nauseated.

He is not here, Esther said.

He's not? Can you tell me where he is? I want to find him so very much.

Esther felt as if she were a girl again, just this girl's age or a little
younger, even, pregnant herself, but by her old father, not a boy near her
own age she'd met and had a romance with. I've never had a romance, she
thought. I'm one of these children again, no one to help us, give us a place
to stay, none of us where we're supposed to be, none of us with our mother,
our father, our sisters, just wandering all over the place, bumping into and
off of one another with no place to head to and no place we can stay.

Can you tell me where is he? Bridget said.

I have no idea in the world where he is. I was hoping you—

And now Esther had to stop for a moment, too, and take a deep breath
because she was about to weep, too, and she bowed her head to collect herself, Again, again, she thought. She thought, Here I am all these
years later, again bowing my head every hour, it seems, to hide tears that
don't pay a second of attention to any of my vows not to cry anymore.

Esther raised her face and looked at Bridget and said, I was hoping
that you could tell *me* where Ethan is. We thought he was coming back
home to us.

So, here is another arrival on our little island, Esther thought. Our
little island on this little earth. This little earth, hung somewhere deep in
the fathomless heavens. Here is another arrival—this girl, this child—
ripening within her own body the seed of another arrival, another child,
each and every life comprehensive, each peculiar, each priceless, and
each less than the shadow of a shadow, all cherished or despised, cele-
brated or aggrieved, memorialized or entirely forgotten.

A SULLEN, SODDEN, SHROUDED day on the island, dark, humid, foggy. Barometer low. Migraines. Arthritis. Nosebleeds. Clouds low, liquescent, balderdashy. Heavy stones lay on every heart.

Rabbit Lark crawled on all fours, slurping witch butter from green puddles. She shimmied on her belly into a tapered cleft in the bedrock usually submerged under the tide and laid the side of her face on the smooth stone, cheek to damp sandy cheek with the island, and whispered to it—not words—quiet, hoarse breaths in time with the rise and fall of the water outside the periodic den. She waited and the fog lifted and the sun broke over the ocean. A finger of quartz shone and fossil shadows of fan-shaped and turbinate shells appeared in the stone in front of her and she reached forward and ran the tips of her fingers across them, deciphering. She found a narrow groove in the rock with her big toe and gently flicked it and laughed into the island's ear. No naïf; she knew and loved the island as any child knows and loves its mother. She was the crown princess of Apple Island, she its rightful heir because girl and island were one another's dearly beloved.

EHA MEANDERED OVER to the Larks' place. Theo was outside the front door swabbing the inside of a blue and white teacup with a rag.

Eha.

Theo.

A moment passed.

What lack ye, friend?

Thought I might help you bundle up some.

Thank ye, Eha, but I suppose I'll mind shop awhile still.

Well, I guess that's right, Eha said. He mumbled on his plug of chew. I guess that's right.

Mr. Theophilus Lark, ca. 1911. Crayon on paper.

This drawing is believed to be of an islander named Theophilus Lark. Mrs. Josephine Rivers, of Providence, RI, granddaughter of Charlotte Honey, grandniece of Ethan Honey, recalls her grandmother telling stories about the Lark family, including the fact that Mr. Lark habitually wore a gingham dress and shopkeeper's apron, both of which had been his mother's. Honey's figuring of Lark's full head of hair, his attentive expression, the evident care with which he is polishing a plate—stand in stark contrast to the accompanying photograph, taken sometime soon after Lark's admission to the State School for the Feebleminded, in which his head has been shaved to prevent lice and he wears a loose, linen shirt of the kind issued to all male "students" at the time, meant to accommodate what contemporary documents describe as the "vernal excitement" experienced by the population during the warm months of spring and summer. Records indicate that all but one of the Larks died within six months of admission. Millicent Lark, one of the daughters of Theophilus and his wife, Candace, stayed at the school until its closing in 1972, at which time she was transferred to a state hospital facility, where she lived until her death in 1980. A footnote to Millicent Lark's biography is that, whenever asked, she swore she knew nothing about and had never lived on Apple Island.

ALL THE ISLANDERS were clustered in a circle around the Larks when the gang from the mainland—that's what Iris and Violet called it—came to take them. They huddled together in the morning chill, except for Zachary Hand to God, who stood aside, with his hands on his hips and his face toward the rising sun behind the trees on the main as if prospecting the weather for a journey.

Two launches came across. In one were the sheriff, two men he'd brought along in case there was any trouble, which he was certain there would not be, and a doctor and assistant from the state hospital. In the other rode a pair of orderlies and an administrator from the School for the Feebleminded, along with three members of the Governor's Council, one acting as a clerk to record that the institutionalization went properly.

As the officials approached and caught sight of the settlers coming into view through the morning mists, against the still night-shaded trees on the island, the paupers looked like not just castaways but deportees from another century, the refugees of another century's misfortunes recrudescing into this one. They looked like apparitions, phantoms standing on the strand, indistinct as sand blowing over sand, ghosts sighted on some shipwrecked expedition to the top of the world. Huddled together the people struck the sheriff as impossibly thin and small, undersized and malnourished. Their clothes were old and threadbare and shabby, as much now dirt and salt as cloth, and it struck him that certain patches of the women's dresses might be scraps from the clothes worn by the first women who'd taken up here in 1793. He wanted this business over as quickly and smoothly as possible.

The family they were to take—the Larks, the clerk said and the hospital assistant confirmed—stood together in the middle of the congregation of islanders. They looked ghastly to the sheriff. Drained, bloodless, pale as watered milk. There were the two parents, brother and sister, he knew, although he did not like to hear or think about it, and four children, two girls and two boys. As the mainland men reached them, the squatters all began to hug and kiss the Larks, parents and children both. Two women, who looked like sisters, crouched to the level of the children and hugged them and stroked their hair and kissed their foreheads and cried despite themselves. The children accepted the affection but did not return it, staring at the people fawning and lamenting over them without expression, except one of the daughters. She cried openly and hugged two other girls the sheriff knew were Eha Honey's daughters, so the trio made a knot of wailing. Eha Honey, the man people sometimes called King Eha, stood facing the parents, head bowed, his hands in the pockets of his coveralls, not speaking. His mother, known to the sheriff as Esther Honey, sat in a rocking chair next to her son. She swatted Eha's pants and he turned to her. She beckoned him down and spoke in his ear. He straightened and took his derby hat off, held it in his left hand, and offered his right hand to the Lark father. The men shook hands then Eha offered his hand to the Lark mother and shook hands with her.

The sunlight broke over the trees and spread over the people and the boats and the beach. Zachary Hand to God watched a flock of sparrows take flight from a bush. They roared like lions and burst into flames. The morning was cold and clear. Sparse mare's-tail clouds trailed high and still at the very top of the sky. It would warm later and be a fine day on the water and in the fields.

THE SHERIFF PICKED UP the colored girl and marched down the beach toward the boat. The colored girl weighed less than a handful of kindling wrapped in a dishrag. Her face was colorless and gaunt and hard. She had long straight colorless hair. Her skin looked bleached from something darker, like sunburned but drained of color except from certain angles a slight green, and she curled her hands against herself like bird claws. She stared at the sheriff, face blank, intense, unwavering.

You'll like it at the school, he said.

The girl stared at him.

I've seen the menu they have. They've got good hot food and lots of it.

The girl looked so thin, hollowed. He'd seen the school's menu, but only for the employees—the nurses and caretakers and men who tended the grounds. One of his wife's cousins worked in the kitchen.

They have pancakes and maple syrup and doughnuts for breakfast, and lamb and mint sauce and pie for dinner, and soup and hot rolls for supper, and fresh milk and hot coffee at every meal, he said. He imagined the girl sitting in a chair in the middle of a big room with big rectangular windows covered with wire grates and radiators five feet high and ten feet wide along the brick walls, clanking and hissing, and steam pipes and water pipes running overhead bracketed to the ceilings, and a line of other girls and women running out the door, and one of the female attendants cutting off the girl's long thin hair until it looked like all the other female students' hair, blunt and cropped in the back, short bangs in the front.

His wife's cousin had said during a visit to their house one Sunday afternoon, It's the little ones I worry about. They're in with the grownups, and some of *them* are sick. Violent. Sometimes they hurt the little ones. There was this one poor little fellow, once—

The sheriff wondered why he thought of the school's dormitories and cafeterias in the winter, warm—overheated sometimes in one place, or freezing, like in the actual places they slept, in others—but full of good hot food. The morning was still coolish but by the afternoon, maybe right when they got the islanders to the school, it would be hot.

He said, I'll bet they have ice cream, too, although he did not know why, because he did not know whether they had ice cream or not. The girl stared at him and he could not tell whether she had heard or understood anything he had said. He wondered if she was deaf. Or an imbecile. He lifted her higher and stepped into the water to put her into the launch.

Candace Lark watched the man carry her daughter into the water toward the boat. Something turned in her stomach at the sight of the man carrying Rabbit. Her insides went rotten. She marched into the water and reached her hand out to tap the man's shoulder to get his attention, to turn him around and take Rabbit into her own arms. Instead, she stumbled forward in the surf and put her arms out to break her fall and pushed the man carrying her daughter so that they almost fell into the water.

Hey, now, what's this, one of the other men with the group barked and ran into the water after Candace. From where he'd stood, he thought Candace was a slight, bowlegged man with a wind- and sun- and gin-burned face, short hair bleached by the sun. He grabbed Candace by the back of her shirt and hauled her up. Sputtering Candace could not find her balance and swallowed seawater and could not see with the salt and sun straight in her eyes. She swung her arms around and tried to grab on to the man to get her balance. The man staggered back as if feinting blows. He made a fist and punched Candace on the side of her head then punched her nose as hard as he could. Candace's nose split with a crack and she collapsed into the carbonated water, her nose spurting blood, echoes of the punches clattering in her head.

Iris and Violet McDermott cried out and rushed toward the water with Theophilus Lark. Even Eha Honey, uncertain as he was about exactly what was happening and what he should do about it, started down the sand. The deputies and orderlies blocked their way, telling everyone to stay calm, now, let's keep this orderly.

The sheriff turned around with Rabbit in his arms. God damn it! he yelled, What's all this? One of the deputies, a man named Scott LeFleur, turned from the islanders and lumbered into the water to separate the two men, who looked to him like they were in a fistfight. He did not have a gun with him but he had a club, an old, heavy, dense, dark wooden police club he'd brought along without thinking much about it, almost like a prop or part of a costume.

Candace grabbed blindly in the surf and caught the man who had punched her around the waist, as much to raise herself up as to stop the man from punching her again, but the man took it to mean that she was fighting back so he boxed her on the ears and punched her on the side of the head again, near her brow, and split the skin open over one of her eyes. Candace panicked and thought she was drowning and thrashed all the more even as she began to lose grasp of her consciousness. It looked to Scott LeFleur that Candace was in a rage and about to pull the man down underwater and drown him dead, so he clobbered Candace on her neck and shoulders with the club. Candace raised her hands to fend off the blows. Candace, Scott LeFleur, and the other man fell over one another in a gasping, bleeding tangle onto the sheriff, who stumbled backward into the water with Rabbit Lark. Candace got hold of the end of the club to stop it from hitting her again. Scott LeFleur yanked the club from Candace's grip and it glanced off Rabbit's head. As a block of ice splinters at the tap of an awl, Rabbit's brain broke inside her skull. Her eyes rolled backward then closed and she died.

Theophilus Lark pushed past the stunned orderlies and slogged into the surf strong and steady. He yanked the blustering sheriff up by his collar and hauled him off his submerged daughter, whom he lifted from the water and carried back to the beach. He knew his child was dead before he lay her on the sand. The men in the water had stopped brawling and floundering and watched the father carry the child to shore. None of them was aware that Scott LeFleur's billy club had struck Rabbit, but watching Theophilus kneel and place the girl on the smooth strand, the sheriff, too, saw that the child was gone.

Zachary Hand to God suddenly screamed.

God damn it is *right*! he cried. God damn it *all*! he wailed.

Zachary rent his tattered shirt and it tore open down the front. He grabbed at it by the shoulders and snatched it off over his head. He threw it down and stared at the soaked and exhausted, grim crowd. He stomped on his shirt in a circle and ground it under his heel. As he turned, everyone saw the livid pink stripes crisscrossing his back.

Look at her! Zachary pointed to Candace, bloodied and sprawled on the sand. Just look; all *you!* he spun around and cried at the officers and clerks and ministers of the council.

And look at them! Zachary pointed to Theophilus on his knees, holding Rabbit.

I've held my tongue, but no more. My patience is gone. *Shot*, he shrieked. He looked down at the length of rope cinching his pants to his waist and clawed at the knot and looked up again at the deputation. He kicked the worn leather soles he wore as sandals off his feet and at the men.

Go to hell; all of you! I mean to *hell;* the *pit*; Sheol; lakes of *fire*; eternal torment! He yanked the rope through the belt loops on his pants and it snapped like a whip and he threw it at the men as if it were a live cobra. The pants dropped from his waist into a pile around his ankles. Zachary stepped out of the rags and stood fully naked on the bare sand.

Look at them. Look at us all. Look at me! Just *look*! Can't you *see?* *Shame* on you! Wrecking these families. And me, a bare-assed, half-starved old man! 'Stead of pants and bread you'd give me twenty lashes and fry the collops for bacon!

Islanders and deputation stared, stunned, at naked old Zachary. The waves broke and the water swashed up the beach and over their feet and died out and the backwash returned to the sea.

Sweet Jesus! Christ harrowed hell for *you?* I just can't stand it; I just can*not* stand one more *second*! You lousy, low-life, Johnny-come-lately *stinkers*! *You* always got some fancy talk that proves we're no good, but it's always the same old recycled happy *horse*shit! Hounding folks till you kill them right down dead! You're a bunch of *murderers*!

Now, Zachary, look here. . . .

That's right, *murderers*! he cried again, voice hoarse, shredded. Take your calipers and your slide rules and *eat* 'em! If you want *me* you got to do what it really is; you got to *kill* me right here, right now, or get the hell off *our* island!

Spindly and knuckled, stark as a branch, Zachary pulled a breath deep into his lungs to cry murder again.

But then he saw Esther Honey.

Esther sat in her rocking chair, her two granddaughters on either side of her, their arms around her, cheeks pressed against her bowed head, the young and certainly pregnant Irish girl, who Zachary hoped Esther might help as he had helped her, behind them pale, shocked, clearly terrified. She wept—not quietly, not gently, but with shuddering sobs that sounded the more awful because they sounded like those of a young girl. Esther, who had murdered her father and almost murdered her son, dear Eha, who was over with Matthew Diamond ministering to Candace Lark. Esther, who he'd begged to abide the issue of time, urged to endure, pleaded with to spare herself and her son from more injury, from more murder, from suicide, implored to forbear, to be patient, to be calm, to have no fear, most of all when the ghost of her father might bedevil her thoughts and blight her dreams. And she had.

Esther had been all those things Zachary had prayed for her to be, all these years, or so he liked to believe, had good reason to believe, and now after all that here he stood before her, naked and deranged, poisoned by the very rage, disfigured by the very anger, bemonstered by the very violence he'd taught her to resist and which she had. Here he stood in front of his beloved Esther, a shabby old spectacle, while she wept like a child.

Suddenly, like a marionette released from above, Zachary crumpled to the ground, where he lay, limp and panting on the sand. Annie Parker knelt next to him and caressed his head.

After a wordless, stunned moment the sheriff murmured, Okay, okay, now, everyone. This is a hard day on everyone, now. I know. Let's all just do what needs to be done so no one else gets hurt, and he and the men from the town got the Lark family up and into the boat.

Two men helped Annie Parker to her feet and swaddled her into a kind of papoose with a blanket. Zachary still lay on the sand. He looked up at her. She smiled at him.

Dear Zachary, she said. My dear old Zach.

The two men took Annie to the edge of the water, picked her up, and hoisted her into the launch. The sheriff propped her up in his arms. She stared at the Larks, her head trembling, muttering words no one could understand.

Their job completed, the sheriff gave the stunned islanders on the beach an absurd little wave farewell because he could not think of what else to do. Theophilus Lark sat in the stern next to sprawled and bleeding Candace, cradling slack Rabbit against his breast. The three other Lark children surrounded their parents and their sister, rubbing Rabbit's arms, stroking her hair, petting her cheeks.

Theophilus kissed his daughter's cold ear and whispered into it, What lack ye, my girl? What lack ye, my little salted cod?

IRIS AND VIOLET McDermott usually came to Esther when they had time to sit and smoke and drink tea and talk together, but with Bridget's help Esther picked her way to the sisters' place at first light the morning after the Larks were taken away. Her feet and legs ached. Her knees were stiff. She had some difficulty gripping the cane Eha had made for her. But she did not want to spend the day sitting in her own yard, nor did she want to spend it sitting on the bluff looking at the same old view, contemplating the same old sins, those she regretted and those she exalted.

The morning was cool and large, the world self-possessed and extensive. The short path Esther knew so well seemed deeper, quieter, fuller with shadows and sharp new light, more densely trimmed with lush overhanging sea grass, intricately laid with mineral schist, purple and gold sand and purple and cream lozenges of seashells, sifting layers, and the rank smell of ocean and grass. The sense of it all widened and captured her within it, the pains in her body, the pizzicato stings in her neck and spine, the sustained, ongoing ache of tendons bowing over the sharp edges of brittle bones, the contrabass drone of her sorrows and anger and joys, integrated with the light and shadow and color and smell, contrapuntal, syllabic, orchestrated, high and whole.

The image of Zachary on the sand and Rabbit Lark, limp in her father's arms, surrounded by her grieving family, dead, she knew, punctured the instant and woe flooded through her again.

Fitzy trotted up the path behind her, scooted around her in the grass, skipped back onto the way and continued as if she were not there. The ammoniac bite of Iris's and Violet's lye and the smell of the small fire they rekindled from banked ashes each morning to heat their tea and the water for washing reached Esther. She turned off the main path toward the sisters' homestead. She heard Iris yell at one of the Sockalexis children to bring her that here and someone thunked a washtub onto the roof of the pilothouse. Esther came around the bend and saw Norma and Scotty Sockalexis scrambling around with water buckets and the teakettle and a basket of laundry for washing. Emily Sockalexis sat on an old cobbler's stool, studying a math book. Iris stood in the hatchway of their schooner-cabin home, hands on her hips, watching the children. Violet called out from somewhere above and Iris looked up into the foliage of the huge oak tree that stood next to the house.

Okay, send it down! Iris shouted. The oak's foliage shivered and a massive wooden pulley rove with dark old Manila rope lowered from the leaves.

That's good! Right there! Iris said. Hold on. She climbed out of the hatch and one by one hitched four lines fixed to the corners of the pilothouse roof onto the metal hook hanging from the bottom of the pulley.

Okay, pull up the slack! Iris said. The pulley and tackle rose and the four lines tightened into a pyramid beneath it. That's good; that's good! Stop! The foliage above the boat swished and snapped. Violet appeared out of the leaves walking across a thick limb like a tightrope walker, using the surrounding branches hand over hand to help keep balance. She reached the trunk and looped a length of the rope around it below the limb. She tied the rope around her waist, leaned backward and out from the tree, her bare feet planted against the trunk, and walked herself down.

Auntie Esther, what in the world? Violet called out. Come, come, sit down. Why you come all this way over? Sit. What do you need? Scotty! Get Auntie Esther some tea! Emily, put down that math book and fetch the chair! Violet unknotted the rope and removed it from her waist.

Good thing you remember how to do all that, Esther said.

Practically the first thing I remember Daddy teaching us, Violet said.

We used to recite it together falling asleep at night, Iris said, taking the rush seat Emily had fetched and setting it in a shaded spot near the fire.

Day's bound to come, he always told us. Just a matter of when. Norma! Come fix Aunt Esther a fresh pipe and rub her feet. I know how much your feet hurt, Auntie. Let Norma rub them for you.

Norma took Esther's pipe and sat on a rock and stuck her tongue out and concentrated on filling the bowl with mugwort she took from a wooden tea box.

Just the pipe is fine, my good child, Esther said. Eha and the girls are getting the old tent from the schoolhouse and I didn't want to sit all by myself with my mind.

Violet gripped the rope and pulled on it and the slack lines at the corners of the pilothouse tautened and the pilothouse grated and creaked. She said, Well, you're at the right place for feeling like hell, Auntie. It's good, Iris; it'll work good.

Violet let the rope go slack. She looked at her red palms, opening and closing them, satisfied she'd be able to hoist the pilothouse from its mooring on the granite. She turned and went to Esther and crouched in front of her and held both her hands and said, You're at the right place for feeling like hell together, Auntie Ess.

Esther felt how hot Violet's hands were from the friction of the rope. Rage and anger burned in both women's hearts but there were the children to think of and work to be done and anger only ever turned to fear and both recalled the prophets' calls for calm and fearlessness so each was quiet and gentle with the other and so both remained composed, if only just.

Clay Pipes, Porcelain Teacups & Dishes, Fragments. Fishhooks, Buttons.
These items represent examples of the nearly forty thousand artifacts

archaeologists from the State University discovered during a survey of Apple Island, conducted in part to recognize the 100th anniversary of the settlement's dismantling and to memorialize the terrible episode in the state's history so that such a thing may never occur again. They were retrieved from within the footprints of the houses that once stood on the island, as well as from tidal flats and shell heaps. Islanders did not have money for tobacco and the recovered pipes mostly contain mugwort ash. Likewise, no islander would have possessed a full set of Chinaware, so the fragments here have a variety of designs, such as Dutch windmills, gilt fleur-de-lis, and other common motifs. These items serve as reminders of what everyday life was like on the island in spite of the prejudice the islanders suffered, and show that it was nearly identical to that of any other nearby community at the time.

THE HONEYS NEEDED someplace to stay so that Eha could break down their house and pack it on the old barge raft and take it with them when they left the island. So, Eha took Tabitha and Charlotte and fetched Zachary Hand to God's old Union Army tent from where he'd stored it in the schoolhouse supply room. He dragged the heavy canvas pile from its corner. The tent smelled moldy and stale and of Pennsylvanian mud. Mice fled from the folds on all four sides.

Here, he said to Tabby. Put out your arms like for firewood.

The girl held her arms out, crooked at the elbows, hands cupped toward her. Eha lay two tent poles across her arms.

Catch 'em up good, he said. Got 'em? Can you take 'em?

Yes, Dad, Tabby said. The poles upended on the right and tipped onto the ground left. Tabby lifted the poles level then frowned and shimmied them a little and found their balance, then they tipped over the other way. She looked at her father, serious, concentrating. She stuck her lower lip out and blew a strand of hair away from her face.

Good girl. That's it, Eha said. Lotte, here. Stick out your arms, like a scarecrow. Like this. She wanted to be as useful as her older sister, and she solemnly stuck her arms out. Eha took the gray coils of tent rope and passed them over the girl's arms and rested them on each of her shoulders.

Hold them good and snug against your chest. Catch 'em at the ends so they stay tight and don't come undone. Lotte grabbed at the coils and leaned forward to counter the weight.

Got it? You alright?

I'm alright, Da, Lotte said, imitating her sister's tone.

Okay, Eha said. He heaved the canvas pile up and onto his head, staggering slightly as he found its balance. Takes some doing, don't it? he said and the girls smiled, pleased to be doing what he was doing and doing it with him. They knew it was important work.

Yes, Da.

Alright, leave us go, he said. He started across the meadow path. Tabby followed, balancing the poles. Lotte came next, grappling with the coils of rope, which began to loosen and unloop almost as soon as she took a step. Twice, sudden gusts breaking over the meadow caught the odd headgear and blew Eha off his course and nearly capsized him. But he leaned into the wind and corrected himself and the dark birds of his thoughts wheeled quiet and wordless, compassing the larger task of which fetching the tent and pitching it and getting his mother and the girls installed inside the boat were smaller parts.

THE SUN ROSE and set every day. The moon, too. The tides went out and came in. The seasons turned in order. Some of the trees lost their leaves in the autumn and grew them back in the spring. People ate breakfast and supper when they had food and smoked and drank their tea. They had babies and raised them. They worked and slept. They sang and laughed and yelled and wept and fought and coupled. But from the first time she'd heard it, Esther Honey understood that if the man Jesus had died and been buried then really and truly rose, it was the only time such a thing had ever happened and that meant everything else in the world took its real meaning from that young man lying dead in his grave and awakening back to life and rolling the stone away from his tomb and saying goodbye to his friends and helpers not in spirit but actually in that body that had died and come back to life.

THE SUN SET and the heat of the day abated and a breeze off the ocean brought some relief. Esther and Bridget and the girls slept on the bluff, or Esther sat in her rocking chair, smoking and looking out at the ocean and Bridget sat across from her, wrapped in her shawl, hugging her knees, and the girls lay between them, wrapped in old blankets, curled up with Grizzly and Fitzy and Sulky, who had come up the path together in single file and joined the girls as they began to settle for bed.

The night was bright with stars but the moon was new, which pleased Eha because he would have felt exposed working under a full moon, as if he were stealing his own home. As he had built his house from the ground up, so he took it apart from the top down. He worked across the roof, starting at the ridge, smoothly and rapidly prying shingles up along with their nails with a notched shim he'd made himself by copying the one he'd seen Zachary use, which Zachary had in turn, he'd claimed, copied from Benjamin Honey's original and called his *scrammer*, stacking them in immaculate bundles he secured with twine and lowered to the ground in piles of one hundred.

Eha recognized every plank of the house as he took it apart. He remembered hammering nearly every nail, what time of day he'd driven it, what the weather had been, whether he'd been tired or spry, aching or strong, where Zachary had been and whether he'd been hammering, too, or planing, or sawing a board to size. Except for his age and that he could not scramble around the roof or leap from it, or climb around the framing as nimbly, but had to move more slowly, on account of his creakier knees and back—it amused him to think of his lean younger self who'd raised the house laughing at the stout gray-haired man he'd then have thought of as a codger—Eha moved about the structure with perfect certainty and sureness, undoing it piece by piece from the roof down in the exact reverse order he'd put it up, as if time, too, were reversing and the old man were greening farther back into his youth with each nail he levered from the pine. It was as if his old and young selves would work toward each other until finally they touched back to back and when the old man packed up the last puncheon log that had been the first laid of the foundation, the two would join and Eha would be a young boy again, poised at the fulcrum of raising and dismantling his home, anticipating equally with joy starting to build with Zachary and with dread taking apart what once had been so graciously given to put together.

Eha lashed the stacks of shingles and floor boards and framing and the two doors and the two windows, which he'd bundled in burlap padded with pine branches and seaweed to protect the glass, and the keg of nails and his box of tools and chest full of pots and kettles and Ethan's drawings rolled up and placed in the middle of the blankets, and the old curtains and the hardware from the olden boats and the buckets and fence slats and posts and the single bed frame and the three chairs and the kitchen table and the wooden cross made of driftwood and the little bit of flour and cornmeal and two cans of milk and a small wicker basket the girls had filled with strawberries and raspberries the day before for breakfast that morning. His hands bristled with splinters that he could not feel stuck in the callouses. An hour before sunrise Eha had the entire house perfectly bundled in a single shook on the deck of the raft.

In the predawn dark Eha hiked up the bluff to where Gram sat in her chair, smoking, quiet. Tabitha and Charlotte and Bridget lay sleeping with the dogs on the grass nearby. The dogs raised their heads when he approached and lowered them once they saw it was him. Eha stood behind his mother, silent. He looked at his daughters and Bridget, then out at the invisible dark vastness of the ocean, then at the diminutive figure of his mother, looking out at the ocean, too, wrapped in the wool blanket, the smoke coming from her pipe snatched away and dispersed by the sharp wind. He wondered what she saw. Not what she saw, but what she was thinking as she saw what she saw, what he saw. He wondered just how old she was and how old he was and about his father, who he'd never met. He wondered what Ethan was doing at that same moment, down in Massachusetts.

Esther braced her hands on the armrests and lifted herself from the chair. She stood for a moment, still looking across the water. She turned and looked at her son.

Back to the wilderness, she said. Eha put a hand on her shoulder. She held a hand out and he took it and she held his hand and squeezed it. Mother and son stood on the bluff, hand in hand. Light began to glow in dim, spectral bands across the sky.

Eha roused Tabitha and Charlotte, who both sat up and began scratching the dogs' ears even as they scowled and looked around, confused about where they were. Bridget awoke and sat up, too, and in the faint light it was impossible to distinguish which of the three girls was which. Eha upended the rocking chair and lifted it over his head and lowered its seat onto the top of his derby hat. He offered his free arm to his mother, who took it, and they all descended from the height down the path across the meadow to the water and the waiting raft piled with their dismantled home, Eha and Esther at the front of the file, Charlotte and Tabitha next, the three dogs, Sulky, Fitzy, and Grizzly following behind, and Bridget at the end, struggling with her bag and her bundled painting.

Eha boarded the raft and set the rocking chair down at the center of the deck. Tabitha and Charlotte sat huddled side by side on the sand, Grizzly and Fitzy almost standing guard on either side of them. They picked single berries from the basket and ate them one by one and passed the self-portraits Ethan had given them back and forth, threatening each other not to stain them with berry juice, saying, He looks like a captain in this one, and, He looks sad in this one. The girls offered neither berry nor sketch to Bridget, who sat on top of her bag, hugging her legs, her head bowed and resting on her knees. Sulky nosed under Bridget's arm, trying to get her to look up, but she would not. Esther stood behind the three girls, still, waiting for her son's instructions.

Eha laid straps of wood perpendicularly over the chair's rockers and nailed them to the deck, then wedged shims between the rockers, straps, and deck, tapping around at them all with a mallet until he was convinced that the chair was secure. The girls helped Esther board the raft and make her way to the chair. Bridget struggled with her bag and the painting and lost her footing as she tried to board the raft. She fell forward onto the painting and felt and heard its frame snap and break beneath her weight. The crack of the breaking frame seemed to bring Charlotte and Tabitha out of their private family grief for a moment, and both girls rushed to help this third, not much older than them, friend of some sort to their lost brother, soon to be mother of their nephew or niece, though neither girl remotely suspected she was pregnant, only somehow sickly, only somewhat ill, it seemed, but with what neither Honey girl had any idea.

While the girls helped Bridget, Eha circled a length of rope around Esther's middle, threading it in and out of the chair's backrest splats.

Smooth seas today, but I don't want you to tumble, he said.

She said, Might rather.

But you've always said you weren't born to drown, he said, fixing a knot in front of her and pulling it tight.

Something I read once, she said. I always thought it was clever. But it was just silly.

Sulky leapt on board the raft as soon as Tabitha called him, but no matter how much the girls threatened, pleaded, pushed, pulled, or tried to lure them with food, neither Grizzly nor Fitzy would come along. Both dogs sat side by side on the sand, waiting to see the Honeys and Bridget off but refusing to leave their duchy. Sulky stood at the edge of the raft, looking at them, and it was as if the three dogs had held a council and decided which of them would remain and which go with the family to watch over the girls.

The incoming tide lifted the rear of the raft and set it back down. Eha wrapped the blanket around his mother's shoulders. Usually Esther remained bareheaded in all but the coldest or wettest weather, but she drew the blanket over her head like a cowl and held it together under her chin as Eha stepped off the raft and began to push at it and rock it back and forth and up and down, and the tide washed up over his feet and knees, and the raft inched out from the shore then beached again then lifted and inched out a little more then floated free on its own for a moment and the girls thought they were launched and both began to cry but the raft beached once more then the tide swelled up again and Eha pushed the raft loose from the island and it floated free on the water and he raised himself from the water onto the deck and took up the twenty-foot sapling he'd cut and trimmed himself and started poling the raft out along the contours of the island toward the mouth of the bay and Esther bowed her head and looked at the seawater sliding to and fro over the deck and between the joined logs and found that she did not have the heart to look up and watch the island recede. She held out her hands and the girls each took one and it looked to Eha like they were praying together.

Tabitha looked up from her drawing of Ethan. I miss Ethan! she cried.

Me, too, Charlotte said.

I don't want to go!

Me neither! Both girls broke into fits of weeping.

Esther squeezed hard on both girls' hands and shook them like she was testing the strength of their grips. Bridget was as she'd been on the sand, hugging her legs to herself, head bowed and resting on her knees, now half-slumped sideways against the stack of their disassembled home. In that moment, Esther saw that however her and her granddaughters' sorrows overlapped with those of this girl who was, it occurred to her, the last orphan to arrive on Apple Island seeking refuge, and quite probably its briefest resident, she and they had their own sorrows, possibly the last things she and they could at this moment call their own, so she let the girl be. Esther saw them all on the raft as they might be seen from the shore, or higher, from over the water, from above the ocean, castaways, a bitter old harridan and her grown brother son and two granddaughters, a mutt, and a pregnant stranger, adrift together on a raft piled with their home in pieces, the house a gesture toward and persistence at the kind of home they'd all wanted for themselves since they'd come to the rock, the island, and clung to it, always knowing that sooner or later they'd be noticed, for the worse, and be expelled back out onto the waters. Esther lifted her face and looked back at her home.

That poor island, she said. That poor little island of such poor dear souls. Driven from our home, our ark, our little basket in the bullrushes. All for some kind of hotel, they say.

Iris and Violet McDermott's refitted schooner appeared from the inlet. Iris piloted with one hand on the wheel and an arm across the shoulders of Norma, Emily, and Scotty, who were huddled together against her. Violet moved along the deck, low, sure-footed, pulling and securing lines. The sails swelled and snapped full. The boat hove to and surged northward abreast of the sun.

ESTHER HAD HEARD a visiting relative once talk about going to a big reunion on her husband's side of the family. There were more than a hundred people, she'd said. Many of them looked exactly alike, but many of them you'd never tell were related. A family so big you had to have special reunions of them, they'd spread so far and wide. What it must have been like to have a family that large and get back together with them like that. Their family on the island was always so small and seemingly getting smaller, compacting, members converging into one another, so few of them they'd begun to be more than one relation to one another at a time, men being their daughters' fathers and husbands, too, mothers being their sons' sisters. The family condensing, imploding, fewer and fewer people, becoming heavier and heavier, until one last woman would stand, dark and wholly compacted, herself begat, she her own mother. She her own daughter and sister, all in her one, impossibly condensed and sorrowful body, leaden and involute so when she lay down to die no one would need to bury her. She would just sink into the ground like a millstone plunging through silty water.

Not now, though. Now they were scattered, to the sea, the asylum, the poorhouse, Ethan God knew where but not coming back, she was sure, although she'd never say so to Eha.

What a sight it would have been, Esther thought, looking at the island as if it were slipping away and not she, to see that last, self-begotten woman, darker than pure dark, heavier than the whole world, standing on the bluff, and what a sight to see the island give way beneath her, as if to her impossible weight granite and bedrock suddenly could give no more support than a silk scarf to a statue cast in lead, plunging from the spangled sparkling surface back into the lightless pith of the only womb left strong enough to bear her away to her next and truest birth. She knew how holy it was that only one family went into the ark and came forth from it. And she knew how terrible it was, too.

The whole world had gone out of joint the moment Esther had killed her father. She'd thought it had gone crooked when he made like she was her mother, like his wife, made her pregnant with Eha, but she'd found that was nothing compared with murder. Her whole life since she'd shoved him off the bluff had been like one long-held breath. She could never really say to anyone what she really knew because she could never say to anyone why or how she knew it. Her father haunted her. He appeared every day, in Eha's face, flaring, only for an instant but clearly, brooding, glowering, foul, so much at first that she'd have rather nursed a snake than her child. Eha had not spoken until he was eight or nine or ten years old, and not all that much since, and she was grateful that he had a slow tongue, because she heard her—and his— father's voice in his, inflections, syllables, fragments she did not even have to put together to know what dismal things they said. For months she planned to stab out her eyes and augur her ears with an awl. She even practiced tending Eha and the house with her eyes closed and her ears stopped with moss, but light and shadow still chased one another behind her eyelids, and it was louder inside her head with her ears plugged. That was how she came to know that she would still see without eyes and still hear without ears. There had been the natural day and night, the sun and moon, the summer and winter of things before she murdered her father, and afterward there was the strange, haunted, hallucinatory time she'd lived in since. Only the thinnest skin separated the two realms, and she had had to practice not to address her father's ghost when she saw it, or speak back to it when it she heard its voice, so that people would not think she'd gone mad or become suspicious, not that there weren't people on the island who talked to themselves and their ancestors and departed friends and enemies all the time, and not that anyone missed her father or would have blamed her much if they'd known she'd killed him. But no one talked to the ghosts of murdered men. No one talked to the ghosts of the men they'd murdered. For all she knew and felt, Esther figured she'd probably kill her father again, and maybe again and again if time proved a carousel and she spun around and around, forever returning to that night on the bluff, because what else could she have done? Been his wife? Had more of his babies? Absolutely not. There had been no one to stop him, so she had improvised. And taken revenge. And she would still avenge and avenge and avenge herself again, every time. What a sad gesture, murder, though. What a foul, cowardly little gesture. Her father had led her into that temptation and she had given over to it.

Esther had never told Eha his begats, but she assumed that at some point he had known, or had almost known and then stopped himself from knowing, because what was done was done and he had a mother and she a son and who else did they have and what were they supposed to do, walk off the edge of the world? And soon enough someone would and now had made them sail off the edge of it anyway. So there they floated, a splintery little pile of wood and metal slipping the stocks of the continent, bobbing in the Atlantic, a little man moving to this side of the raft then that, with no more than a length of old dried straw to push the pile a little this way then that as the waters moved them along as they would, and a little old lady lashed to a chair lashed to the pile of splinters and sticks, holding on to her granddaughters who were practically orphans already it seemed, and this other orphan, pregnant, who would soon have to make her own way because the Honeys could not do anything to save her whether they were inclined to or not, all like insects on a bobbing square of cork, not human persons floating away on their house that had been shuffled and squared up like a worn deck of cards.

Could we spend the day out here, on the water?

Esther could not bear landing the raft on some rock and being carried to shore, Eha and the girls getting soaked, her half-soaked, her wet clothes too heavy for her old body to stand up in, to warm back up in, when they got her to the land, an old woman awful and obscene on the ground, too weak to lift herself or scramble up the embankment or lean herself up against a pine tree, too frail for the weight of her own frail body inside her wet rags, for Eha to drag her up by her arms.

I'm too tired to find a dry place on land. Could we just stay out here?

Yes, Mama. Eha said. He squinted out at the darkness. We can stay out here.

When Eha said they could stay on the water it was like the world let go of its breath, and Esther's hearing and her sight and her sense of smell returned and the raft rose and fell on the calm roll of the sea and the light sharpened into that pale morning light she loved so much and the smells of the pine trees not far away on the shore came out over the water and mixed with the salt and clean wind and soothed her. The motion of the water and the sound of the breeze and of the surf breaking and retreating on the shore, stirring and shushing, lulled her and she closed her eyes and slept a little, still holding the girls' hands.

Bridget began to sing to herself, softly, *Seothó, seothó lo.*

Esther heard the lullaby as part of a dream and it seemed to her she was with her mother and sister and all her old aunties and cousins again, coming back from gathering, singing together in the quiet evening.

Envelope with three drawings, pencil and charcoal, September 1914, addressed to Mr. Diamond, Apple Island, Maine, U.S. of A.

Ethan Honey apparently fled the Hale estate the day before Bridget Carney did. His reasons for doing so are unclear. He left all his art supplies behind. The last evidence of his life is this envelope, addressed to his family

care of Matthew Diamond dated September 1914, one year after he disap-
peared. It is not known how the parcel came to be in the Hales' possession, but
Phoebe Hale recalled that her grandfather, Thomas Hale, repeatedly tried
but failed to locate any Honeys over the next years, to whom he might deliver
the communication. The post was preserved, unopened, for decades with the
rest of Honey's work. With Phoebe Hale's permission, the envelope has now
been opened as an important source in the study of the people and settlement
on Apple Island. The envelope contained the three drawings found displayed
at the end of the exhibition. They render what have been tentatively identified
by Prof. Steven Hoffs of the State University Art History Department as bat-
tlefields in Ardennes, France. No information has come to light about why,
how, or even if Ethan Honey was in France.

EHA WORKED THE RAFT and estimated how far they might try to get
up the coast before landing. He had an idea that maybe they could turn
inland, not too far, though, but to somewhere near where he and Zachary had cut the tree down for the house so long ago. If they found someplace good, he could make a trip back to the island, in secret, and leave
a sign of some sort for Ethan that he'd see when he came back. The
sign could point across the channel and when Ethan crossed back to the
mainland there'd be another sign, this one a blaze like the ones Zachary
had made through the woods so they knew how to get back to the tree
he'd chosen for the house. Eha could go through the woods and chip
marks that Ethan could follow to where they'd resettled. < | >. Eha
hoped Ethan would remember about Zachary's marks that led to the
tree. He hoped his son would come back and, once the shock passed
at finding the island empty, think things through and realize his father
would leave a sign for him, would leave the kind of blazes his father had
told him Zachary used a long time ago, find and follow them to their
rebuilt house, once a tree in the woods, then a house on an island, now

packed on a raft, by then remade. Eha saw Ethan in the woods, worried, but every mark bright and catching his eye, leading him back until one morning, when Eha and Lotte and Tabby were in the yard doing chores, Ethan would appear from the trees and they'd cry out and drop bucket and broom, washboard and hammer, and rush to him and embrace him. And Esther, sleeping in her rocking chair in the house—as she did now, lashed to the deck of the raft—would awaken at the commotion and know it was Ethan come back and cry out, Is that our boy? Bring him here! Bring him here so I can see his beautiful face!

4

In a year it will be nearly impossible to tell that they were ever here. Apple Island lies in the Atlantic, belted in night. The graves where the island dead once lay are open and empty and listen like ears.

The morning after the islanders left, a dozen men assembled at the launch on the main in the predawn cold. Nine of them were laborers, following a day's work, digging postholes one day, hauling lobster traps or picking potatoes the next. There were three sailors, too, by the look of their pilot coats, who had drifted or possibly fled from Bath or Portland or Portsmouth. Some of the other men knew one another from previous work, but the sailors, after nodding to the others, stood slightly apart, dark, speaking what one of the other men muttered was Portuguese when another asked what the hell was that talk.

The sound of a wagon and single mule pulling it preceded by several moments the appearance in the opening in the trees of what two of the non-seafaring laborers recognized at once from previous stints assisting him at his melancholy chores as the sexton, Barney Kramp. The wagon hit a stone in the road and the clatter of what the same two men knew was a dozen probably borrowed spades and three or four paupers' coffins ruptured the last of the receding night and suddenly it was day and the birds cried and swooped up and the trees and the wind awoke and the waters, too, and the men themselves roused anew into the new day. The sexton pulled up to the group of men, who broke and ranked themselves in a semicircle in front of the wagon.

Good morning, you filthy gang of scoundrels, the sexton said. Good morning to you groundlings, plowboys, and villains.

Grave digging, one of the men muttered.

Diggin' 'em *up*, said another.

NONE OF THE workers saw him arrive, but an hour after they started digging up the cemetery on Apple Island they noticed Zachary Hand to God leaning against the trunk of a nearby tree watching them.

Who's this old bluegum? said a thin, pale white boy with big ears and a shorn head who looked barely old enough to be away from home.

Got me, said the man digging next to the boy.

Hey, Uncle, who the hell are *you*? the boy yelled.

Zachary did not answer.

Hey, lazybones, why don't you grab a shovel and give us a hand, do some honest work, the boy called out. Who the hell are you, anyway?

I'm nobody, Zachary said.

Sure, sure. Salt of the earth, said the white boy.

God has mercy on the meek and the poor, one of the other men said, thrusting his shovel into the ground.

Ha! the white boy said. Then he sure must love all these colored old half-breeds.

Zachary Hand to God stared at the ocean and, as if he couldn't care whether the boy or anyone else heard him or not, as if the big-eared pale white boy with the shorn head weren't even there, as if the bones of his neighbors and lovers and maybe even Benjamin and Patience Honey, too, and even, he thought, of Esther Honey's father, Grant Howden—who he'd known Esther had murdered the moment he'd found the broken-necked, broken-backed body in the rocks below the bluff that morning—as if every one of the souls who'd died and been buried on

Apple Island were not being dug up right in front of his own eyes, said, Well, He surely walked among us on this earth as one of us.

What was that? the boy said, bolting upright. What'd you just say?

Zachary sighed and looked at the four raw empty coffins then at the sea then directly at the pale white boy with big ears and shorn head. I said that, for my sake I hope He does, because I'm the last sorry old half-breed left on this rock.

Here, here! Enough of that blaspheming, you grimy bilge rats! Barney Kramp called from the wagon. Back to digging!

The pale white boy threw his cigarette onto a pile of freshly dug dirt. He shook his head to himself, for Zachary and the sailors to see. He looked at the man digging next to him and snickered.

Beat this, he said.

The other man wiped his bright pink, balding head with a handkerchief. What was left of his hair hung limp from where it grew over his ear, down the side of his face, to his jawbone, thin, sweaty, sparse blond and gray. The man pasted the loose skein back over his pate and tucked it behind his other ear. He sighed, picked up his shovel, and stuck it back into the dirt. A pluff of wind lifted his hair again and flopped it over to the other side of his head.

The sailors returned to digging.

Zachary turned away and walked across the island toward where his house and the others were nearly done burning. The men from the mainland had missed Zachary's tree so he went to it and got inside. He closed his eyes and ran the pads of his fingers across the carvings as if to decipher them by touch. He opened his eyes and followed the radius of each band of pictures. Really, they were crude. Most of the intricacies and nuances of expression and gesture and architecture and decoration had been those of his thoughts while he'd carved. Very little of the finesse of his ideas had made its way into the wood, he saw now. He gathered his candle and cross. He knelt and cupped up a cone of wood shavings and set it burning with his flint and steel. Smoke rose into the darkness of the hollowed trunk then refluxed and began pulsing from the opening. Zachary watched the fire grow until he was certain it would not smother, then headed for the water.

EARTH IS THIS SURFACE. Earth is this solid stratum. Earth is the hole or hiding place of burrowing animals. Earth is the soil suitable for cultivation. Earth is the medium by which a circuit is completed. Earth is the ground. Earth is a place for burial. Earth is the present abode of humankind. Earth is wordless and patient and suffered the grave robbers' spades in silence.

THE TWO MEN from the town who had been put in charge of burning the remaining buildings on the island could not get the Larks' shanty lit. The schoolhouse burned just fine, and so did Zachary's shack and Annie Parker's heap, but the Larks' home only smoldered and sent out smutty fumes. Whether it was too moldy with rot or soaked through with water or what it was the men could not really tell. After half an hour of repeatedly setting torches to various piles of rags and nesting and debris, the men soaked the entire shack inside and out with kerosene. They stood ten yards back and one of them threw his torch at the home like a tomahawk (he was an out-of-work part-time lumberjack, who'd won cash and pocket watches and wedding bands throwing actual tomahawks at saplings from thirty paces after dinner, often after half a bottle of whisky, on log drives down the West Branch Carry on the Penobscot River). The torch spun through the air end over end, fizzling flames and sparks like a Chinese firework, and disappeared into the shack through the open doorframe and the men heard the torch strike the back wall.

Nice throw, there.

Smoke uncoiled from the windows and stovepipe then a torrent of flames gushed from the doorway and up into the sky like a river of fire in spate.

Like the house was upside down, one of the men thought. Like the fire was pouring out of the house upward the way water would pour through a sluice. The men smoked and the shanty barely worthy of the name smoked and burned and crumpled to one side first then toppled, like an animal, almost, dropping to its front knees as the flames swarmed and felled it.

Like wolves on a steer or something, one of the men thought.

The other man thought it looked like the time he'd seen a woman on fire walk out of a burning house, the way she staggered like the fire was heavy and she couldn't stand upright under its weight. The men put their hands on the tops of their rake handles and rested their chins on their hands and smoked their cigarettes.

A mastiff and a terrier had come up behind the men and sat watching the fire. The mastiff let out a single deep bark. The man who had thrown the torch like a tomahawk and had seen a burning woman drew his revolver and shot both dogs between the eyes.

EVENTUALLY ONE OF the Portuguese sailors struck bone. He levered up a pelvis, sacrum dry and crustacean.

Aye! he yelled to Kramp.

That's it, you mangy, flea-bitten dogs, Kramp called, coming to the pit. He shaded his eyes and peered into the hole and looked at the hipbone resting on the shovel blade the Portuguese sailor held as far away from himself as he could without dropping it and scrambling out of the ditch.

God save us all, you rogues, Kramp said, and the pale white boy with big ears scooped up a skull missing its mandible.

I got a head! he declared. Look at it! he said, staring. Just look at that, he said, his smile disappearing. His voice quieted. Just look at that.

The men shoveled up femurs and fibulas, ribs and radii.

Put them in the boxes, you scarecrows, Kramp said. Start with the left one. Don't get too much dirt in with them. There mightn't be enough room, otherhow.

Three hours later the man with the woebegone comb-over paused digging. He stood hunched over, shovel in his two hands, panting. He grunted and stabbed the shovel into the ground and pulled himself upright by its handle. He was the only man left. The sailors had walked away across the low tide two hours earlier, without pay, passing oaths back and forth in Portuguese. Even the pale white boy with big ears had gone sulky and silent. He'd slowed more and more with each scoop of bones to the box until, after flipping a tiny, be-cracked ribcage into the third box, he'd stood looking at the crates full of the mixed-up remains and the last crate yet to be filled and had spat on the ground and cursed.

Aw, shit. I ain't no grave digger, anyway, he'd growled. He'd pitched his shovel against the cartwheel and said, I'm through. Give my pay to the goddamn orphanage.

Each time a man quit, Kramp nodded and sighed and rowed him back to the main in a dinghy that had been left behind by the islanders and said, Farewell, you good-for-nothing, Farewell, you filthy beggar, Farewell, you dirty peddler, and returned to the work. He knew from experience that all but the most desperate or ruthless men would not finish the job, that he would not have to pay the wages he'd promised, which he had not even brought with him, and that he would have to do much of the job himself, alone, through the night, by lantern.

The white man with the sorrowful hair was named John Thorpe. He lived where he lay down each night. He had no money, no regular work, and could not afford to walk away from this cursed job, even though he gave himself fifty-fifty odds at best that that foul-mouthed man who'd hired him would pay him when he was done. He dug all morning and all afternoon and figured he'd probably dig all night, too.

Barney Kramp returned from taking the pale white boy with big ears and shorn head across the inlet, grabbed a shovel, and joined him.

As the light left the sky, John Thorpe saw Zachary Hand to God wading away from the island across the channel, chest-deep in the water. Zachary held what looked like an old faded and patched flag bundled and knotted together by the corners above his head. His silhouette cut through the invisible current of the tide and to Thorpe he looked like a threadbare angel abandoning the wrecked ship over which he'd once been guardian, light fanning across the water behind him as he pushed against the incoming flood.

ACKNOWLEDGMENTS

The author wishes to express his deepest gratitude to Ellen Levine and to Alane Salierno Mason.